Praise for Stephen J. Cannell

ON THE GRIND

"Cover to cover, [*On the Grind*] never lets you up for air. Read it!"

—Michael Connelly, bestselling author of *The Brass Verdict*

"A hard-boiled cop and really scuzzy bad guys... Cannell is the gold in crime fiction."

—Stephen Coonts, bestselling author of *The Assassin*

THREE SHIRT DEAL

"Cannell's brand of thriller is served straight-up...and he knows how to cut to the chase."

—*The New York Times*

"The white-knuckle climax is one of the most exciting ever." —BookReporter.com

WHITE SISTER

"A very satisfying thriller written by a born entertainer."

—*New York Post*

"A strong piece of fiction that leads readers...through the harrowing underbelly of L.A." —*Daily News*

MORE...

"A terrific read." —*New York Sun*

"Cannell dishes out the action in forklift-sized servings." —*Publishers Weekly*

COLD HIT

"As the case spirals outward from local crime to international espionage dating back to the 1980s, the action rarely lets up. When it does, we're reintroduced to the back story that is one of the pleasures of reading the Scully series." —*Los Angeles Times*

"The action rarely lets up." —*Chicago Tribune*

"A thriller, a procedural, and an indictment of the Patriot Act in the wrong hands. Scully, the plots, and the characters get better with each book."

—*Sunday Oklahoman*

"An intriguing, torn-from-today's-headlines premise on his fifth Shane Scully outing."

—*News Press* (Fort Myers, FL)

VERTICAL COFFIN

"Readers will enjoy watching [Scully] puzzle out the twists and turns of the plot and watch breathlessly as he undertakes a climactic high-speed chase."

—*Publishers Weekly*

"Cannell certainly knows how to tell a story...You'll probably read the entire book with a smile on your face."
—*Cleveland Plain Dealer*

HOLLYWOOD TOUGH

"Cannell, creator of such TV shows as *The A-Team*, clearly knows the ins and outs of the entertainment industry, and the detective story, with its wry, subtle humor, doubles as Hollywood satire...the cops-and-robbers sequences hit the mark as well. Well-drawn characters and keen observations on the similarities between Hollywood and the mafia make this a winner."
—*Publishers Weekly*

"Scully has ample opportunity to prove how 'Hollywood tough' he is...veteran writer/TV producer Cannell has concocted his special brand of reader candy."
—*Kirkus Reviews*

RUNAWAY HEART

"A cop thriller with a futuristic, sci-fi twist...Cannell has a genius for creating memorable characters and quirky, gripping plots...this is a fun read."
—*Publishers Weekly*

THE VIKING FUNERAL

"Stephen J. Cannell is an accomplished novelist."
—*New York Daily News*

"Stephen J. Cannell's *The Viking Funeral* is the sort of fast and furious read you might expect from one of television's most successful and inventive writer-producers." —*Los Angeles Times*

THE TIN COLLECTORS

"I've been a Stephen Cannell fan since his remarkable *King Con*, and he keeps getting better. *The Tin Collectors* is an LAPD story that possesses both heart and soul; a fresh and different look at the men and women who, even more than the NYPD, are the most media-covered police force in the world. Stephen Cannell has the screenwriter's fine ear for dialogue and great sense of timing and pacing as well as the novelist's gift of substance and subtlety. Cannell likes to write, and it shows." —Nelson DeMille

"Cannell turns out another winding, suspenseful thriller." —*New York Daily News*

"Readers who enjoy cop novels by Robert Daley or William Caunitz will find Cannell right up their dark, dangerous alley." —*Booklist*

"Compelling, frightening, and...very moving. Don't miss it. Cannell is a first-rate storyteller and *The Tin Collectors* never stops." —*Janet Evanovich*

St. Martin's Paperbacks Titles
by Stephen J. Cannell

On the Grind

Three Shirt Deal

White Sister

Cold Hit

Vertical Coffin

Runaway Heart

Hollywood Tough

The Viking Funeral

The Tin Collectors

THE PALLBEARERS

STEPHEN J. CANNELL

St. Martin's Paperbacks

THE PALLBEARERS

For information address St. Martin's Press, 175 Fifth Avenue, New York, NY 10010.

Library of Congress Catalog Card Number: 2009033519

ISBN: 978-0-312-53245-1

Printed in the United States of America

St. Martin's hardcover edition / March 2010
St. Martin's Paperbacks edition / October 2010

St. Martin's Paperbacks are published by St. Martin's Press, 175 Fifth Avenue, New York, NY 10010.

10 9 8 7 6 5 4 3 2 1

This is for Ivan Weinburg, my teammate and friend since youth—a promising novelist in his own right and a pretty damn good wideout on our high school football team.

THEN

CHAPTER 1

IN 1976 AMERICA WAS JUST coming out of a protracted depression called the Vietnam War, but back then I was still deep in the middle of mine. I was twelve years old, and, boy, was I pissed.

It was early in May on that particular spring morning and I was huddled with some other children on Seal Beach around 9th Street. We were staring out through a predawn mist at the gray Pacific Ocean while consulting Walter Dix's old surf watch to time the AWP—which is what Walt called the Average Wave Period between the incoming swells. Walt called swells the steeps.

The beach we were on was about fifteen miles from the Huntington House Group Home, which was in a run-down neighborhood in Harbor City, a few minutes southeast of Carson. There were four of us gathered around Walt, all wearing beavertail wet suits with the sixties-style long flap that wrapped around under your crotch and left your legs uncovered. We were his lifers. The yo-yos. The kids who kept getting thrown back.

All of us knew we would probably never get another chance at a foster family or adoption because we were too ugly or too flawed or we had lousy county packages, having already been placed too many times and then returned with bad write-ups.

But there were other reasons we didn't make it. We were an angry group. I held the Huntington House catch-and-release record, having just been sent back for the fifth time. My last foster family had called me incorrigible, unmanageable, and a liar. Probably all pretty accurate classifications.

The four of us had been specifically chosen for different reasons by Walter "Pop" Dix for that morning's sunrise surf patrol. Of course we had all desperately wanted to be picked, but it wasn't lost on any of us that we'd earned the privilege because of a variety of recent setbacks. Pop understood that even though we'd failed, it didn't mean we were failures. He also understood our anger, even if nobody else did. Pop was the executive director of Huntington House and was the closest thing to a father I'd ever known.

"Okay, cowabungas. Big rhinos out der. We gonna bus' 'em out big time," he said, glancing up from the watch to the incoming sets, speaking in that strange-sounding Hawaiian pidgin that he sometimes used when we were surfing. "We pack large dis morning. Catch us one big homaliah wave, stay out of de tumbler and it be all tits and gravy, bruddah."

He grinned, kneeling in the sand wearing his Katin trunks, displaying the surfer knots on the tops of his feet and knees—little calcium deposits caused by a lifetime of paddling to catch up to what Pop called the wall of glass.

Pop was a tall, stringy, blue-eyed guy with long blond hair just beginning to streak with gray. He was about forty then, but he seemed much younger.

There was an Igloo cooler with juice and rolls in the sand before us, packed by Walter's wife, Elizabeth, for after surfing. We'd take our clean-up set at around seven thirty, come in and shower by the lifeguard station, eat, and change clothes in the van. Then we would pack up and Walt would drop us at school by eight thirty.

Pop had been born on the North Shore of Hawaii, which he said made him "kamaaina to da max." His parents had taught school there and he'd ended up in L.A. after the army. That was pretty much all I knew about him. I was too caught up with my own problems to worry about much else.

Because he'd been raised on the North Shore and taught to surf by the old-timers there, Pop was a throwback surfer, what the Hawaiians called a logger. His stick was a nine-foot-long board with no fins and a square tail—very old school. On the nose, he had painted his own crescent symbol, an inch-high breaking curl with the words "Tap the Source" in script underneath. Pop said the source was that place in the center of the ocean where Kahuna, the god of the waves, made "da big poundahs"—double overhead haymakers with sphincter factor.

Other than a couple of Hawaiians and one or two

Aussies, Pop was one of the few surfers left who rode a cigar-box surfboard, a 1930s Catalina Hollow made by Tom Blake. Once it had water inside from too many rides, it got heavy in the nose and was a bitch to stay up on. The rest of us had new polyurethane shorties with a dolphin-fin skeg for speed. The boards and wet suits belonged to the Huntington House Group Home and were only used for special occasions like this.

We were sad children whose dark records were clinically defined in the terse cold files kept by Child Protective Services. But our nicknames were much crueler than our histories because we bestowed them on each other.

Nine-year-old Theresa Rodriguez knelt beside me, holding her short board. She had been set on fire by her mother shortly after birth but had miraculously survived. Terry was damaged goods, with an ugly, scarred face that looked like melted wax. Everyone knew Theresa was a lifer from the time County Welfare had first put her in Huntington House at the age of five. She was chosen for this morning's field trip because she had no friends and never got much of anything, except from Pop. We called her Scary Terry.

Also kneeling in the sand that morning was Leroy Corlet. Black, age eleven. Leroy's dad was in prison, his mother was dead of a heroin overdose. He had been sexually molested by the uncle he'd been sent to live with until a neighbor called Child Protective Services and they took him away. We called him Boy Toy behind his back, but never to his face because Leroy wasn't right in the head anymore. He was a violent nut-case who held grudges, and if you pissed him off, he'd sneak into your room in the middle of the night while you slept and beat you in the face with his shoe. He couldn't stand to be touched.

Pop had picked him that morning because he had just failed a special evaluation test at elementary school and was being held back for the second time in four years. He'd been sulking in his room for the last two days. No foster family wanted him either.

Next to Leroy was fifteen-year-old Khan Kashadarian. Half-Armenian, half-Arab or Lebanese. He'd been abandoned at age ten and was living in an alley in West Hollywood when he was picked up and shoved into the welfare system. Khan was fat, and a bully. We had given him two nicknames: Sand Nigger and Five Finger Khan, because he stole anything you didn't keep locked up. I didn't know why Pop picked him to be with us. As far as I was concerned, we'd have all been better off if he was dead. Even though he was three years older and a hundred pounds heavier, I'd had six or seven violent fights with Khan. I lost them all.

I was small back then, but I didn't take any shit. I was willing to step off with anybody at the slightest hint of insult. I got along with no one and had convinced myself that my five ex–foster families were a bunch of welfare crooks who were milking the system.

"No floatwalling," Pop said, his blue eyes twinkling. Floatwalling was paddling out beyond the surf but never going for a wave, not to be confused with backwalling, which was acceptable behavior because you were treading water, waiting for the big one.

Then the sun peeked above the horizon, the sign that it was time for us to paddle out.

"Let's go rhino chasing, bruddahs!" Pop said.

We picked up our boards and started down toward the early-morning break. I was fuming inside. I couldn't believe nobody wanted me, even though I insisted I didn't want or need anybody. Before we got to the water, Pop put out a hand and turned me toward him, as the others moved ahead. He lowered his voice and dropped the Hawaiian pidgin.

"Get your chin up, guy. There's a place for you, Shane," he said softly. "Sometimes we have to wait to find out where we belong. Be patient."

I nodded, but said nothing.

"Until you get picked again, you've always got a place with me." Then he flashed his big, warm grin and switched back to pidgin, trying to get me to smile. "I always want you, bruddah. What's a matta you? Your face go all jam up. You no laugh no more, haole boy?"

I glanced down at the sand, shuffled my feet. But I didn't smile. I was too miserable.

"Come on then." Pop put a hand on my shoulder and walked with me to the water.

I was Shane Scully, a name picked for me by strangers. No mom, no dad. No chance. I had nobody, but nobody messed with me either. My nickname around the group home was Duncan because I was the ultimate yo-yo.

All any of us had was Pop Dix. He was the only one

who cared, the only one who ever noticed what we were going through and tried to make it better.

And yet we were all so self-involved and angry that, to the best of my knowledge, none of us had ever bothered to say thank you.

NOW

CHAPTER 2

"THIS HOTEL IS GONNA COST us a fortune," I said, looking at the brochure of the beautiful Waikiki Hilton. The photo showed a huge structure right on the beach in Honolulu. "You sure you got us the full off-season discount?"

I called this question inside to my wife, Alexa, while sitting out in our backyard in Venice, holding a beer and warming my spot on one of our painted metal porch chairs. Our adopted marmalade cat, Franco, was curled up nearby. He looked like he was asleep, but he was faking. I could tell because he was subtly working his ears with every sound. Cat radar. The colorful evening sky reflected an orange sunset in the flat mirrored surface of the Venice Grand Canal. It was peaceful. I was feeling mellow.

Alexa came out of the sliding-glass door wearing a skimpy string bikini. She looked unbelievably hot—beautiful figure, long legs, coal-black hair, with a model's high cheekbones under piercing aqua-blue eyes.

"Ta-da," she said, announcing herself with her own chord. She stood before me, modeling the bathing suit. "You like, mister? Want kissy-kissy?"

I grabbed her arm and pulled her down onto my lap.

"You are not wearing that in public. But get thee to the bedroom, wench." I grinned and nuzzled her behind the ear as I picked her up to carry her inside.

"Put me down." She laughed. "We'll get to that later. I'm trying to pack."

We were leaving tomorrow for Hawaii. It was our annual two-week LAPD-mandated vacation. I could hardly wait to get away. As usual, we'd timed our vacation periods to coincide, and for fourteen glorious days I'd have no homicides to investigate, no gruesome crime-scene photos or forensic reports to study, no grieving families to console. Only acres of white sand and surf with my gorgeous wife in paradise.

Alexa had worked twelve-hour days for a week to get her office squared away so she could afford the time off. Alexa is a lieutenant and the acting commander of the Detective Division of the LAPD. She's about to make captain, and the job will then be made permanent. That makes her technically my boss. I'm a D3 working out of the elite homicide squad known as Homicide Special, where we handle all of L.A.'s media-worthy, high-profile murders. It's a good gig, but I was feeling burned out and needed some time away.

"Put me down. That's a direct order, Detective," she said, faking her LAPD command voice.

"You can give the orders in that squirrel cage downtown, but at home it's best two out of three falls, and in that outfit, get ready to be pinned."

"You brute. Stop making promises and get to it, then." She kissed me.

I was trying to get the sliding-glass door opened without dropping her: I barely made it, and lugged her across the carpet into the bedroom, which was littered with her resort outfits. It looked like a bomb had gone off in a clothing store. Bathing suits, shorts, and tops scattered everywhere.

"What happened in here?" I said and dropped her on the bed, then dove on top of her.

Sometimes I can't believe how lucky I am to have won her. I'm a scarred, scabrous piece of work with a nose that's been broken too many times and dark hair that never quite lays down. Alexa is so beautiful she takes my breath away. How I ended up with her is one of my life's major mysteries.

I reached for the string tie on her bikini and she rolled right, laughing as I grabbed her arm to pull her back. Just then, the phone rang.

"If that's your office again, I'm gonna load up and clean out that entire floor of gold-braid pussies you work with," I said, only half in jest.

The phone kept blasting us with electronic urgency. It was quickly ruining the moment. Alexa rolled off the bed and snatched it up.

"Yes?" Then she paused. "Who is this?" She hesitated. "Just a minute."

She turned toward me, covering the receiver with

her palm. "You know somebody named Diamond Peterson?"

"No, but if she's related to Diamond Cutter, tell her she's killing her little brother."

"Stop bragging about your wood and take this." Alexa grinned, handing me the phone.

I sat on the side of the bed and put the receiver to my ear.

"Yes? This is Detective Scully."

"You're a police detective?" a female voice said with a slight ghetto accent. She sounded surprised.

"Who is this again?"

"Diamond Peterson. I'm calling from Huntington House Group Home." The mention of the group home shot darkness through me. Memories of that part of my life were negative and confusing. I now only visit them occasionally in dreams.

"How can I help you, Ms. Peterson?" I asked cautiously.

"It's about Walter Dix. Since you're in the police, I assume you've heard."

"Heard what? Is Pop okay?"

"Not hardly." She hesitated, then let out a breath that sounded like a sigh and plunged ahead. "Pop's dead."

A wave of feelings cascaded through me. When they settled, the emotion on top was guilt. I had left Walt and the group home in my rearview mirror decades ago. I had been studiously ignoring the man who had injected the only bit of positive energy into my life growing up—the man to whom I probably owed a large portion of my eventual survival. Pop provided a thread of hope that had been all that was left when I hit rock bottom eight years ago.

Even during my lowest days, because of Pop, I clung to the belief that there was still some good in the world despite the fact that by the time I reached my mid-thirties, I'd managed to find almost none.

It was hard to know the complete mixture of events that had finally led to my salvation. The easy ones to spot were Alexa, and my now-grown son, Chooch, who was attending USC on a football ride. But Pop was also there in a big way. He had somehow convinced me that it was possible to survive a horrible start where I was left unattended in a hospital waiting room, a nameless baby with no parents, who was then shuffled off to a county infant orphanage. Child Protective Services had finally placed me at Huntington House at the age of six, but by then I was already starting to rot from the inside.

It marked the beginning of a life of loneliness, which was only occasionally interrupted by a parade of strangers. Once or twice a year I was forced to put on my best clothes and stand like a slave waiting to be purchased. "This is Shane, he's seven years old. This is Shane, he's nine. This is Shane, he's twelve."

All the rejection, all the rage—Pop had seen me through it with his crinkly smile, the weird seventies surfer lingo, the sunrise surf patrols. "Shane, there's a place for you. You have to be patient." All these years later, it turned out he was right.

But once I'd survived it, I'd turned my back on him. I'd moved on. It was too painful to go back there and revisit that part of my life, so I hadn't. I'd left Pop behind as surely as if I'd thrown him from a moving car.

The memory made me feel small as I stood in our bedroom scattered with Alexa's colorful clothing. I'd been getting ready to run off to paradise but had just been pulled back with one sentence from a woman I didn't know.

"Dead?" I finally managed to say.

"Suicide. He went into his backyard yesterday and blew his head off with a shotgun."

Diamond Peterson was talking softly, trying to mute the devastating news with gentle tonality. It wasn't working. I knew from years of police work in homicide that there is no good way to deliver this kind of information.

My stomach did a turn. I felt my spirits plunge.

"I've been meaning to stop by and see him," I said. It was, of course, completely off the point and pretty much a huge lie.

"He left a note in his desk," she said. "It was written a week before he died. He wanted you to be one of his pallbearers."

CHAPTER 3

DIAMOND PETERSON TOLD me that the funeral was going to be at the old Surfers' Church located on Cliff-side Drive, overlooking the public beach at Point Dume. It was scheduled for the day after tomorrow, when we were planning to be in Hawaii.

I hung up and turned to face Alexa, who could read my devastation. She knew bad news was coming.

"Problems?"

"Yeah." I stood there, trying to get the right words.

"Come on, buddy. Just lay it on me," Alexa said. "Something go wrong with one of your current cases?"

"You remember Walter Dix?"

She frowned slightly, found the memory, and nodded. "From the group home?"

"He's dead."

Her expression changed, saddened by sympathy. "I'm so sorry, Shane. I know how important he was to you growing up."

"Suicide," I said, trying to fit that idea into a mosaic

of things I knew about Pop. Some guys are suicide types—brooders, drinkers, mood flippers, tight winds. Pop was none of those. He was the perennial optimist, a hang-loose guy who loved to laugh.

Even though he ran a foster-care home packed with depressing social casualties, he saw the world as a place of constant opportunity. There was always a party wave out there. He knew it was coming and would be large enough for all of us to ride. He believed in miracles.

He didn't seem to me like someone who would commit suicide. But then, how did I really know? I'd ditched him like a bad date. I hadn't been back there to see him in years. And the few times I did go, I'd been awkwardly subdued. We'd been on the same page when I was a kid, but we struggled to communicate as adults. I'd told myself the reason for this was that all we had in common were bad memories of my childhood, which neither of us wanted to revisit.

This excuse suddenly seemed like an artful dodge to avoid a painful self-evaluation. I suspected the real reason I didn't go was because Walt was a witness to a different Shane Scully, a mean angry bully who I no longer liked. I'd been staying away because he knew about parts of me that I was trying to either eliminate or forget.

If I thought about it, I didn't really know Walter Dix as he was today at all. I knew who he said he was, but sometimes there's a big gap between that and the real thing. Maybe under those crinkly smile lines and the surfer disguise, something darker was hiding. I couldn't trust my recollections as a child and hadn't invested enough interest as a man to have a valid opinion.

"When's the funeral?" Alexa asked, getting to the meat of it before I had a chance to bring up that problem.

"Day after tomorrow."

"You need to go," she said, instantly knocking three days off a vacation we'd carefully planned and had been desperately looking forward to.

"Yeah," I said.

She took a step forward and held my hand. "It's okay, honey. Ten days in paradise is still nothing to complain about. It'll give me time to refine my wardrobe selections."

"He left a note. He wants me to be a pallbearer."

She stood there thinking, remembering the few things I'd told her over the years. "But you . . ."

"Yeah. Shallow, selfish bastard that I am, I've barely talked to him in twenty-five years."

"Come on, Shane, stop it."

My thoughts suddenly started shooting all over the place. The Huntington House home; the early morning surf trips to the beach; toys Pop had bought for us with his own money; coaching our baseball and soccer teams; a sad memory of him sitting next to Theresa Rodriguez's bed one night, holding one of her horribly scarred hands while she cried.

"Where's the funeral?" Alexa said, trying to jog me out of what she could see was a developing funk.

"Surfers' Church in Point Dume. Never been there. She said it was on a cliff overlooking the steeps."

"Steeps?"

"Surfer talk—what Walt called waves. He also called them glass walls, cylinders, the green room. . . . Everything was surf lingo with him." My voice was dulled by emotion.

"How 'bout I fix us a drink? This mess in here can wait. I've got plenty of time to pack now."

She put on a robe, fixed me a light scotch, and got one for herself. We went back outside and sat on the patio. I could still feel remnants of my body heat coming off the iron chair from before. My world had totally shifted before the metal even had time to cool. Things were different. A little piece of my past had been torn out and had just floated away. Some things lost can never be retrieved. I had lost my chance to say thank you, and now all that was left to do was carry Pop's coffin and say good-bye.

Again, Alexa read me. "He understood, Shane."

I turned and looked at her.

"How could he?"

"It wasn't all about you. Some of it was about him."

Of course, she was right about that. But he'd been there for me when it counted and if he was so desperate he'd committed suicide, why had I not been around to know that and repay the favor? I'd been in the military when his wife, Elizabeth, had died. Stationed far away. No help. I sent him cards at Christmas, paid one or two visits. Not enough. But the reason was simple. I just didn't want to go back there. I couldn't. So I rarely had.

Alexa and I sat in silence until the sun went down. I

said very little because I was deep inside my own head. I saw her shiver slightly in a descending ocean mist.

"You go on in. I'll be there in a few minutes."

She got up, kissed the top of my head, and went into the house.

I began letting the thoughts I'd pushed aside for all those years flood back.

I remembered old feelings. The anger, the hatred, the need to strike out and hurt someone. I thought about living in a group home full of angry, similarly rejected children. None of us trusted or liked the others.

There had only been Pop to lean on.

CHAPTER 4

THE CHURCH LOOKED LIKE IT belonged in Mexico. It was white stucco, small, and almost exactly square. It had an old-fashioned steeple with three bells. Ropes attached to the clappers hung down the front face of the building so the bells could be rung by people standing on the ground. A primitive system.

There were about forty surfboards leaning against the outside walls, a silent tribute to Walt from a bunch of long-haired, toes-on-the-nose mourners. Hibiscus and jasmine grew wild in a field overlooking the ocean and choked the little stone path that led up from the dirt parking lot.

The view was spectacular, sitting right on top of Point Dume, just off Cliffside Drive, overlooking the ocean almost a thousand feet below. The three-foot incoming swells were diminished by the height where we stood and from up here looked like tiny ripples heading toward shore. The setting was quaint and beautiful. A perfect place to say good-bye.

I pulled in next to one of several Huntington House vans. There were already about thirty or forty cars, all shapes and sizes parked in the lot—some clunkers, a few pricey models, and a scattering of rusting surf wagons.

Alexa and I got out. I was wearing a black suit and sunglasses. My face felt hot in the afternoon sun. I moved slowly as we walked toward the church and a very dark, African-American woman who appeared to be about twenty-five. She was big-boned—large, but not fat—and wore a black dress with padded shoulders. She had a friendly, if unremarkable, face. As I approached, she put out her hand and flashed a bright smile.

"I'm Diamond," she said. "Hope you're either Shane or Jack."

"I'm Shane." We shook hands. "This is my wife, Alexa."

"Nice to meet you. If that's the right thing to say under such terrible circumstances."

It was always like that at funerals. Even common pleasantries seemed out of place.

"We're having a preservice pallbearers' meeting in the rectory building over there beside the church. There's only one who hasn't showed yet. Hope he doesn't duck out."

"Who's missing?" I asked, thinking maybe it was someone from my days there.

"Jack Straw. He's coming from Long Beach. Do you know him?" I shook my head. "I don't know him either, but like all of us, he once lived at Huntington House and was on Walt's list. He said over the phone that his boss wouldn't let him off 'til noon." She frowned at her watch. "He should have been here by now."

"I'll just go on into the rectory and introduce myself," I said.

"Good. I'll be there as soon as this guy Straw shows."

Just then a shiny, red-and-black, custom Softail Harley came roaring up the hill, pipes blaring. I could tell from the deep growling sound that the engine was a big V-twin. Astride the brightly painted bike, arms outstretched to clutch shoulderwide ape hangers, was a young guy with no helmet, long black hair, dirty jeans, and leathers. Not what I'd choose to wear to a funeral, but Huntington House wasn't exactly an Eastern finishing school, so you had to be ready for anything.

The rider pulled to a stop in the parking lot, put down a foot, shut off the bike, and racked the kickstand. Then he climbed off and walked up the path toward us.

"Jack Straw. Sorry I'm so late," he said, addressing Ms. Peterson. "You look pissed, so you must be Diamond."

She looked at his outfit then flicked her gaze at me. "That's what you're planning on wearing?"

"All I got, Toots." When he smiled, he showed us one gold-boxed tooth in front.

I'm a cop. My job is to read people, and from jump this guy was coming off as dirt. He had a career criminal vibe. If I ran him through the system, I was sure his package would contain a fat list of priors. At least, that was my instant take. He was twenty-eight or thirty and handsome in a greasy, Tommy Lee way. His attitude suggested he thought he was pretty damn hot.

Then he took off his heavy leather biker jacket. Underneath, he had on a white tank. Tattoos covered both arms and confirmed my suspicions—spiderwebs at each elbow, crude drawings, and the names of old girlfriends written on both forearms. A walking billboard. It was mostly prison work, done in that hard-to-miss, strange, green-blue ink that the California penal system uses.

He turned and looked me up and down.

"You a cop?" he asked, making me as quickly as I had just made him. Cops and cons can do that.

"Yeah, but I'm only here as a friend of Walter Dix," I said coldly. "I won't tell your P.O. you skipped out of work early."

"Hey, come on. Don't bake me, dude. I just asked." Then he put his hand out to me, and since I had no choice, I shook it. He turned back to face Diamond.

"I work at a motorcycle shop in Long Beach. My boss is a dick and made me finish a ring job I was doing on a flathead Harley." He looked over at Alexa.

"This is my wife, Alexa," I said. He held his appraisal for a few seconds too long. A frank sexual inventory. He'd made me as a cop quickly, but seemed to have missed the fact that, besides being gorgeous, underneath her simple black sheath Alexa was also LAPD blue. I watched as he mentally undressed her. If Mr. Straw didn't cut it out, he was soon going to be keeping that boxed tooth in a tooth box.

"Let's go inside. We need to pick our spots," Diamond said. "Mrs. Scully, you can wait inside the church. It's starting to fill up, so you better get a seat."

Alexa nodded and moved toward the little chapel.

I followed Diamond Peterson and Jack Straw into the small rectory beside the church. Three other people were waiting. Apparently, there were just going to be the standard six pallbearers.

It was a strange bunch, all veterans of the group home. We were all dressed differently, and all of us were from different time periods at Huntington House.

The oldest was a stocky Hispanic man in his early fifties with a low forehead and a full head of thick black hair, silvering at the temples. He must have been from Walt's early years at the home in the late sixties. He was wearing an inexpensive off-the-rack black suit. His knuckles were scarred and looked like long ago he'd had old gang tattoos removed. They were big bony hands that could hurt you.

He introduced himself as Sabas Vargas and said he was an attorney in East L.A. My guess from the scraped knuckles and the hard-line set of his mouth was that his practice in the barrio probably involved getting vato killers their prison walking papers.

Standing next to him was a woman in her mid-to-late thirties. Trim body, short hair, conservative print dress. She was very mannered, tightly wrapped, and efficient looking. Her name was Victoria Lavicki. Diamond made the introductions and said that Victoria was a CPA with the well-known downtown accounting firm of Kinney and Glass. From her approximate age, I figured we'd probably just missed each other at the home. She said she'd been at Huntington House for six years in the eighties, which was a long stay, but I still held the record.

The last introduction was Seriana Cotton, an imposing specimen about six feet tall and twenty-three years old. She was African American and wore an Army corporal's dress uniform with a row of campaign ribbons. The uniform patch on her shoulder identified her as a soldier in the Third Armored Cavalry Division. Seriana was physically fit and had a no-nonsense demeanor. She was one of those rare women who could accurately be described as handsome. Corporal Cotton did not smile as she met us but said that she was about to return to Iraq for her second tour.

"Okay," Diamond said. "We'll put the men on three of the four corners because that's where the weight is. I need one woman to take the last corner. You look like the best bet, Corporal," she said, smiling at Seriana Cotton.

"I'm good for it, ma'am," Seriana replied.

"Victoria and I will take the middle."

I didn't know who put Diamond Peterson in charge, but she was organized, so no one was complaining.

"You can decide who takes the front and who gets the back, but let's do it now because the service needs to start. Once it's over, the hearse will be waiting out front. Carry the casket out the door and the driver will instruct you on how best to slide it into the hearse. He told me there's rollers in the back to help get it inside."

We spent a minute lining up in our correct places, around an imaginary coffin, then nodded to each other. We were ready.

It was strange looking into their faces. All of them had started right where I had, all had come out someplace completely different. Six graduates of Huntington House. Pop's favorites.

Or at least that's what I thought at the time, even though I couldn't understand why he'd picked me. Why else, I reasoned, would he have wanted the six of us to carry his coffin?

CHAPTER 5

THE CATHOLIC PRIEST WAS Father Mike Leary. He was a surfing buddy of Walt's, and he kept the service loose and unstructured to go with Pop's hang-ten personality. He started with a benediction and a few prayers, then launched right into a free-form discussion.

Memories of Walter Dix. Old surf stories, starting with the one about Pop almost getting eaten by a tiger shark just outside the break at Rincon. After the tiger's first pass, Pop had started stripping off his wet suit, throwing it in the water. The suit ballooned with air and the tiger shark hit it hard, taking it to the bottom.

"That bad boy musta been shitting rubber for a week," our priest joked.

That loosened up the atmosphere and got the ball rolling. One by one, members of the congregation came up and added to the memories.

Jack Straw told a story about stealing candy out of a market two weeks after he was put in Huntington House. Pop found him hiding in his room that night, chowing down. He made Jack go back to the store and stood there while he confessed to the manager, who was so impressed, he gave Jack a part-time job as a box boy.

"After that, I was stealing so much candy, I went into business selling it to the rest of you jerks in the rec center," he joked.

We laughed at the stories. I had no funny stories to add. Pop had saved me, but there was nothing humorous about it. He had done it by steadfastly looking past my anger and giving me support and counsel. So I kept quiet and listened. The service was a trip into the past. Happy memories—pure Walter Dix.

After the stories, Father Leary pulled down a screen and turned on a video projector. Shots of long-ago Christmas parties flickered on white acetate. Lots of little kids sitting around in the rec center while Pop, as Santa, handed out presents.

Then it was Easter-egg hunts on the old dirt athletic field, which I assumed was gone now because Pop had told me on my last visit years ago that it was being replaced with expensive rubberized turf. There were pictures of half a dozen Halloween parties over the years, with twenty or more kids dressed for trick-or-treating. Pop was leading the festivities, an unlikely surfing Elvis in a black wig, high-collared Hawaiian shirt, and board shorts. He was helping kids into the vans to be taken to the rich neighborhoods, where we always went because the candy was safer and more plentiful.

The video shots were cobbled together from years' and years' worth of these events. Some in the chapel were crying at the loss, some were leaning forward, trying to catch glimpses of themselves. In the video, Pop's hair and clothes changed with the years, but he never seemed to get any older. In all of them, he looked just as I remembered him—happy, full of energy, involved in making our lives more bearable. It was hard not to marvel at the energy he had put into us.

One thought kept bugging me. *How could a man so devoted decide to go out into his backyard and blow his head off with a shotgun? How could Pop have done that?*

Alexa must have sensed my mood because she took my hand and squeezed it. I looked over, trying to find myself in all this, trying to come out of it more or less the way I went in. But my betrayal, if that's what it was, kept weighing heavily on me, causing emptiness and reevaluation.

After the service, I got up from the pew and, along with my fellow pallbearers, grasped the chrome rails of the heavy mahogany coffin. We lifted it up off its stand and, while a young man with stringy blond surf hair played a mournful song on the harmonica, carried the flower-laden box slowly out of the crowded church, making our way down the stone path.

I was on the left front, across from the badly dressed Jack Straw in his frayed tank top. I was keeping my eyes up, trying to give Walt's last journey the respect that I'd failed to provide during his life.

We stopped at the hearse, and under the instructions of the black-suited driver, Jack and I set the leading edge of the coffin into a chrome tray on rollers. We then stepped aside as the next two behind us pushed the box into the shiny, humpbacked black Cadillac. Seriana Cotton and Sabas Vargas pushed the back end of the coffin into the hearse and stood with the rest of us as the driver closed the door.

"That's it," Diamond said. "There's no graveside service, so we don't go to the cemetery." She handed each of us a slip of paper. A computer printed invitation that read:

Please join us in celebration of a magnificent life.

"There's a reception following this back at Huntington House," she said. Then for some reason she turned to me and asked, "Do you need a map to find it?"

I didn't know if it was a cold shot or just a friendly question.

"I can find it," I said stiffly. "I lived there on and off for ten years."

I could see one or two others up by the steps also handing out invitations as the rest of the mourners left the church.

"See you there," Diamond said to all of us.

I said good-bye to my fellow pallbearers and headed with Alexa to our car.

We were just getting inside when I heard a woman call my name. I turned. Theresa Rodriguez was hurrying across the lot toward us.

"It's Terry," she said, as if anyone could ever forget that face.

"Hey, Terry. God, it's so good to see you," I responded, trying to enjoy the reunion, although back then we'd not been close. Back then, I made no effort to know anyone. I leaned forward, and, for the first time in our lives, we hugged. She felt thin under her dark-green pantsuit. She'd always been skinny, and in thirty years, that hadn't changed.

"This is my wife, Alexa," I said, nodding to Alexa. "Terry and I were in Huntington House together."

"Old buddies, then," Alexa said, smiling, not reacting at all to Terry's melted face. In twenty-five years, because of her scars, Theresa Rodriguez hadn't changed or aged. She looked just as hideous today as she always had.

"You going to the reception?" I asked.

"Yeah." For the first time since I'd known her, I realized that under all that scar tissue her brown eyes were dark and richly beautiful. *Why had I never noticed that before?* Then she said, "You're a cop now, right?"

"Yes, Terry. I am."

"Somebody inside said you work in homicide."

"That's right."

"You believe this suicide nonsense?"

I looked at her, trying to come up with just the right answer. I felt myself hovering on the edge of something. I felt Hawaii slipping slowly away.

"Hard to say," I hedged.

"I think it's bogus," she stated flatly.

I thought about it, not giving her much more than my street-hard cop face.

"Pop wouldn't voluntarily take a sand ride," she said.

"We don't know that, Terry."

She stood right in front of me, her scarred face making her expression impossible to read.

"What are you doing now?" I asked to change the subject.

"I work for Child Protective Services. Never got out of the system. I'm trying to make it better for the ones that follow."

"That's very cool," I said. "Well, see you at the reception, I guess."

"Okay, see you there," she answered.

I got into the car next to Alexa, feeling the heat from the sun-cooked interior. I was still struggling to gather my feelings. To put them back in some kind of order.

"What's a sand ride?" Alexa asked, interrupting my thoughts.

"It's a shore break that slams you down on the beach. Surfers call it unassisted suicide."

"Oh," Alexa said. She waited as I sat there thinking about what Theresa had just said. Then I started the car and drove us out of there.

CHAPTER 6

THE FEW TIMES I'D GONE BACK to visit the Huntington House before, I'd had the same reaction. It always looked smaller and grimier than I remembered. My room had been on the second floor of Sharon Cross Hall, a big two-story Spanish house on the east side of the four-acre campus. I didn't know why it was called Sharon Cross Hall. I had never bothered to ask.

When I was a kid, the hall had seemed huge and imposing, looming majestically over my head. Now it just looked like a plain but badly maintained house that needed a new roof and rain gutters.

The athletic field had always been dirt and I'd acquired an impressive collection of skin burns sliding around on it. As I walked the campus after the funeral, I'd been expecting to see the new rubberized turf that Pop had told me about. It wasn't there. The same dirt playground greeted me. It also looked much smaller than I remembered.

Diamond led the five other pallbearers and Alexa on

a short tour of the grounds. Nothing had changed but my recollections.

"What happened to the field?" I asked as we stepped out onto the hard dirt baseball diamond. "Pop told me you were putting in rubberized turf."

"Pop always had his dreams," Diamond said sadly. "You know how he was. We couldn't afford stuff like that. There was no money to even run this place. It's been a struggle month to month."

Shortly after we arrived at the reception, I found out from one of the other mourners why Diamond Peterson was put in charge of the funeral. It turned out that she was the current secretary-treasurer of Huntington House. After two years as a foster child here, she'd been taken by a family that eventually adopted her. She graduated from a high school in the Valley and had gone on to community college, where she took sociology. Diamond told us she'd stayed in touch with Pop and wanted to help him, so she'd come back and, for the last six years, had been working on staff. Pop made her the secretary-treasurer two years ago. It was a paid appointed position that, according to the California Department of Social Services, didn't require any special certifications or accounting degrees.

We walked through the milling mourners and finally rounded the corner of the boxy, gym-sized, seventies-era addition known as the rec center. The bungalow that had always served as the office used to sit behind the recreation building, but now all that was left was a charred hulk. The fire looked recent. Ash and debris were everywhere.

"What happened here?" Jack Straw asked as we looked at the small house, now burned to the foundation.

"It accidentally caught fire the same day Pop died. He was so distressed, I guess he must have . . ." Diamond stopped, then changed her thought. "I guess we don't really know what happened."

I looked over at Alexa. She didn't give me much, and, like me, she had on her cop face. She was thinking what I was thinking. *Too many bad things in one time and place.* It was starting to look like more than a suicide and accidental fire. It made us both suspicious.

Diamond must've picked up the vibe, because she quickly added, "The arson investigators haven't quite finished. We don't know yet if it was deliberately set."

"Really?" It was the first time Sabas Vargas spoke since the tour began. But that one word was packed with skepticism. "I wonder if this is connected to why he called me," he added.

"He called you?" I asked the middle-aged Hispanic man. "You do criminal law, right?"

"Yeah. But he called a couple a days before all this happened. He wanted to have a meeting. He wouldn't tell me what it was about. I assumed he wanted a donation for the home. We set it up for next week."

Why would Pop call a criminal lawyer? I wondered.

"Pop didn't do this," Vicki Lavicki said, refuting his unstated accusation. She was standing with her arms crossed defensively, glaring. "He loved this place. He wouldn't burn it down. That's pure bullshit."

"Nobody said he did," Sabas Vargas said softly. "But

come on, the office burns and he kills himself on the same day? Maybe he was so depressed he just snapped."

"What if the office accidentally burning was like the last straw that pushed Pop over the edge?" Vicki challenged, glaring at him. "Ever think of that?"

"He's dead," Diamond said, heaving a sad sigh. "Even if he did set this fire, who are you gonna prosecute? I'm trying to get the arson investigators to do us a favor and just close it. We desperately need the insurance check."

I looked over and noticed Seriana Cotton standing next to Jack Straw. They were wearing flip sides of the same expression. Seriana had a slight frown, Jack a slight smile. Both expressions said, "What the hell is going on here?"

We went into the rec center, where the staff had set up three card tables with refreshments. It was a meager feast. Cheese squares with Triscuits and Dixie cups half full of supermarket wine.

After an hour, Alexa wanted to leave. Because we'd pushed our trip back, she said she had a few more things to do at Parker Center downtown. But I wasn't ready to go just yet, so I told her to take the car. I'd get back to Venice some other way.

Vicki Lavicki was standing nearby and overheard us. "I live in the Marina," she said. "I could drop you, Shane. I go right by there."

"Sounds good," I told her and handed Alexa the keys to my MDX.

"You sure?" Alexa said.

I could tell she really wanted to get me out of there.

She could see I was still beating myself up. I smiled at her brightly. Since we were locked in this mild marital deception in front of a witness, there was nothing Alexa could do but agree to leave me there.

"I just need a little more time," I said.

She nodded and, ten minutes later, took my car and left.

I don't know what I was thinking, what I was looking for, but like Sabas Vargas, I didn't believe the story here was as simple as it sounded. Or was I just trying to play catch up, making myself feel useful after it was really too late to help Pop at all?

I found Diamond Peterson by the serving table and asked if I could have a minute. We walked out of the building and sat on one of the wood benches that lined the athletic field.

"You really think Pop set fire to the office bungalow?" I asked.

"No," she said softly. "I can't imagine that. Besides, if Pop did this, if he intentionally set the fire, then we won't get the insurance. He wouldn't do that because he knew we desperately need that money."

"So who did it then?"

"I don't know. Maybe nobody. Maybe it was bad wiring. The arson cops couldn't find an accelerant or even isolate a point of origin. The building was wood. It went up fast."

We looked out at the sad, ramshackle campus of Huntington House Group Home. It was run down, but stumbling on. Tattered, limping, fiscally unhealthy. The evidence of neglect was everywhere. In the poor condition of the rusting vans parked out front, in the deferred maintenance that was visible all around us.

"This place looks terrible," I finally said.

"Yeah." Then Diamond's lip started quivering, and she put her head in her hands and began to cry. I put my hand on her shoulder and then held her as her large body was wracked with sobs. Finally, she struggled to pull herself together. We sat and waited until she was back under control.

"Sorry," she said.

"Don't be."

"I don't know what to do anymore," she admitted. "We have so many problems."

"Tell me."

"I don't know how much you know about how the foster-care system works."

"Almost nothing. When I was here, I was pretty locked up. It was just about me."

She looked at me, tears still on her cheeks. Then she rubbed them angrily away, took a deep breath to settle herself down, and began.

"Okay, well, starting at the beginning, you probably know Walt doesn't own this place anymore. After Elizabeth died it was taken over by a nonprofit corporation that kept him on as the paid executive director. Huntington House is currently owned by an outfit called Creative Solutions. Creative Solutions gets money for each child in residence here, then deposits the funds into our account and acts as a short-term bank for us if we run low. But we have to zero out with them at the end of each fiscal year. Also, the amount a group home gets per child can vary greatly."

"How's that work?"

"There's something called an RCL, which stands for Rate Classification Level. It's given by the California Department of Social Services and it's made up of a lot of stuff. How well-maintained the home is, the ratio of staff to children, how many staff have advanced degrees, rate of foster-home placement or adoption . . . all kinds of things."

She looked right into my eyes. "The higher the RCL, the more the state pays. It can go from as low as four thousand a child per month to in excess of six."

She struggled again to hold back her tears. "Walt was such a dreamer," she continued. "Like him telling you we were gonna get that Astroturf, or rubberized grass, whatever the hell. That was gonna cost us over two hundred thousand to buy and install. There was no way we could afford that.

"We'd been getting almost six thousand per child, but then we lost Dr. Logan to a better job, and our clinical psychologist quit to have a baby. We were running short of money from the state. I know six thousand a month for each kid sounds like a lot, but there's a lot to maintain. There's plain overhead—staff salaries, insurance, food, schoolbooks, medical . . . it goes on and on.

"Anyway, we didn't want our RCL lowered, so we stupidly didn't report the drop in staff positions to the CDSS. Two of the staff we lost had doctorates and that figured big in our high RCL rating. At the same time, we lost one or two other people, so our staff-to-child ratio took a big hit as well. We were trying to keep it a secret 'til we worked our way out of it.

"Then, last Christmas, they retroactively lowered our RCL and the state auditor came after us. They demanded a repayment check of almost half a million dollars. We didn't have it. Worse still, with our lowered RCL, we went from six thousand to four thousand per child. This place just couldn't run on that.

"Like I said, Creative Solutions is a nonprofit and didn't want to take the loss. They were thinking about closing the home. Just a few days before Pop died, the California Department of Social Services notified us that because of us not telling them the truth about our staff changes, they'd become suspicious of everything and CDSS was about to do a full audit. Walt knew there were even more problems that a state audit would discover. He just couldn't deal with it."

"And that's why he burned the office before he committed suicide," I said. "To destroy the records?"

"Maybe." She wiped another slow-moving tear away. "I don't know. I don't want to believe he'd burn this place. I also don't want to believe he'd kill himself."

"Me neither."

"But what can we do about it?" she said, shrugging her shoulders in a gesture of defeat.

"Let me mull it over. I'll come up with something."

Good-bye Waikiki.

CHAPTER 7

HALF AN HOUR LATER, I FOUND myself on the second floor of Sharon Cross Hall, looking into my old room at a scowling black kid who was about nine. He was sitting on a bunk holding a first-baseman's glove and wearing his Little League uniform. Across his chest, it said "Astros."

"Looks like you had a game," I said.

"My team had a game. I didn't get there 'cause all the vans were at the funeral. They wouldn't let the young kids go to the church to see Pop off. Some county shrink thought it was bad for our emotional development."

I wandered into the room and he stood up immediately. He didn't want me in here. His posture was confrontational, even menacing.

"This is my crib, Chuck," he said. It wasn't quite a threat because I outweighed him by a buck fifty. Call it a statement of fact, fiercely delivered.

"This used to be my room a long time ago," I told him, trying to ease the tension with some common ground. "Lemme show you something." I walked over to the painted wood cabinet. I opened it and looked for some words I'd carved in the paint on the back of the door over a quarter of a century ago. Of course they weren't there anymore. I looked over at the Astros' first baseman. "Guess it got sanded off," I said stupidly. "It used to say, 'Fuck everybody. S. S.' S. S. is me, Shane Scully."

"Fact that you lived in this room ain't nothing to brag about," he said sourly. "Just tells me you're another fucked-up loser like the rest of us."

I let that go and turned to face him. "So how 'bout you?" I asked.

"How 'bout me, what?"

"You think Pop killed himself?"

"No way."

"You seem sure."

"Hey, Scully . . . That's what you called yourself?"

I nodded and he continued. "Only cowards take that ride. Pop was no coward. 'Sides, he's been helpin' me look for my real people. My mom and shit. Two years we been doin' it. He even spent some of his own money on a lawyer guy who wrote up some papers. We were gonna make the court tell us where I came from. He wouldn't check out, leaving me holding dirt."

I nodded. "Probably not."

I turned to go, then stopped in the door and looked back. "What's your name?"

"What's it to you?" he scowled. " 'Cause I don't need no new friend. Friends are just people who hang on ya and drag ya down."

I left the little cynic standing there. He was a living, breathing example of my own anger when I was his age. The Little League player in my old room had finally pushed me over the edge. I was now absolutely ready to get away from here.

I started looking for Vicki Lavicki to take me home and found out from Diamond that she'd received a call and had to leave.

"How do I get home then?" I wondered aloud.

"She set up another ride for you before she left," Diamond informed me.

"Who's that?"

"That'd be me, dude," a voice said.

I turned and found Jack Straw standing right behind me, grinning insolently.

CHAPTER 8

I FOLLOWED STRAW INTO THE parking lot and over to his red and black Harley Softail.

"You know how to ride one of these?" he asked.

"I've ridden Harleys," I told him.

"No helmets. Sorry, but with you being Five-O, I'm figuring, we don't get busted."

"That what you're figuring?"

He smiled, giving me another look at the boxed front tooth.

"Venice, right?"

"Yeah."

"Lotta freaks live in Venice," he said, straddling the bike and straightening the ape hangers as he stuck the key in the ignition just above the gas tank.

"They got worse freaks in CCI," I replied. "At least in Venice you don't have to shower with your back to the wall."

"What makes you think I was in California Corrections?" he asked, smiling slightly.

"Don't tempt me, Jack."

He laughed and said, "Okay. Hop on then."

I got on the bike behind him and told him, "Quickest way is to take the 110 to the 405 and get off on Venice Boulevard."

"Just hold on and try not to fall off. I'll get us there." Then he jacked the starter.

He ignored my instructions completely and took side streets almost all the way to Venice. The Pacific Ocean stayed on our left, winking in and out of view as we headed northwest. I leaned back on the chickie stick to keep his long hair from flapping in my face and tried to enjoy the ride. But Jack was having fun with me and kept swerving abruptly to pass cars so I had to grab on to him or the seat rail. Occasionally when he turned the ape hangers, I could see him in the handlebar mirror. He was either smiling or trying to catch bugs in his teeth.

We finally made it to my house in Venice. He pulled into the alley in back, then shut down the bike and dismounted. I climbed off and straightened my rumpled suit jacket.

"How 'bout a beer?" he said, inviting himself in.

"What'd you do your time for?" I asked.

"Home invasion. Couple a armed robberies. I pled them out and both got kicked down to straight burgs."

"And you think I'm gonna invite you into my house?"

"Listen, Scully. If I was gonna rob a place, I wouldn't choose some clapboard shoe box on a sewage canal."

I could see that Alexa hadn't made it home yet because the MDX wasn't in the drive. She was still at Parker Center polishing her already-clean desk. She's compulsive about her job. Even so, I didn't want to invite Jack Straw inside. I'd had more than enough of him already.

"Thanks for the ride, but I've got stuff to do."

"Pop didn't gonk himself. You know it. I know it. Anybody who knew him knows it. This is bullshit."

"Okay," I said. "You through?"

"No."

He pocketed his keys and walked around his bike. "Gimme ten minutes to make my case, then I'll book."

"Shit," I said softly, but after taking a moment to think it over, I relented and led him to the front door.

We went inside and I left him in the entry but kept an eye on him while I got two beers from the fridge in the kitchen. Then we walked through the house and out into the backyard. He followed me, his neck on a swivel, looking around, checking the place out.

"You're right. Lotta pricey shit here. I love the papier-mâché Mexican dolls in the living room. Where'd you buy those, Sotheby's?"

I handed him a beer. "You're on the clock, Jack." I pointedly looked at my watch.

"Jesus, Scully. Ease up. I haven't even removed this twist-off cap."

"What joint?" I asked. "Where'd you cell up?"

"Soledad. Got six years, gavel to gravel. Only did four. Two years were knocked off for good time. That's what I wanted to talk to you about. Pop helped me get out. He was on my parole sheet. He's the one who got me the job at the cycle shop in Long Beach so I'd qualify for early release.

"I have a one-month hearing coming up with my P.O. next week. Guy's a real Barney. Walt was gonna go to my parole evaluation hearing and do my character stuff. We talked the day before he supposedly blew his head off. The man was not suicidal, okay? No way he went out in his backyard and did the Dutch. He was upbeat. He told me things were getting better at Huntington House. He sounded real pleased about something. Wouldn't tell me what, but he was flying, man."

"Ever heard of extreme mood swings?"

Straw put down the beer and looked out at the canal.

"This is kinda restful back here. How does a guy who lives in such a peaceful setting get such a puckered asshole?"

"Okay, I guess that's it then." I started for the sliding-glass porch door to show him out, but Jack held his ground.

"Hey, Scully. Answer me one thing. If you won't do it for me, then do it in Pop's memory."

"What?"

"You're a cop. You know how this is gonna come out. The burn squad will say he torched the office or whatever, then killed himself 'cause that closes the case so they can get it off their desk and move on. You can't really think that's what happened."

"Apparently there was a state audit coming. Money was missing. That's what Diamond thinks."

"I don't care what Diamond thinks. I want to know what you think."

"I don't know what I think."

"You're kinda close to the vest, ain't ya?" He smiled. "Or maybe you're just a pussy."

"Yeah, maybe that's it." I took a step closer.

He backed up and put his hands out saying, "Come on, let's try to be adults here."

He picked up his beer, almost draining it in one shot. Then he looked at me.

"So now we got Pop, the embezzler who sets fire to the office bungalow to burn the evidence of his crimes, then kills himself with a shotgun. What's next, child rape?"

"Okay," I admitted reluctantly. "I agree it feels wrong."

He nodded. "So we just say, too bad. Let the fucking cops pin this fire on him. Blow the home's insurance policy away. Whatever Arson says, that's it?"

I couldn't answer him. I just stood there feeling impotent.

"You're a cop, man. You could . . . y'know, raise some questions, make some trouble. I asked around at the church. Talked to some scary-looking chick. Theresa Gonzales."

"Rodriguez."

He nodded. "She said back then, you were a scowling, ugly presence with five or six throw backs. No chance you'd ever make it in life. Look at what you got now. I don't have to ask if Pop had anything to do with it, 'cause I knew the man. You owe him, dude. Why don't you fucking pay up?"

He pinned me with hard gray eyes.

"Okay," I said. "Here's why I can't do anything. The

police already investigated. They didn't find evidence pointing to anything but suicide. The city medical examiner did an autopsy of the body. Same result. Coroner listed it as a probable suicide. There was a suicide note sealing the deal.

"The body was released for burial with the classification self-inflicted gunshot—'death by his own hand.' No homicide number was assigned by the department, so there is no crime. Unless Arson finds a crime and puts a burn number on it, there's nothing to investigate.

"I'm a homicide detective, but I can't work a case unless the department assigns it a number. What about this don't you get? No homicide number—no case. Got it? I start messing with this I'll get gigged."

"Bunch a words," Jack said.

"You wanta get outta here, now?"

"Sure."

He picked up his leather jacket, slung it over his tattooed shoulder, and then walked back through the house. I heard the front door slam. The Harley growled and roared away.

I stayed in the backyard for a long time after he left, just sitting there while I waited for Alexa to get home. She made it just before dinner and came outside to find me in my chair, looking in the direction of the ocean two city blocks away. In my mind I'd been picturing Walt out there waiting for that perfect set, searching for just the right steep. In my memory I saw him in the curl, shuffling up to the nose of his old cigar-box board in that weird Quasimodo stance of his, hair flying, riding the down rail. Why the hell had I deserted him?

"You okay?" Alexa asked.

"Can't go to Hawaii," I said sadly. "I've gotta stay here and work on this."

CHAPTER 9

ALEXA MUST HAVE SEEN IT coming. She didn't argue or try to change my mind. Instead, she put her arms around me and pulled me close. I was choked up with emotion, not handling it well. She could feel my heavy breathing and maybe sensed I was close to tears.

So much of this was complicated in a way that I couldn't even describe. You can cut yourself some slack as a child because all children start out being selfish. But you want to believe something better of yourself as a man.

I understood why I was so angry when I was at Huntington House. I even understood why I'd had the feelings I'd had about not wanting to go back there. But that didn't excuse the fact that I hadn't gone. Sometimes in life you have to make hard choices. There's going to be some pain along the way.

Alexa held me for a while, then she brought us each a beer.

"You've had two already. Might as well go all the way," she said, handing me a fresh bottle.

"I only had one." Then I saw Jack's empty sitting on the glass-topped table. "Oh, that. That was that biker guy, Jack Straw. He ended up bringing me home on his chopper. What a fuckhead."

"You gonna run him?" she asked me, knowing as surely as I did that he was dirty.

"He already told me he got sentenced to a long nickel for burglary. Went to Soledad. Got out in four."

"Figures." She sat beside me and held my hand. We sipped the beers.

"What'd you think of Huntington House?" I finally asked.

"Truthfully?"

"No, I want you to lie to me."

"I thought it looked pretty shabby."

"They were having money problems."

I told her what Diamond said, including the suspicion that Pop had set the office on fire to cover up records of missing funds. When I got through, she sat there thinking.

"It sounds to me like he could have burned down that bungalow," she finally said. "I know you don't want to hear that, but it's certainly a possibility."

"Yeah, it's gotta be looked at," I agreed, trying not to let her see my eyes, keeping my head turned away, not trusting what I might do or say.

Then, because I wanted to change the subject and because Alexa is one of the best I ever met on cold reads, I asked, "Give me your take on the other five pallbearers."

"Why?"

"I'm trying to understand why Walt picked me. I had barely spoken to him in years and yet, out of hundreds of kids who lived in that place, I'm one of six."

"I've got a take on that."

"Let's hear it, 'cause I'm completely lost."

"Five of the six of you share one major and very uncommon trait." She looked at me. "This is just instinct, so treat it for what it is."

I nodded.

"You're kamikazes. Nonconformists who aren't worried about actions that might cause a bad result. You're also all uncompromising and stubborn."

"That's it?"

"Give me a psychologist and two weeks, I'll flesh it out for you. This is after only a few hours, not really trying." She smiled. "Of course, the biker is easy. Straw wouldn't follow a stripper upstairs after a lap dance. Complete renegade."

"Agreed."

"The Army corporal, Seriana Cotton, never smiled, and those eyes were always evaluating, always adding and subtracting. Her eyes are just like yours sometimes. She's armor plated. She'll take orders, but not blindly. She'd rather follow her own counsel. That's you, buddy."

"And Vargas?"

"The lawyer?" I nodded. "Rarely talks, never shows you what he's thinking. But when he does speak, he's willing to say the unpopular stuff. Vicki La whatever her name is . . ."

"Lavicki."

"She looks like a summer pastry in her little print dress and sensible shoes, but that's one very tough brass cupcake. She'll cut you no quarter. She will go down swinging, Shane Scully style.

"Diamond Peterson is the only one who doesn't fit. She's a den mother. But she worked with Pop, so she probably got there on a pass."

"You're saying, except for Diamond, they're all like me?"

"Not exactly. But they share your trait of suspicious nonconformity. You're all walk alones who don't mind breaking the pottery."

I thought about that for a long time.

"Comments?" she said, looking over at me.

"I guess I can see it," I said. "So why did he pick us?"

"I don't know. Maybe he wanted you to do just what you're doing. Study this and wonder. Maybe, for some reason, he didn't want a bunch of organization drones carrying his coffin."

We sat there for a while longer. Then she said, "You want me to make you something for dinner? I got the makings in there for a great casserole."

"I looked in the fridge. Cheese and noodles isn't a great casserole."

She slapped my arm playfully. "Stop complaining. We were going to Hawaii so I didn't go to the market. At least it's not peanut butter and jelly." Then she got up and went inside.

I wondered if that was it. Pop knew us better than most. He'd been there when the raw material was being molded. He knew how hard our centers were. We'd all known him well and none of us thought he'd committed suicide because it wasn't in his DNA. Pop just wouldn't shotgun his head off alone in his backyard. He was a party-wave guy. As Theresa had said, he wouldn't take a sand ride.

Did he pick me because I was such a stubborn uncompromising son of a bitch that I would never let go of this even if everything and everybody told me to? Was that the endearing quality that had earned me a place at his coffin rail?

Had he chosen four of the other five for the same reason?

It seemed pretty far-fetched. Pretty mystical. Anything with more than a ten percent bugga-bugga factor usually had me laughing, but I wasn't laughing tonight. Tonight I wondered if Walt was stuck in some heaven rip, backwalling beyond the break, watching and waiting for the six of us to do something.

I wondered if we were supposed to somehow avenge his death so he could ride that big rhino out of limbo and finally make it back to shore.

CHAPTER 10

THE MEDICAL EXAMINER'S OFFICE is on North Mission Road, not far from Parker Center. It's located on the top two floors of an ugly rectangular building that always reminds me of a large cement shoe box.

I pulled into the lot at seven the next morning and looked for Ray Tsu's brown Toyota. I'd already called ahead and found out that Ray's ME section had done the police autopsy on Walter Dix.

Ray is one of three chief coroners working under the L.A. medical examiner. He currently supervises the midnight to eight shift, which is the busy one because most murders occur after midnight. After his shift ends, Ray usually goes to breakfast. That's why I was down here so early.

I spotted his car on the east side of the lot in a marked row of spaces reserved for the ME's staff, so I parked in visitors and went inside.

Mission Road is not one of my favorite places, but a lot of my favorite police work gets done here. It's the morbid pall that overhangs a building devoted solely to death that always pulls me down.

I called upstairs from reception and offered to buy Ray breakfast if he'd bring a photocopy of the Dix file with him. No crime had supposedly been committed, so I didn't think he would have a problem sharing the death report. Ray did, however, ask me why.

"Walter Dix ran the group home where I was raised as a foster kid," I told him over the lobby phone. "We buried him yesterday and a lot of the people who also grew up there didn't believe he would kill himself. I told them I'd look at the file. Get some kind of closure for us or something," trying to low key it.

"Where will we be dining?" Ray said in his soft, almost effeminate voice.

"How about the Breakfast Bagel?" I suggested because it was close and cheap.

"How about the Pacific Dining Car?"

"Jesus, Ray. You seen the prices on the menu there?"

"You want a cheap date, call Hairy Mary in forensics." He paused, then asked, "You want this file or not?"

"God, you're such a whore."

"Be right down."

Ray was a rare piece of meat, a rail-thin Chinese American with fine black hair, which he wore long and parted in the middle, tucked behind each ear. A hairstyle that always reminded me of tie-back drapes. He spoke in such a soft voice that he'd been nicknamed Fey Ray by the homicide detectives who dealt with him.

But Ray knew his stuff. He'd started out as a crime-scene criminalist, then went to medical school. He now supervised a staff of ten medical examiners and dieners. But Ray wasn't content to be an office jock. He was a devoted cutter who, despite his management position, still did a good bit of table work.

We snagged a booth at the back of the original Pacific Dining Car on 6th Street, which is a great L.A. landmark restaurant, close enough to the downtown financial center to be a stockbroker hangout. The interior is done in red leather with green upholstered walls and brass fixtures. A polished oak bar dominates the Grill Room, where we were seated.

Ray Tsu didn't weigh much more than a hundred pounds, but he ordered a big enough breakfast for two or three NFL linemen.

"You planning on brown-bagging that to nibble on throughout the week?" I groused.

"I'll get it all down, just watch."

After our food came we got around to Walt's autopsy.

"It was a standard do-it-yourself shooting," Ray said between bites of steak, hash browns, and eggs. He slid the file across the table to me. "Of course, unless we have video or pictures of the actual capping, we can only call it a probable. But there was nothing that indicated any unusual circumstances."

I opened the file and thumbed through the ME's pictures of Pop. He was laid out on an autopsy table under harsh lights with half of his head missing. I'd seen plenty of similar shots over the years, but these knotted my stomach and shot a bolt of emotional guilt through me.

"You did this one yourself?" I asked, putting the photos aside and looking at ten pages of small print and Latin medical phrases.

"No. We usually give our newbies the slam dunks, which include most of the obvious suicides like this one."

He reached over and spun the file around so he could read it. "This was done by Barbara Wilkes. She's only been with us for six months, but she's thorough. Does great work."

"So I won't have to translate all this Latin, give me the top line."

Ray looked down at the report. "Twelve-gauge shotgun blast took the back of the deceased's head. The load hit him on the right side at the mastoid bone. The weapon was a Winchester Speed Pump Defender with an eighteen-inch barrel registered to Walter Dix. It was found on the grass just off the back porch, lying at a forty-degree angle, barrel away from the back of the chair he was on, which was tipped over with him still in it. He was holding the Winchester with his extended right hand, the barrel resting on his shoulder, head turned away. When the shotgun kicked, it threw itself over his right shoulder, onto the back lawn behind him. That would be the correct general position for what this looks like. He turned his mastoid area and the back of his head into red sauce and pasta. Blew his arithmetic all over the grass."

I winced and Ray smiled sadly.

"Sorry. Forgot you were his friend. He obliterated everything from his brain stem to the left side of his skull at the occipital bone. No other way to say it."

"Okay. How about the body cavity? Any blunt-force trauma?"

"No evidence that he was beaten before he died, if that's your question. No body contusions, bruises, or bone breaks. The blood-tox screen was normal—no drugs or alcohol. The homicide dicks have a file with his suicide note. I looked at it before I assigned Barbara to the autopsy. The standard 'Sorry, but I can't go on, my life is over' riff but full of surf lingo." He looked down at his ME report. "It was investigated by Kovacevich and Cole. It's not on here, but I think they said they were on the homicide desk over in Shootin' Newton."

I couldn't understand why Newton Division homicide dicks would answer a call in Harbor City, which is out of their basic car area, but I didn't argue. I'd check that myself.

"It reads as a straight suicide, Shane," Ray continued. "Guy did himself in."

I sat thinking about this while Tsu shoveled down his entire breakfast as promised. I had no appetite, so I'd only ordered a fruit plate, but hadn't touched it.

"You want that?" Fey Ray asked softly, pointing with his knife at my still-pristine plate of sliced grapefruit, strawberries, and oranges.

"Help yourself," I offered.

He pulled it over and dug in but was glancing up at me from time to time while he ate, checking me out.

"Listen, Shane. Nobody knows what goes through another guy's mind. You remember Richard Jeni?"

"The comedian?"

"Yeah. I did his postmortem. One of the funniest

comics ever. Seemed like a happy guy. Sense of humor like you wouldn't believe. The guy was a total rip, but, despite that, he did himself. Tragic. You can't judge by outward appearances. I've seen too many of these that seem wrong on the surface but aren't. You and your friends should let it go."

"Yeah," I finally said. "You're probably right."

After breakfast, I drove Ray back to Mission Road and dropped him.

I kept Walt's death report on the seat beside me.

CHAPTER 11

OF COURSE, I WASN'T GOING to just let it go as Ray had suggested. The LAPD is worse than a sewing circle when it comes to gossip, so I didn't tell him what I was really thinking. I didn't want anybody to know yet, but I was on a mission.

I drove the short distance to Parker Center, parked in my assigned space in the underground garage, then took the elevator up to five.

"What are you doing here? You're supposed to be pulling little umbrellas outta fruit drinks," my partner, Sally Quinn, said as I draped my jacket over the back of my chair and sat behind the desk opposite her in our cramped cubicle at Homicide Special.

Sally doesn't look anything like a cop. She looks like she should be teaching kindergarten or first grade. Short, bobbed, reddish-brown hair, a pixie nose. But she's a no-nonsense hard charger. We've only been partnered for a couple of years, but despite one rough spot last year, we were turning into a good team because she's smart, diligent, and follows the rules, which helps balance out my long list of negative traits.

"Not going," I told her as I turned on my computer and waited for it to boot up.

"Not going?" She leaned forward. "Everything okay? Alexa's not sick or anything?"

"Something came up. A business problem. Unfortunately I gotta stick around to deal with it."

"You know once you put in, you can't move vacation time, Shane," fighting to protect my two weeks off. "If you don't go now, you lose it. You can't push it back or change it."

"Don't want me around, Sal?" I said, grinning. "Gonna get a gold shield by clearing all our head-scratch whodunits without me?"

"Come on, that's not it and you know it. Homicide can dark you out. You need to get some fresh air, hear some music."

"How 'bout if I promise to take a quick trip down to Disneyland and listen to some elves singing?"

"Shane, what the hell is going on? And don't give me this 'something came up, business problem' bullshit. I'm your partner, man. I can read you."

She studied me over the top of her computer screen as I logged onto mine, went into the department assignment roster, and found the two primaries who had handled Walt's death call.

Cassie Kovacevich and Burtram Cole were not from Newton, as I suspected, but were detectives out of the Harbor Division in our South Bureau, which patrols Harbor City, where Huntington House is located. I wrote down their badge numbers and logged off the computer. When I looked up, Sally was still staring at me.

I knew she wasn't going to go away. She knew I was up to something and wasn't about to let it drop. An unhealthy moment of distrust festered between us. Since I knew she wouldn't leak and I was probably going to need somebody who could handle the inside if this got rolling, I decided it was better to confide in her.

I stood and motioned for her to follow me out into the corridor. We walked across the crowded squad room, past the cubicles of paired detective teams. I finally stopped in a nook by the windows out in the lobby, just around the corner from the elevators.

"Okay, look, you're right. It's not a business problem. I'm not going to Hawaii because a guy who was very close to me, a father figure growing up, committed suicide four days ago. The funeral was yesterday."

"I'm sorry to hear that, Shane. But if he's buried, what's to keep you from taking your vacation?"

"I'm not reading his death as self-inflicted."

"Murder?"

"I don't know."

"Shane, it's not your case. You can't work it. You'll piss off the primaries. You'll take a write-up from their captain. You know how territorial this place is. Where'd this happen?"

"Two detectives out of Harbor got the squeal, but they didn't look at it too hard and put it in as a suicide. Coroner agrees so nobody's got it now. There's nobody to piss off 'cause it doesn't even have a case number. A perfect vacation murder project," I joked.

She wasn't laughing but had rocked back on her heels and was looking at me like I'd just grown antlers.

"I know, I know. But you had to know this guy," I said. "He wouldn't a killed himself."

"Shane, I don't . . ."

"Sally, you can either help me, or you can get in my way. I've already decided to peel this wrapper. I may need somebody in here to lob information out to me if I can't get in. Wanta sign up to be my inside guy?"

"You mean you don't want to show up here and leave a computer trail alerting anybody to what you're doing," she correctly surmised. "You want me to blind screen it for you."

"Yeah . . ." I said and smiled. "You up for that?"

"I guess," she said, not putting too much energy into it. We both knew if I had a suspicion that something wasn't right and had anything solid confirming that suspicion, I should take it back to Kovacevich and Cole and let them investigate it. Working without portfolio was not professional, and if she got caught doing my unauthorized computer runs, she could end up in the bag with me.

"Tell you what. Use my computer password. I'll deal with the fallout. I don't want this to land on you."

"That's okay. I know how to finesse it." She smiled ruefully. "I've been your partner just long enough to become a devious cheat."

"You're the best, kid. Gotta go," I said, to get her to stop clocking me.

I led her around the corner and was heading toward the elevators when I saw a tall, imposing, six-foot woman in a polo shirt and slacks standing outside Homicide Special with a large purse over her shoulder, looking for a cubicle number on the listing board.

"Seriana?" I said.

She turned and spotted me.

"There you are," she said. No smile. Intense eyes. Just like yesterday.

"Wait here while I get my stuff. I was just leaving." I indicated Sally Quinn. "Corporal Cotton, this is my partner, Detective Quinn." When Seriana shook her hand, it was so large that Sally's slender one disappeared like a hard ball into a fielder's mitt.

"Be right back," I said to Seriana. "I gotta get my jacket." We left her by the elevators and walked back into the squad room.

"That's some imposing woman," Sally said. "What Amazon tribe did you get her from?"

"Third Cavalry, U.S. Army. She's heading back to Iraq for her second tour in a week or two."

"Is she part of this thing too?"

"Yeah." I grabbed my coat and my briefcase with Walt's autopsy report. Then I faced Sally. Concern for me was spread across her freckled face. "I'll be okay, Sally. I've quit rolling gutter balls."

"Since when?" she said.

I left her and headed back to Seriana Cotton and the ghost of Walter Dix.

CHAPTER 12

IT WAS MY SECOND BREAKFAST of the morning. I still wasn't hungry, so I just ordered coffee. Seriana had a bagel and orange juice. We were at a little coffee shop across from Parker Center called the Time Out. The place was full of day-watch officers on Code Seven and the background noise was somewhere between a din and a roar.

"Jack Straw said you didn't want to help us find out what happened to Pop," she said.

"Jack Straw may not be the most reliable person to listen to."

"Mr. Scully, I go back to Iraq in about two weeks. That means I've got to look into this right now, because I need to find out who did it. I know Pop didn't kill himself, but when I was a kid he did keep *me* from killing *myself*. I loved him. I owe him. Now I've got to do right by the man."

"You're sure he didn't kill himself?"

"Absolutely certain, sir. For one, it just wasn't something he'd do. He was religious. A Catholic. He believed suicide was a sin. For another, he promised to be at my going-away party before I redeployed. It's at my foster parents' house in South Central next Wednesday. When he made me a promise, he never broke it. Not once since I was eight years old. He wouldn't miss my send-off. You know how Walt was."

"Yes, I do."

"In my unit, we've got this rule. We always get everybody home. Dead bodies included. You don't leave a teammate or his remains in the field. I gotta be sure I get Pop home."

She was looking at me with those intense ink-black irises, her handsome ebony face showing almost no expression. I was beginning to realize this was her way. Her look. Her features rarely varied, but there was no lack of emotion. In her eyes, I could see pain and sorrow. The eyes said it all.

"You're a cop," she said. "You knew him like the rest of us. He had to have made a huge impact on you. Look how you came from nothing and made something of yourself."

It was exactly what Jack Straw had told me yesterday. Seriana continued. "I know firsthand how hard that had to be. I know Pop helped you get there, just like he helped me. Jack said you agree he wouldn't kill himself. So why won't you help us find out what really happened?"

I reached into my small briefcase and pulled out the ME's report but left the copies of the gruesome autopsy photos behind. I shoved the file across the table to her.

"What's this?" she asked, opening it up.

"Pop's autopsy findings. I went to the coroner's office this morning and got a copy."

"Then you *are* working on it."

I shrugged, but didn't answer. Then I sat back and watched her as she scanned the lead paragraph, which, once you got through the medical babble, said it was death by his own hand. She finished and looked up at me.

"This is a lie."

"No, that's a legal finding. Done by a competent medical examiner. No evidence of a beating. He had no drugs or unusual substances in his blood, and he left a suicide note."

She studied me for a long moment. Her strong gaze was frank, unrelenting, and unsettling. I could see exactly what Alexa had been talking about. Seriana Cotton was definitely somebody who made up her own mind about things.

"Are you saying you agree with this, sir? You agree with this medical examiner that Pop killed himself."

"I didn't say that. I said the ME report said that."

She looked at me, trying to figure me out. "I guess I don't understand," she finally said.

"I'm going to devote a little time to it and shake this tree. See what falls out."

"Good." Her mouth shifted slightly. It was probably as close as she usually got to a smile. "We're having a pallbearers' meeting at six tonight," she said. "We've also all decided we're going to work on this. I want you to attend it with the rest of us, sir."

"The Pallbearers' Murder Club. Slick. Who's got the movie rights?"

"Don't make fun," she admonished.

"You're all amateurs, Seriana. You're just going to slow me down."

"You weren't the only one who loved him, sir," she said without expression.

"Who said I loved him?" I shot back. "When I was at Huntington House, I wasn't capable of love. Back then, and for most of the last twenty-five years, I was running from my past. I barely ever went over there to see what he was up to. I never helped him. I have no idea why he wanted me to carry his coffin. But I'll grant you one thing, Corporal. I sure *do* owe the man. So I'm going to take some time and see if I can put a case on somebody. If not, then it's like that report says. Suicide. We suck it up and all go on with our lives."

"Bullshit," she said softly.

"What about that sounds like BS?"

"You loved him, sir. I can see the truth in your eyes. I see the pain and loss."

Of course, she was right. But admitting to her that I loved Walt made my betrayal seem even more devastating.

"I'll tell you why he picked you to be a pallbearer," she continued. "It was because he also loved *you*. He saw past the cruel stuff we all did. He understood our selfishness. That's what made him so special."

I felt about six inches tall. I knew all this. It's why I had already decided to look into his suicide. But I didn't need their help. Didn't want it. The idea of doing this with my fellow pallbearers was way too Agatha Christie for me.

"Come to the meeting at six tonight," Seriana said. "It's at Sabas Vargas's office in East L.A. Here's the address." She slid a piece of paper across the table. I glanced down at it.

She had neat, careful handwriting. Sabas's office was on Whittier Boulevard in the twelve hundred block in Boyle Heights. The Hispanic hood.

"I'm not sure. I've got a lot to do," I said.

Seriana leaned forward and studied me. "Please come, sir," she said. "I promised the others I would convince you because you're a homicide detective. You're the only one who knows how we should go about this."

I sat there looking at her. A very imposing woman. I don't know exactly why, but my resolve suddenly weakened. "Okay, but you have to stop calling me sir."

"Shane, then." She finally smiled. It came and went so quickly I almost missed it. But it lit her face, turning it beautiful for a brief second before it fled.

CHAPTER 13

HOMICIDE DETECTIVE CASSIE Kovacevich was a pretty, thirty-year-old blonde who looked like she should be employed as a party planner, not a cop. Her partner, Burt Cole, was your standard old-school LAPD burnout—a hammered-down skeptic from his bad crew cut and exploded face capillaries to his orthopedic shoes. He looked twenty years older than his partner and about half as smart, which turned out to be an elaborate disguise.

"There was nothing to investigate," Detective Cole said, after I'd asked them about Walt's death.

We were standing in the lobby of the brand-new, forty-million-dollar Harbor Community Police Station. I'd waited for almost half an hour for them to appear. The clean cop-shop lobby was a sharp contrast to the victimized people who came and went, dragging improbable tales of violence, their faces etched in misery.

"Nothing to investigate?" I asked, sounding concerned and judgmental. I was trying to get them to defend their conclusion so I could draw out more facts.

"Shotgun blast, so there were no ballistics," Detective Kovacevich said, taking the bait. "Suicide note left on his computer, no forced entry, no sign of a struggle. Just a wooden chair tipped over on the back porch with him still in it. A small lawn painted red with blood, brain splatter, and cerebrospinal fluid.

"We get ten rollouts a week and we're shorthanded. We gotta put the easy ones down fast or we'll choke on the caseloads." She sounded defensive and a little angry. My party-planner take quickly shifted. Kovacevich was as hard and cynical as her slumping, ready-to-retire partner. Just better hair, legs, and posture.

"You got the suicide note?" I asked. "I'd like to see it."

Cole looked at Kovacevich and the two of them had a silent conversation. They had a good rhythm like most seasoned police teams and had learned to communicate without talking. You struggled to get to that place with a partner. I'd just recently reached the plateau with Sally Quinn.

"Okay, why?" Cole asked. "What's going on here?"

Kovacevich stood with her arms crossed, waiting for my answer.

"Look, you guys. I do this same job. I'm not trying to embarrass anyone. This guy was my friend." Then I went through the same "some of us at the group home need closure" story and waited while they processed it.

"We must look like a couple of slow, fat Guernseys to you," Kovacevich said. "You're not down here looking for closure. You're looking for clues. You want to reverse this finding, 'cause you don't think your dearly departed friend could have possibly capped himself."

"She's right," Cole agreed. "If we give you our case file and you find a way to reopen this, we look like a couple of enema bags."

"I'm not gonna do anything but try and convince my friends there's nothing wrong here. I know you got it right," I lied. "It's just so they can get over this, mourn his passing, and move on."

They exchanged another look. More telepathic information passed between them.

"Okay," Cole answered. "Out of professional courtesy, we'll show it to you because we're dead certain we got it right and Dix was a suicide just like we wrote it up. But on the off chance you kick up something we missed, you gotta promise to bring it back here first and don't put me and Cassie in the blender."

"Fair enough. But I won't find anything. I agree with you. I just have these other people who . . ."

"Save it for *The Today Show*," Kovacevich interrupted.

We went to their homicide cubicle. It was a lot like mine. The desk was newer, the chairs softer. "Wanted" flyers covered every available surface. "Asshole wallpaper" we called it. Cole found the folder in his desk's bottom file drawer, pulled it out, and handed it over to me.

"We dusted the victim's personal computer," he said. "Only his prints on the keyboard, so he typed the suicide note himself."

The case file was thin. They'd worked it fast, closed it in twelve hours, just like they'd said. There was nothing in the folder I didn't already know. Just ten short entries along with some crime-scene photos that showed Pop sprawled on the lawn in a tipped-over chair with that brutal head wound, the shotgun on the grass behind and just to the right. I forced myself to study them. There was a copy of the ME's report, which I already had, and Walt's suicide note, which I didn't. I pulled it out. Walt's last earthly communication was only seven lines. Short and sweet.

To Whom it may Concern,
I caught a bad wave. Got pulled down by leash drag.
I wasn't trying to hurt anyone.
Sorry about the yard sale, but it was the only way off the ride.
Don't hate me for what I did.
If you need the reason, tap the source,
Walt

I looked up from the note, into the stone-cold eyes of the two detectives.

"We had to get somebody who surfs to translate," Kovacevich said. "Leash drag is like getting held under by the ankle leash. A yard sale is a brutal wipeout. 'Tap the source' was painted on his board and his surf stuff. Apparently, it's the place where good waves come from."

"Yeah, I know what it all means," I said. "That's the way Walt talked."

"Don't fuck us up," Cole said, telling me with that sentence that he'd grown tired of me.

"There's nothing here," I assured them. "You guys got this exactly right. Suicide, pure and simple."

They watched me with suspicious eyes.

"Can I have a copy of this?" I asked, holding up the note.

"You can have that one. We still have the computer with the original. We had a guy in the electronics division do a computer dump. Nothing useful." Cole dropped into his chair and kicked his file drawer closed. Meeting over.

I drove out of the parking lot and headed east. I had almost two hours before the six o'clock pallbearers' meeting in Boyle Heights. I decided to use the time to stop by Huntington House. I had a few more questions, which I hoped Diamond Peterson could answer.

The suicide note was open on the seat beside me as I drove. At traffic lights, I kept looking down at it, rereading the seven lines. It certainly sounded like Pop, but somehow it felt bogus. I don't know what about it made me suspicious. Maybe it was because it had been written on a computer. I would have trusted it more if it was handwritten. But Kovacevich and Cole said only Pop's fingerprints were on the keyboard, and we get a lot of electronic suicide notes these days, so that in itself wasn't enough.

Maybe it was all the surfer babble. Would Walt choose surf lingo for his last communication? Could it be that someone else had written it and was trying to make it sound like Pop, or was I just grasping at straws again, trying to find something where nothing existed?

I had agreed to go to a meeting with five people who

didn't know what the fuck they were doing and were expecting me to solve this for them. I was the police expert. The professional. Yet I kept hoping they'd be able to explain it to me because I didn't have a take.

I was as confused as I was all those years ago when Pop first rescued me.

CHAPTER 14

I GOT TO HUNTINGTON HOUSE at four thirty, pulled into the parking lot, and walked around the side of Sharon Cross Hall to the rec center, where Diamond told me yesterday she'd set up the temporary office.

As the dirt playground came into view, I stopped for a moment and watched ten boys playing baseball on the diamond. Five up and five in the field. Not enough for two full teams. This was a take-no-prisoners game where you needed to hold your ground on the baselines, put a shoulder down, and watch out for your nuts if you wanted to survive.

The kids seemed angry. They swung from the heels trying to pulverize the ball. With each crack of the bat, they ran on skinny legs, pumping their arms. There was a lot of shouting, way too many violent collisions on the base paths, one or two of them always on the verge of a fistfight.

For a second, I was back on that diamond with them.

Little Shane Scully finding a few minutes away from my loneliness as I tried to get rid of my anger by knocking the shit out of somebody, the violence more important than the game.

"Shane, whatta you doing here?" Diamond's voice interrupted my thoughts. I turned and found her standing behind me. She had just come out of the rec center and was carrying several thick folders and a clipboard with a list of some kind written on it.

"Hi," I said. "I thought I'd drop by for a minute to talk before the six o'clock meeting at Vargas's office. I assume you're going."

"I think we're wasting our time with that, but yes." Like me, she seemed resigned to the exercise. "What did you want to talk about?"

"You keep saying you don't think Pop killed himself, but I get the distinct feeling you don't really believe that. I wanted you to go over your feelings again and see if you could explain why."

The sun was lowering directly over my shoulder, forcing her to squint into it as she studied me. She glanced down at her watch.

"Let's go inside," she said.

I followed her into the rec center. She led me across the large basketball court into a temporary office that was located in a coach's room. They had set up brand-new metal filing cabinets that still had the Staples stickers on the sides. I could read the price tags—one hundred and forty-nine dollars apiece. Diamond saw me studying the cabinets.

"We're trying to rebuild our financial records. It's slow going, but with this state audit coming, we'll need to show them something."

She sat behind a card table that served as her desk. It was stacked high with papers that looked like accounting spreadsheets.

"I'm sort of looking into Pop's death on my own," I told her. "I need to know what you really think. You were around him the most, and I keep picking up this vibe that you disagree with the others."

She took a moment to consider this before answering.

"You're getting that vibe because you're right. I hate to admit it, but I think it's real possible he killed himself," she said flatly. "It's an unpopular opinion, but like you said, I was close to him. I saw how much stress he was under. God knows, I don't want to believe it because he also had a life-insurance policy for half a million dollars. He had no surviving relatives. The beneficiary was Huntington House. It doesn't pay off on a suicide, so obviously, I desperately wanted it to be something else because we need that life-insurance check.

"With that money we could have gotten straight with the state and out of debt with our nonprofit owner, Creative Solutions. . . . It would have made a huge difference. But since the police listed Pop as a suicide, it's not coming.

"Same thing happens to the insurance if the Arson cops say he burned down the administration building. For all those reasons, and because I don't want to believe he was so tortured inside he'd kill himself, I don't want this to be a suicide. But, damn it, I was there. I saw how messed up he was at the end. How out of control. Besides, who would have murdered Pop? Everybody loved him." She rubbed a hand on her forehead, then leaned back in the chair. She looked exhausted.

"Are you okay?"

"No," she said softly. "Creative Solutions has just appointed me to be the temporary executive director of the home. I don't want the job. It's more than I can handle. But somebody has to run this place, and I guess I'm the best choice. But it means I have to step down as secretary-treasurer because, according to California nonprofit law, I can't hold both the executive director and secretary-treasurer positions at the same time. It's to protect the home from the possibility of fraud, so I can't write checks to myself or something.

"That means I need to get a new secretary-treasurer, like immediately. Nobody wants the job, and with all this financial turmoil, I don't blame them. I got this damn state audit coming. I'm way shorthanded as it is, and now I've got the head of Creative Solutions all over me to reassemble these fiscal records for the state auditor. I'm not sleeping, my stomach is on fire. I think I'm getting an ulcer or something. So no, I'm definitely not okay."

She almost seemed upset enough to commit suicide herself. When I lived here, it never occurred to me how much stress was involved in running this place.

"Can't Creative Solutions send somebody over to step in as secretary-treasurer?" I asked.

"That's what I'm trying to get them to do. But they think we're about to crater and they manage other foster homes, so they don't want to get their fingerprints on anything that could cause legal problems for them with the state."

Just then, a very large, tattooed, fair-skinned, muscular man with reddish-blond hair stuck his head into the office. He was about thirty years old and had a cruel flat-nosed face, and shoulders like a water buffalo.

"Diamond, I'm waiting," he snapped. "I've been standing over by Sharon Cross Hall for ten minutes. Whatta you doing?"

"Mr. O'Shea, this is Shane Scully. He dropped by unannounced and I . . ."

"We need to go through this physical inventory," the man interrupted. "I have to get out of here." He moved into the room, and I saw that he had a trim thirty-inch waist to go with those huge shoulders. He was wearing a short-sleeved shirt, and his elaborately tattooed arms rippled with muscles that you can only get with an intense workout routine.

"I'm Shane Scully," I said, standing to greet him, putting out my hand.

"Good for you. Come on, Diamond. Let's do this." He ignored my handshake and left abruptly. Diamond stood up.

"See what I mean?" she said, glowering at the door he'd just gone through. "It ain't easy."

"Nice guy. Who is he?"

"That's Rick O'Shea. President of Creative Solutions." She sighed. "My boss."

I was looking at the empty doorway where, moments before, two hundred and thirty pounds of tattoo-enhanced gristle had been standing.

"That's the president of your nonprofit corporation?" I said. "Kinda not what you'd expect, is he?"

"He's a very difficult man." Diamond sighed again. Then she gathered up the folders she'd been carrying before, grabbed the clipboard, and turned to face me in the doorway.

"Listen, Shane, I gotta go. I'll see you at Sabas's place at six."

"Great."

We both left the rec center together, and I split off to go back to my Acura. Before getting in, I walked the lot. I was looking for a car that didn't belong here. The kind of ride a thirty-year-old tattooed gym rat might drive.

It was easy to spot. A one-year-old, custom-painted maroon Escalade with expensive chrome spinners. I looked in the passenger window and saw a gym bag. On the side, it said: *RICK "RICOCHET" O'SHEA*. I walked around to the back of the SUV and wrote down the plates.

O'Shea was about to get a little piece of my unofficial investigation.

Then I got into my car and, even though it was early, headed on out to the twelve hundred block on Whittier Boulevard in Boyle Heights.

An hour ago I'd been feeling like this case was loose. But something had just shifted. At the beginning of any investigation, what you're looking for are the little inconsistencies that may be hiding an important fact. Tiny pieces of the puzzle that don't quite fit. You're looking for the slight but unmistakable odor of deceit.

Like Alexa, I'm also pretty good on cop reads. Rick "Ricochet" O'Shea was definitely coming off as a false note. He didn't belong in this picture.

Besides that, he was an asshole.

CHAPTER 15

AS I DROVE TOWARD THE SIX o'clock meeting in Boyle Heights, I checked in with Sally Quinn. She wasn't there so I left her a message to call me. I was going east on Whittier Boulevard, heading deeper and deeper into East L.A. Tagger art announced the gang blocks. MS-13's graffiti gave way to East Side Surenos, then 18th Street Locos, and finally to Latin Kings. The letters were angry black slashes made from thousands of Home Depot spray cans.

If you're uninitiated, this jagged tagger script can be almost impossible to read, but after a few weeks in a squad car, you get pretty good at it. Driving the East L.A. ghetto was a little like riding through hostile Indian country in an open wagon. If you didn't want an arrow in the back, you'd better scan the rocks for signs of danger.

Since many of these Hispanic gangs had different countries of origin, their cultural differences tended to define their behavior. Knowing which bunch you were up against could affect your survival.

I finally pulled up in front of the address Seriana had given me. I had been expecting an office building, but instead found a small, badly maintained Spanish-style bungalow in the middle of six blocks tagged as Latin Kings turf. I looked at my watch. It was still early, and I didn't see Jack's Harley or any other car I recognized from before. I figured I was the first to arrive, so I sat at the curb and cased the run-down block and house. A small sign propped in the window read:

SABAS VARGAS

ATTORNEY AT LAW

A few minutes later, I saw a white woman dressed in a tailored cream-colored pantsuit, carrying an expensive-looking, oversized shoulder bag, walking up to a porch six houses away. She looked completely lost.

I watched as she knocked, waited for the door to open, then spoke for a moment to somebody inside. The door was abruptly slammed in her face.

I knew even before she turned that it was Vicki Lavicki walking around down here in her summer suit and sensible shoes like a Jehovah's Witness who drew the short straw.

Then a lowrider with four young thugs inside glided by, pulling to a stop where she was standing. She stupidly crossed to the lowered Chevy and started asking for directions.

The four teenaged vatos in the lowrider didn't seem

to be paying much attention to what she was saying. They were busy taking inventory of her jewelry.

They got out of their axle-dragging mother ship and surrounded her on the sidewalk like a pack of wild coyotes about to shred a defenseless poodle.

I couldn't hear what was being said, but Ms. Lavicki didn't seem to appreciate the danger she was in. She had one hand in her purse fishing around for a pen or something, while four Latin Kings in black and gold head wraps were fanning out, going into attack mode.

"Shit," I muttered and got out of my car, pulling my badge, while moving quickly up the block toward her.

"Hey, Vicki!" I called out to distract them, holding up my creds as I ran. The four vato thugs spun to check me out, trying to decide whether to add me to the party or just roll on. I pulled back my jacket as I ran, showing them my sidearm in its clip-on holster. Because they were just teenagers, I didn't want to draw down on them. I was pretty sure they were all packing but was trying not to initiate a gunfight. I kept my right hand near my gun and my left holding the creds high as I ran to let them know they'd be firing on a cop.

They hesitated for a minute, decided they didn't want that kind of trouble, got back into their lowered hood mobile, and pulled slowly off. They took the corner at the end of the block at an insolent five miles an hour.

"My hero," Vicki said dryly as I approached. "Very John Wayne, but I had that handled."

"You were seconds from getting unzipped," I told her, but she waved this off as she glanced down at an address in her hand.

"I must've gotten the wrong street number from Diamond," she said. "Where the hell is Vargas's office?"

"Listen, Ms. Lavicki, in the future it might not be such a good idea to wander around down here alone."

Her hazel eyes cut holes in me. "I was okay. You were the one causing the problem."

"You were *not* okay. Those guys were packing."

"Me too." Then she pulled her right hand out of the purse. The whole time she'd been holding a snub-nosed .44 caliber Charter Arms Bulldog with a wood-checked grip, aiming it at them from inside her purse.

"You're supposed to be a damn accountant. What kind of adding machine is that?"

"It subtracts to five, but there were only four, so you do the math," she said. Then, because I frowned deeply, she added, "Get over it, Scully. I sometimes carry cashier's checks for my firm. I have a permit."

"You were gonna shoot them?"

She stuffed the Bulldog back into her purse and smirked at me. "That was just a little chest bump. Those guys were only sniffing."

"And you're some kind of expert on street action," I shot back.

"Before I got put in Huntington House, I was raised in South Central," she replied. "I was the only white face on my block. The shit jumped off in that hood almost every night. We didn't have bars in our windows, we had MAC-10s." She seemed tired of discussing this and abruptly changed the subject, showing me the slip of paper in her hand. "You know where Vargas's office is? These all look like houses. I was expecting a building."

"I'm glad you're not doing my taxes. This three should be an eight." I pointed to the bungalow half a block away.

Alexa had called Vicki a brass cupcake, and she was right. I now had a tough-talking pistol-packing CPA and ex–South Central hood rat from Kinney and Glass to worry about. I got my briefcase out of the MDX, and we walked up the path to the front door of Vargas's bungalow and rang the bell.

A minute later, a tough-looking male teenager opened up. He was dressed in Latin Kings colors, wearing a black and gold New Orleans Saints football jersey, a hairnet, and four-hundred-dollar Air Jordans. He also had a big *LK* emblazoned on the side of his neck and two teardrop tattoos under his right eye, indicating that, despite his tender age, he'd already lost two homies in the street.

The man-boy stared at us insolently but made no move to step out of the way. His attitude wasn't going to do much for the walk-in trade.

"We're here for the six o'clock meeting," Vicki said, not wavering under his malevolent stare. "You wanta go tell Mr. Vargas we're here or just stand there acting like a dickhead?"

Jesus . . . I thought. But he just stepped aside and let us in.

I followed Vicki into the house. The bungalow looked to be entirely devoted to Sabas Vargas's legal practice. There were several hard-looking Hispanic women in their mid-twenties to thirties typing legal documents on computers and answering phones. Most of them also had teardrop tattoos. It wasn't like any law office I'd ever been in before. This staff looked like a bunch of parolees. Then one of the chica warriors stood and confronted us.

"What is it?" the tall, angry presence demanded.

"We're here to talk to Sabas." I fished out my trusty badge again. She glared, shrugged, then turned and, without a word, left us there, heading into the back.

"Put that thing away," Vicki whispered. "Nobody cares."

A moment later, Sabas came down the hall in shirt-sleeves. Without the jacket and with his cuffs rolled up, I could see that he was heavier than I had originally thought. A roll of fat pressed at his belt line, a faded marine tattoo decorated one forearm.

"I'm just wrapping up a client conference," he said, and I noticed a very slight Mexican accent that I'd somehow failed to detect at the reception. "Some of the others are already gathered in the conference room. Follow me." We headed toward the back of the house.

I could see into the guest bedrooms that opened off the hall. They were full of records and supplies. One was outfitted with a copy machine and file cabinets. He led us into a den, which looked out over a small weed-choked backyard that surprisingly contained a cracked and empty kidney-shaped swimming pool. Then he left us, heading back down the hall to finish his meeting.

The room contained a fold-up conference table and ten metal chairs. Jack Straw was lounging in one, tipped back insolently. Seriana Cotton was sitting with rigid military posture in another. Diamond Peterson hadn't made it yet.

"I didn't see the Harley out front," I said.

"We both parked around back in Sabas's driveway," Straw replied. "You'd have to be brain dead to leave your ride out front."

I had a sudden mental image of my MDX jacked up, missing all four tires, radio, and airbags.

"This is quite a setup," I said, indicating the reception area out front. "I could probably make my arrest quotas for the week by just running this guy's office staff."

"Sabas told us he takes a lot of pro bono cases," Seriana explained. "His clients and their families work in the office to settle out their legal expenses."

Before I could respond, Sabas Vargas came into the den and closed the door behind him. "Let's get started," he said, taking control of the meeting. "I just talked to Diamond and she said she had some inventory lists to take care of at Huntington House and will be a little late."

He pulled up his chair and sat at the edge of the table. "Okay, let's talk about how we go about proving Pop didn't kill himself so Huntington House can get this life-insurance check." He looked directly at me. "Shane, why don't you start by giving me a police take on that."

CHAPTER 16

"I'M NOT SURE I HAVE A TAKE," I said, trying to duck him. What I really wanted to do was to get the hell out. I already knew that coming here was a huge mistake.

Sabas Vargas had a deep bass voice that he used to control the room. "I know we're not all on the exact same page, but the idea of this meeting is to discuss whether or not it's feasible that Pop would go into his backyard and blow his head off. A lot of you feel he wasn't that kind of guy."

"We don't know that," I said. "Diamond was the closest to him recently. She says he was stressed, worried about missing funds."

"Seriana tells me that you got the ME's report," Sabas went on, not reacting to that. "Anything in there that looks off?"

"No." I looked around at the room of Huntington House grads. None of them seemed too happy with me.

"Usually when I'm trying a death case, there's *some-*

thing in the ME report worth quarreling with," Sabas said suspiciously.

"Nothing," I repeated. "It was pretty standard. Pretty cut-and-dry." *How the hell did I allow myself to get dragged into this?*

"If you don't want to help, why did you bother coming?" Vicki Lavicki said, anger reddening her freckled, schoolgirl complexion.

"I came because Seriana asked me to," I defended. "It doesn't mean I think we're going to find anything."

"You also told Corporal Cotton you were looking into Pop's death on your own," Vicki pressed. "So it's okay for you to check it out, but it's not okay for the rest of us."

I glanced over at Seriana who held my gaze silently, never blinking.

"I was checking a few things because I agree it wasn't Pop's style or in his general demeanor to pull something like this. Also, I agree that the bungalow fire seems a bit much on top of the suicide, so I spent twenty minutes to check out the coroner's autopsy. Not much there. You can read it for yourselves."

I took the report out of my briefcase, again leaving the grisly autopsy photos behind, and slid the file across the table. Seriana had already read it, so she passed it on to Vicki, who passed it to Sabas, who passed it to Jack. Once they had all finished, they returned it to me.

"So you find nothing was done inappropriately at the coroner's inquest? Nothing wrong with the police investigation?" Sabas asked. "You're absolutely sure?"

"I'm sure. I talked to the cops who got the original rollout. Nothing in their investigation suggested anything but suicide. They gave me a copy of Walt's suicide note. It was written on his computer, only his prints on the keyboard. I have it here."

I also put that on the table, and it followed the same path as the ME report, going hand to hand around the room. When they finished reading those seven lines, each of the pallbearers looked up. I could see frustration on Vicki's face, anger in Seriana's intense black eyes. Jack was tipping back, arms folded, flashing forearm art. Sabas Vargas seemed to be losing energy for this as the pieces I'd gathered started to paint a depressing picture of suicide.

"Pop didn't write that," Vicki suddenly blurted. "It's not in his handwriting, just a computer printout. He wouldn't say he got pulled down by leash drag or did a yard sale. What kind of BS is that?"

That was sort of my take too, but I didn't say anything. I wasn't going to stop working on this, I just didn't want to do it with them.

"You're sure nothing in the ME's report seemed out of the ordinary?" Sabas said skeptically. "Not even one little detail?"

"Well . . ." I stopped. They all leaned forward. I knew in that second that I'd just made a major blunder. They knew I had something, and I didn't want to go down that road. What was I doing? I felt myself being pulled in by a sense of belonging. We'd all been there. All residents of the home. I owed Pop, but did I owe these people?

"Well what?" Vicki said. "What is it? You found something?"

"I didn't find anything. It's just that . . ." I looked again at their expectant faces. What the hell. Since I'd already stumbled, I might as well finish the fall. "The coroner told me they give the obvious suicide autopsies to the new medical examiners. According to the shift supervisor, this Barbara Wilkes person who did Pop's ME report has only been on the job for six months."

"So she could have missed something?" Jack said, smiling, looking triumphantly at Seriana, who, as usual, had no expression.

"I didn't say that. I just said she was new. Not a lot of experience."

"And that means she could have missed something," Jack repeated. He leaned forward, bringing the two chair legs down abruptly.

"It's possible but not probable," I said.

They all looked at me, waiting. For some damn reason, it made me edgy. Or maybe I was just feeling guilty. The moment simmered.

"Whatta ya want!?" I snapped angrily. "Stop looking at me. It doesn't mean anything. Besides, I can't work on this. It's not even a case. I spent a couple a hours and got my hands on a few things, but that's all I can do. No case, no crime. No crime, no investigation!"

"Shane, if you were going to do something . . . if you could take one more step, what would it be?" It was a good question, asked in a quiet voice by Seriana Cotton. Her voice might have been soft, but her black irises were stuck on mine like laser-gun sights.

"I'd try to get an exhumation order and reautopsy the body," I finally admitted. "Sometimes, if an examiner is certain of what the outcome will be before he or she does the autopsy, they could jump to an inaccurate conclusion, especially somebody with little experience. If they already think they know what the finding will be, or if they're rushed and doing it in a hurry, it's possible they might do a quick slapdash job. I'd redo it and look for something that would get Walt's death classification changed from suicide to homicide. Then the department will assign a homicide number to it and a proper police investigation would take place."

"Let's do that then," Vicki said.

"How you gonna do that?" I replied. "I said I'd *try* for an exhumation, but it's not gonna happen. We have no new facts to submit to force one. The coroner doesn't have time to redo this stuff on a whim. They're way too busy over there as it is."

"There are private firms we could hire that perform independent autopsies," Sabas Vargas said. "I've used them to gather my own medical evidence for trials."

"And who's gonna pay for that?" I asked.

"I will," Vicki said. "I'll put up my piece."

"Me too," Seriana said. Jack nodded, so did Sabas Vargas. They were circling the wagons.

"I know who we could get to do it for us," Vicki Lavicki said, smiling. "One of our clients at Kinney and Glass is Oakcrest Pathology and Medical Group. They do that kind of thing. It's my account and I'm friends with the executive director. I'm sure I could get us a quick job at a good price." She glared at me. "I assume you'll also step up for your end of the exhumation and autopsy costs, Shane?" she challenged.

"Yeah, sure," I flustered. "I'm good for my piece."

I couldn't believe how completely I'd been sucked in. Somehow I'd just joined this silly Pallbearers' Murder Club.

"I'll use the phone in the other room. Maybe the director of Oakcrest hasn't gone home yet," Vicki said, getting up and leaving the den.

Jack asked, "How do we get Walt's body exhumed? Isn't that going to be kinda tough to accomplish?"

"Walt didn't have any living relatives," Sabas said. "Nobody but us. I guess whoever signed the final agreement with the mortuary to have him picked up would be the one to authorize it."

"That was me," Diamond said. We all turned and saw her standing in the doorway. She'd finally made it.

"We're thinking we should pass the hat among us and exhume and reautopsy Walt's body," Jack told her. "Shane thinks that the L.A. coroner missed something."

Of course, I didn't say that. But this had already developed a life of its own.

"We can't do that," Diamond said softly. "I thought you guys knew. That's why we didn't have a graveside ceremony. Walt stated in his will that he wanted to be cremated. The body's been destroyed."

CHAPTER 17

WE ALL SAT THERE IN THAT small den overlooking Vargas's empty pool in East L.A. trying to come to grips with that.

"Maybe it hasn't happened yet," Seriana suggested. She had risen to her feet and was now standing at the head of the table, her body a coiled spring.

"It's been over twenty-four hours since the funeral when we released the body to Forest Lawn," Diamond answered. "I think they always do cremations pretty much immediately after the service."

"Not always," Sabas said. "They usually wait a day for legal reasons, to make sure there are no problems or disputes over the last-wish provisions. I've also seen situations where, because of backlogs, it's taken almost as long as a week. Somebody should call Forest Lawn and see what the deal is."

"I'll do it," Seriana said. She quickly left the room. Jack was again leaning back in his chair, an insolent, judgmental little smirk on his lips. I wanted to kick the chair out from under him. I wanted to knock that smirk off his face. Obviously the guy didn't have to do much to piss me off.

"You should not get your hopes up," Sabas said. "Since it's been more than a day, the odds are the cremation already happened." After he said that, he immediately shifted gears. "On the other hand, maybe Walt's body is still sitting in back in some embalming room or something. You never know. I don't think they'd burn the body until full payment's been made. Maybe there were payment problems."

"Walt had his mortuary services prepaid," Diamond said. "He knew he didn't have anyone to handle that for him, so he took care of it in advance."

We all sat there and fidgeted while Vicki and Seriana made their calls. Seriana was back first.

"Mortuary office is closed. Nobody to ask. Can't find out anything until eight or nine tomorrow."

Vicki came back a few minutes later and told us she couldn't get through to Oakcrest either. They'd also closed. She'd left the room before Diamond arrived and didn't know about the cremation. When we told her, her shoulders slumped. "When are we gonna catch a fucking break?" Vicki scowled.

It wasn't going to happen tonight, so we all agreed to meet back at Sabas's office first thing in the morning.

"If the body is still there, I'm gonna have to file papers with the court so Forest Lawn will release Walt's remains to us," Sabas said. "Diamond, didn't you say that Walt left the benefits of his life-insurance policy to the home?"

"Yes, but we can't collect it because of the suicide."

"Doesn't matter," Vargas said. "That's our legal hook. If the body's still there, I'll file papers with the court claiming that a bad city autopsy has potentially denied Huntington House its insurance benefit. As the party at loss, Huntington House can demand a new autopsy. With no family to object, I don't see how the court could deny it as long as we foot all the expense. Diamond, you're the new executive director. I'll need you to be the one to file the papers on behalf of the home."

"Okay," she agreed. "I can do that."

"I'll write up the documents tonight, so we'll be ready to pounce on the off chance that we can still do this. In the morning, we'll know one way or the other."

We left Sabas's office, none of us thinking we had much of a chance. What were the odds that the body was still lying around someplace waiting to be cremated? Pretty slim was my guess.

I walked Vicki back to her car, a Toyota Camry that was parked a short distance away. It had somehow escaped theft or vandalism, which was strange because our auto-theft division lists Toyotas as one of the three most frequently stolen vehicles in L.A. When I opened the door, she turned to me.

"Walt's remains are toast, excuse the pun," she said somewhat harshly. "You and I already know that, even if the others don't. We're majorly fucked."

"Even if Walt's body is gone, there are still other ways to work on this."

She seemed skeptical as she got into her car. I leaned down and looked in at her.

"Listen, Vicki. I think Diamond is in way over her head. She's the new executive director of the home, but she told me she has to give up the secretary-treasurer job because the state says she can't hold both positions at once. She doesn't seem to be able to get anybody to take over that job. You're a CPA, I was thinking you should volunteer to take the position."

She was digging in her purse for her keys but suddenly stopped and was now holding my gaze with hard hazel eyes. I wondered if the hand in her purse had that Bulldog pointing at my crotch.

"Really?"

"Yeah. It would really help Diamond and it would be good to have somebody on the inside, going through the books, trying to figure out what the hell was really going on in that place."

She gave me a slow devious smile. "You're a tricky bastard, aren't you?"

I didn't answer that one.

"I could certainly do that," she said thoughtfully. "Matter of fact, it's something I'd really enjoy. They got anything left to look at? The building was completely torched."

"Diamond said they're rebuilding the files somehow. I don't know how they're doing it."

"Probably calling around to everyone they wrote checks to, getting all their accounts receivable to send them copies of old invoices and billing records, reconciling those against the bank statements. There'd be some holes, but it would be generally accurate."

"See you in the morning. Don't shoot anybody on your way out of here."

She smiled at me, then pulled her keys out of the purse, started the Camry, and left.

As I was driving out of the hood, my cell phone rang. When I picked up, Sally Quinn was on the line. "Just got your message, Hoss. What's up?"

"Sally, I need a little favor . . ."

"I've learned there're no little favors when it comes to you, buddy." She had a smile in her voice, so I knew she was just playing with me.

"I need a records run on a guy named Rick O'Shea. He drives a new maroon Escalade, license number one-Victor-May-Ida-three-six-six. I also need his sheet if he has one, along with his DMV and any current wants or warrants."

"Hang on a minute, gotta turn my computer back on."

While she worked on the information, I drove out of East L.A., heading west toward Venice.

"Got him," she said. "Twenty-nine years old. Lives at 3859 Lupine Lane in Calabasas. I think that's a pretty good neighborhood. I've got an aunt who lives out there, off Pine. He had some write-ups for violent assaults. Mostly ticky-tack—bar fights, stuff like that. Nothing that ever went to trial." She hesitated then added, "He could have a record from somewhere else. Want me to start a federal run, see what I get?"

"Yeah, that might help. And listen, can you check with the prosecutor's office and give me some info on an attorney named Sabas Vargas? His office is in Boyle Heights."

"Done! Talk to you tomorrow," she said quickly. "I gotta run, Jeb's calling." She hung up before I could ask her to run Vicki Lavicki and Jack Straw.

When I got home, Alexa was waiting. She had on a cocktail dress and heels.

"We going somewhere?" I asked.

"Not unless you get rid of that long face," she teased. "Then I thought we'd go to the Tiki Hut restaurant for dinner. Closest thing to Hawaii I can come up with."

"Let's have a drink here first. It's been a long day."

We poured two scotches, then went outside and sat on the porch chairs. Alexa told me about a conversation she'd had that afternoon with our son, Chooch, who was in spring training for USC football and had just suffered a mild hamstring pull. He was on the bench carrying a clipboard, stressing that it could get him knocked down the list in the Trojan quarterback derby.

So Chooch was bummed about that, I was bummed about Walt, and Alexa and I were both bummed about not going to Hawaii. Scully family karma was low.

I told Alexa about the cremation and what we were planning to do if the body hadn't been destroyed, adding that I was pretty sure it already had been.

We went to dinner, then we came home and made love. Alexa held me close. I fought to keep my thoughts out of a negative spin. I had failed Walt and, in failing him, had failed myself. Alexa wouldn't let me go there. She whispered in my ear. She rubbed my back and brought me erect again. I hovered there between ecstasy and pain, strength and weakness, longing and despair.

In the end, I knew I had to get past my sense of failure if I wanted to finally be there for Walt. I had to deal with the fact that, like it or not, I'd run from him. I couldn't change what had already happened.

I can't rewrite history, I told myself. *So get going and start writing the future instead.*

CHAPTER 18

I ARRIVED AT THE TWELVE hundred block of Whittier Boulevard in Boyle Heights at eight forty the next morning. At that early hour, the neighborhood was quiet.

Vargas's staff of case-pending office workers started drifting into his bungalow at a little after nine. The members of the Pallbearers' Murder Club were there, all of us with guarded expressions, not knowing what to expect. Vicki and Seriana were working the phones. Seriana was trying to reach the funeral director at Forest Lawn while Vicki was chasing down the executive director at Oakcrest.

Sabas Vargas had left the room to call a "friendly judge" who had agreed to fast-track his court papers if this ever came to pass.

Then the miracle happened.

Seriana came back into the den and announced that Walt's body had not yet been cremated. It was scheduled to go in the oven at eleven o'clock that morning. A small cheer went up from the five of us. Seriana's face remained impassive, but I saw the fierce spark of victory flash in her eyes.

From that point on, it all went pretty quickly. First, Sabas's judge issued the restraining order to prevent the cremation, then came his order for Forest Lawn to release Walt's body to us for reautopsy.

By nine thirty, we were splitting up. Sabas and Jack were heading out to Forest Lawn to stand by Walt's casket and make sure nobody out there missed the order and put him into the oven by mistake.

The rest of us headed over to Oakcrest in the Valley. Vicki had arranged for the new autopsy to take place at just after noon and led the way in her Toyota Camry.

Oakcrest Pathology and Medical Group was located on the west end of Thousand Oaks. The area was filled with newly built commercial structures, strip malls, and modern office plazas. Oakcrest was in a new three-story, mirrored-glass building.

The director, Lester Shoe, was a bald guy in a suit who had a prominent eagle's beak. He seemed particularly fond of Vicki and gave us what she said was a killer price for a complete reautopsy.

The service included forensic photography; preservation of toxic samples; and a gross, as well as a microscopic, examination, complete with an immediate written report detailing the top-line findings. A full medical document would follow two to four weeks later. The price for all of this was normally five thousand dollars. Vicki had arranged it for three.

Sabas and Jack arrived at a few minutes past noon and reported that the Oakcrest van had picked up

Walt's casket from Forest Lawn and the body was on its way. Then Vicki started passing the hat, collecting personal checks to pay the pathology group.

I wrote mine for five hundred dollars, tore it off, and handed it to her.

"That wasn't so hard, was it, Shane?"

I didn't know if she was talking about my writing the check or the fact that we'd managed to save Walt's body for this second autopsy.

The Oakcrest van with Walt's remains arrived at the medical group at a little past one. Technicians in lab coats took delivery of the body and whisked it off to an autopsy theater. I called Alexa and told her what was going on.

"You see, things are looking up," she told me.

"These people seem very professional. Lots of white coats and everything, but I'm not expecting them to find much," I said. "I know how thorough the L.A. medical examiners are. The chance that they missed something is pretty slim."

"But at least you'll know you did everything possible."

The Hawaii trip lay quietly between the lines of this conversation. It still wasn't too late to go. Neither of us wanted to hope that the Oakcrest pathologists would find nothing so we could jet happily off to paradise, because that would confirm the loss of Walt's life-insurance check and be crippling to Diamond and Huntington House. On the other hand, some part of me, the selfish part that Walt had always scrupulously looked past, wanted this to be over.

We spent the next few hours sitting in the sterile waiting room of the pathology group, looking at bad art and miniature ficus trees. Jack Straw sat quietly opposite me, cycle boots up on the table.

I had watched him write his check for five hundred dollars as if it were nothing, tearing if off, flipping it casually on the table. Where did this guy get five hundred in spare cash? He was an ex-con grease monkey changing piston rings at a cycle shop in Long Beach. He was less than a month out of Soledad, yet money seemed to be no problem.

Vicki Lavicki was pacing. Sabas Vargas was on the cell phone rearranging his court calendar for the next two days, talking to one of the teardrop office chicas.

Diamond was out in the hall, standing alone, looking out the third-story window. Her face was sad as she watched leaves blow off the trees in the parking lot, propelled by a stiff wind. God knows what she was thinking.

Seriana and I sat opposite each other. Her face was impassive as usual, stoic. Once when I held her gaze, I thought for a moment I saw her wink.

Around four o'clock, the chief pathologist, Dr. William Hoyt, and his assistant came out.

"Are we all here?" Dr. Hoyt asked.

"I'll get Diamond," Seriana said, and went to retrieve her from the hall.

Finally, we were all standing together, formed in a half circle around the Oakcrest doctors. Our expressions were guarded.

"Most everything we found lines up exactly with the L.A. coroner's findings," Dr. Hoyt began.

"Most everything?" Diamond asked.

"Except for one thing. The L.A. coroner didn't open the deceased's lungs, probably because there was no reason to. We decided to take that extra step and found aspirated blood inside both lower lobes."

"Is that important?" Seriana asked.

"Yes. You see, the shotgun blast took out your friend's entire brain stem before it obliterated the left side of his skull. In the instant the shotgun was fired, the brain stem was destroyed."

"How's that important?" Jack asked.

"The brain stem controls the breathing reflex. Without a brain stem, you can't inhale."

I immediately knew where this was heading. This was the mistake we'd been looking for. I wasn't going to be heading off to Hawaii.

"I don't understand," Seriana said.

"Aspirated blood is blood that has been inhaled from the mouth, down the trachea into the lungs," Dr. Hoyt explained. "With his brain stem gone, your friend couldn't have inhaled that blood after the shotgun blast. He had to have inhaled it before."

Seriana and Sabas started to nod. Diamond, Vicki, and Jack were still lost.

"What Dr. Hoyt is saying," I explained, "is that Walt had blood in his mouth and inhaled it before his brain stem was blown away. The only reason he would have blood in his mouth is if he'd been beaten in the face before he died. The shotgun blast covered up the signs of that beating."

"That means Pop was murdered," Jack said.

We all stood there, not quite knowing how to react.

"So what the fuck do we do now?" petite Ms. Lavicki finally asked.

CHAPTER 19

IT WAS 5:00 P.M., AND I WAS back in my car on the cell to Alexa as I headed out of the Valley.

"That means Huntington House will get Walt's life insurance," Alexa said after I told her what had just happened.

"They can certainly use it." But what I was thinking was how Alexa had embraced this from the beginning and had not put any of her own disappointment about losing our vacation on me. Sometimes this woman takes my breath away.

"I'd like you to rig this homicide so it ends up on my desk," I told her. "I know it's technically not a high-profile case and shouldn't go to Homicide Special, but there's gotta be some privilege we can claim to get it over there so Sally and I can work it."

"Okay, but the reassignment has to come through channels. First the coroner needs to change his death finding and a homicide number needs to be assigned. Once that happens, I'll talk to Jeb and have him put in for it," referring to Captain Jeb Calloway, my boss at Homicide Special.

"I'm sorry about Hawaii, but I owe this to Walt. I can't let anybody else do it."

"I understand, babe. You don't have to apologize. What are you doing now? You want to meet me for an early dinner someplace?"

"I gotta go back to Harbor Division. I promised the two primaries who handled the original squeal I'd keep them in the pipeline. I want to do it in person."

"How about we meet at the Tiki Hut again around eight? Mai Tais on me."

"Book it."

Kovacevich and Cole were not happy with me, but they weren't exactly pissed off either. They were somewhere in between. Mostly they were just frustrated and angry at the events that had produced their mistake. We were standing in their detective's cubicle on the second floor of the new precinct house in Harbor City. I watched as each of them reviewed the top sheet on the Oakcrest Pathology and Medical Group's autopsy report.

Cole was frowning. "How the fuck did our ME miss this?" he growled.

"It happens. On the surface it looked like suicide. They were moving fast."

After rereading the top sheet for about the third time, Kovacevich finally looked up. "Good work, Scully. It makes me and Cole look like donkeys, but at least a righteous homicide didn't get lost."

"Listen. So this stays in channels and to keep your record clean, I think it would be best for you to be the ones to take this report back to the L.A. coroner. Tell him the private autopsy was ordered by Huntington House because they were the beneficiaries of Walt's life insurance. Talk to Ray Tsu over at North Mission Road. He already knows I'm looking into this and he's a friend. He'll smooth it over."

"Thanks," Cole said.

"The ME's office is gonna want to do another autopsy and establish their own result," I continued. "I've already arranged to have Walt's remains made ready to ship. You should call over to Oakcrest and have them send him back over to Mission Road."

"I can't believe our chop shop missed this," Kovacevich said, frowning again at the report in her hand.

"I got lucky, and I had an advantage that the rest of you didn't." They waited to hear me out. "I knew the guy. I was pretty sure he'd never commit suicide."

They didn't react to that, just stood there frowning.

"By the way, I'm in the process of getting the case moved to my homicide table, so if you could e-mail the file over to me at the Glass House I'd appreciate it."

We all exchanged cards, and then I closed my briefcase and prepared to leave.

"This Walter Dix guy was a close friend?" Cole asked.

"He raised me from the time I was six."

"You sure you're the one to be working on it?" he continued. "You get too close to something you can make different kinds of mistakes. It's also out of department policy for a detective to work a case where he's emotionally involved."

"We're not related so there's no policy issue. He just ran the group home where I was placed as a kid. Besides, that rule never made sense to me. Who better to work it than somebody who cares? With me, this case never goes cold."

When I walked out, they were still holding Walt's new autopsy finding, rereading it and shaking their heads.

Good homicide cops hate making mistakes. This murder had just missed going over the falls where it would have been lost forever, and they were both pissed off about it.

CHAPTER 20

I WAS IN A DEEP FUNK AND angry with myself as I left Harbor Division. I couldn't get past this festering guilt. I was marinating in dangerous self-analysis even though I knew that was no way to work a case.

Suicides are intensely personal. A man at odds with himself looks into his own abyss, not telling anyone about the devastation he feels, pretending to most around him that everything is okay. Usually only his wife or close friends will see evidence of it. Then suddenly and without warning he ends it. Since almost nobody saw it coming, nobody is really in a position to stop it but the victim or the immediate family.

I could almost deal with Walt's death being a suicide. Almost. I could sort of absolve myself from blame if he died by his own hand. After all, he hadn't reached out to me. He hadn't asked for my help, even though I'd not been around to give it.

Murder, on the other hand, was a whole different situation. In a murder, there's a perp. A dark presence who seeks to harm. There's usually a motive. Motives are often transparent, even to bystanders. If you're paying attention, a murder should not be a surprise event.

A good friend, especially if he's a cop, should see it coming. There might have been prior threats of harm, which would have caused behavior modifications in Walt that I could have spotted, asked about, and evaluated. *Method*, *motive*, and *opportunity* are the three pillars of all homicide investigations. I live by those words. I should have known something was wrong, and that's why I was so angry.

I was furious for having been absent without cause from Walt's life. Had I been there, I could have made Pop confide in me. I could have stopped this from happening.

I parked my car at the valet in front of the Tiki Hut, got out, and dragged my guilt-ridden ass through an entrance lit with flaming torches, gave my name to the maître d', and was led through a half-empty restaurant, out to the deck that sat right on the ocean sand, only three blocks from my house. Alexa was seated under an outdoor heater. She had a surprise guest.

My son, Chooch, rose to hug me as I approached the table. I kissed Alexa and, as we sat down, I thought, this is just right. These are the two people I want to be with.

"I thought you could never miss training table during spring ball," I said to my handsome, six-foot-four, half-Hispanic son.

"They let me out because I had to go over and see a doc in West L.A. for deep ultrasound," he explained.

"How's the hammie?"

"It's a bitch. Hamstrings take forever. Fortunately, this one didn't get pulled too bad. If I'm careful and don't reinjure it I should be back on the field in six to eight days." He was smiling, trying to keep it upbeat even though I knew he was panicked about losing position and dropping down on the depth chart. Coach Pete Carroll runs an open program, so everybody always has a chance to move up. Football at USC is a lot of fun, but it's also a tough, competitive hustle.

"You guys ready to order?" Alexa asked, smiling at the guy talk while passing menus around.

Alexa and I had the classic Mai Tai, Chooch had a Coke, and we all ordered the teriyaki-steak special. While we waited for the meals, we talked some more about school and spring ball.

"I was doing great 'til this hamstring," Chooch said. "Coach says you don't lose your position on the depth chart through injury, but my not being on the field can't help. I gotta totally concentrate on getting rehabbed."

It went on like that for a while, until our dinners came. Then Chooch abruptly changed the subject.

"Mom tells me Walter Dix was real important to you. That's why you guys canceled Hawaii."

"Yeah," I said. "He was."

"Then how come you never talked about him?"

I sat for a moment and tried to deal with that.

"It was a mistake not to," I said. "I should have." Alexa reached out and took my hand. "Pop Dix ran the foster home where I lived from the time I was six until I graduated high school. He was the only person back then who cared whether I did my homework or got into fights. Cared if I was hurting or afraid. Walter stood between me and disaster. But when he needed me, I was nowhere around. I failed him, and in doing so I failed myself." The last part came out almost as a whisper.

"If I said something like that, you know what you'd say to me, Dad?"

"No."

"You'd say, 'Suck it up, Chooch. Stop feeling sorry for yourself. It's not the way to solve your problem.' "

"Is that what I'd say?"

"Yeah. It wasn't your fault."

"I can't get past my betrayal," I said. "I'm trying, but it's eating me up."

"Y'know, Dad, you can never pay people back for the favors they do. The best you can usually do is pass those favors on."

I looked down at my plate, then stirred my tropical drink, wondering how the hell to get out of this conversation.

"When we first met, you didn't know that you were my dad," Chooch continued. "But you reached out to me anyway. Got me out of that gang. You cared about me when nobody else did. There was only you between me and disaster, the same way Mr. Dix was there for you. When you saved me, you passed his favor on."

"It isn't quite that simple," I said.

"It is," Chooch replied. "It's exactly that simple."

Alexa squeezed my hand, and when I looked over, she nodded.

Later that night, after Chooch went back to USC and we got home, Alexa and I were again in the backyard.

A low fog had dropped over the coast, and we were sitting in a thick white cloud, unable to even see halfway across the small canal that runs past our house. She held my hand as a distant foghorn blared mournfully miles away out in the ocean.

I thought about what Chooch had told me, how you can rarely pay people back for the good deeds they do. Circumstances almost never align so perfectly that they allow for that to happen. So you drag your debts around instead, feeling bad because you haven't been able to square things. As Chooch had said, the closest you usually come to a payback is some sort of transference. Becoming a cop was part of that for me.

But now that Walt was gone the debt had been prematurely canceled. His death had just turned into a homicide and that gave me a fresh chance. At least I could now go out there and solve his murder.

Alexa was studying me carefully as I sat beside her. "I think you're way too emotional about this," she said, echoing Detective Cole's concern. "You better snap out of your funk or I'm not gonna let Cal assign this case to you."

"I should have been there. I should have seen what Walt was going through," I said softly.

"But you weren't and you didn't. You'll never do right by Walt now if you've got your chin on your chest. You've got to work this like any other murder. Unemotionally and with objectivity. You do it any other way you're gonna screw up."

"Yeah, you're right. I'll pull it together."

She looked over at me, skeptically. "I was thinking,

since I'm on vacation for two weeks anyway and don't have anything to do, maybe I could give you a hand."

"Don't trust me to do this by myself?"

"You want my help, I'm in," she said. "I won't butt in on what Sally does, but I can handle stuff in the background. Then we can go over it and strategize together at night."

"You always were my best backup," I told her. I reached over and we slapped palms. "Partners," we said in unison.

"Since I'm gonna have a little role in this, you want to tell me what we're doing—what our first step is?"

"In the morning I'm gonna take a look at a guy named Rick O'Shea." Then I told her who he was and why he'd caught my interest.

"Sounds like a good thread to start pulling," she said. "What do you want me to do?"

"Put some pressure on the ME's office. This redo autopsy is a loser for them. They already know they're gonna end up looking bad. Don't let them delay it or push it off."

"Done," she said.

"I'm pissed off, Alexa. I'm really angry. How could I have let this happen?"

"Now you're cooking. Anger's good. Now go out and bring us back a collar." The night was turning cool so Alexa decided to go inside.

I sat there a little longer and slowly my anger turned to resolve. Suddenly I felt Walt's unseen presence hovering next to me. It was like the old days, when we'd been in the morning lineup, floating beyond the break, just outside the impact zone.

Without looking, we could always tell when a big one was coming. The energy of the wave building from the ocean floor touched a spot deep inside us, curling our toes with expectation.

I had that same feeling now. A huge swell of energy and expectation was beneath me. I could almost hear Walt shouting encouragement like he did when I was a boy, yelling at me to start cranking and tap the source.

In the old days we'd sometimes take off on the same wave, ride shoulder to shoulder, dropping in together behind the curl. Both of us lighting it up, fully covered, blasting out of the tube, rail to rail, riding the wall of glass all the way into the shore, shouting our excitement into the sky where only God could hear.

CHAPTER 21

AT SEVEN THIRTY THE NEXT morning I was getting ready to leave the house when the phone rang. Alexa was in the shower, so I picked it up.

"Scully?" a deep voice said.

"Yeah?"

"Sabas."

"How ya doing?"

"I need to meet with you."

"That's gonna be tough to arrange this morning," I said. "I'm running late. We can set it up for this afternoon or maybe tomorrow if you want."

"I'm parked outside your house. Let's do it now."

"Now's not convenient."

"I don't care."

This wasn't getting us anywhere.

"You better talk to me, Scully. You don't, I promise you're gonna regret it."

"I'll be right out."

I thought, *Who does this guy think he is*?

I grabbed my briefcase and jacket and walked out the door. A lowered five-windowed '53 Chevy pickup, painted bright yellow with a fifties-style flame job on the nose, was parked in the drive right across my rear bumper, blocking my egress.

Vargas was standing by the truck bed, dressed in jeans and a polo shirt. He had a BlackBerry in his hand.

"I don't have much time, so let's make this quick," I said.

"Scully, I did a little checking on you last night. Some friends of mine who work at the Public Defenders office say you have a very unorthodox style. You don't obey the rules."

"What's that supposed to mean?"

"You run stop signs, create legal messes."

"All that tells me is I musta put a bunch of good cases on your dirtbag friends in the PD's office."

"It's more than that."

"I don't need career counseling right now. Get to it. What's this about?"

We faced off over the bed of the Chevy.

"Where you going this morning?" he demanded.

"None of your business."

"If it's about Walt Dix, then I'm making it my business."

I stood there, trying to decide how to unload this guy. Then I pointed to his truck.

"You want to move that, or do I have to call for a police tow?"

"I know from my friends downtown that you're used to running things on your own, but with Walt's murder, that's going to change. I'm going to be taking the lead."

"It's an open homicide, Mr. Vargas. You hamper my active investigation, you're gonna eat a nice fat obstruction statute."

"Bullshit."

"Try me."

"I'm not like the others," Vargas said. "The law's my beat too. I know how the game works. It's gonna take the coroner two, maybe three days to alter his cause-of-death finding. Until that happens, this is still officially just a suicide. That means you got shit. You got no case for me to hamper. I can do whatever I want."

He was right, of course, but I didn't give him the satisfaction of saying that. I was looking for a plan of action that didn't include letting some East L.A. gang lawyer get in the way on my murder case.

"For the next two days, I'm gonna check into this on my own," Vargas said. "There's nothing you can do to stop me."

"That would be a mistake. We could screw the case up, not coordinate on a witness, create future havoc for the DA."

"That's why I came over," he said. "I cleared my court calendar. I'm willing to cooperate with you. I'll meet you halfway. I have some unique street contacts that could be very helpful in a pinch."

"Sabas, I know you're a tough guy. I see the old scars on your knuckles. What'd that used to say, *DEATH*?"

He looked down at both his hands as I went on.

"I checked you out too. I got a call from my office at eight this morning. You used to run with the Latin Kings as a kid. Word I get is you've got a thick sealed file in juvie."

"Si, lo sabes," he replied softly. The words rolled off his tongue. It was obvious that Spanish was his native language. "You're right." He held up both hands. "I had *DEATH* on my right, *MATAR* on my left. I could kill you in two languages."

"I don't want your help," I told him. "If I see you anywhere around this case, I'll find some charge that works and lay it on you. Now move your truck or you'll have to pick it up in police impound."

He hesitated for a moment before moving to the driver's-side door. Then he stepped up on the running board and faced me over the roof of the cab.

"I talked to Diamond. She said you never came around, that you barely ever talked to Walt the last couple of years."

"See ya."

"Sounds to me like you're probably dealing with a heavy load of guilt right now because after all Pop did, you dissed him. Why was that? You been running away from your past and now you feel bad because you still owe him big and he's gone. That why you don't want to share this case with the rest of us?"

He'd come pretty damn close.

"Hey, I get it, Detective. Remember when I told you that Pop called me a few days before he died? That he wanted to set up a meeting?"

I looked at him and waited.

"He wanted to see me right away, but I blew him off. I was in court on a murder trial. Too busy. I told him I'd see him in a week. If I'd met with him right away like he wanted, then maybe he'd still be alive. Like you, I fucked up and didn't help him when he needed it. I'm not sleeping over it. Shit's been killin' me."

I only took a moment to think about it before I said, "Park your truck on the lawn over there, we'll take my car. I'll tell you what we're doing on the way."

Vargas moved his Chevy truck. Then he grabbed a worn leather briefcase from the front seat and climbed into the Acura beside me.

I put the MDX in gear and pulled out heading toward the 101 freeway and Rick O'Shea's house in Calabasas.

CHAPTER 22

AS WE DROVE, I TOLD VARGAS that I didn't really have anything solid except for a strong feeling that Rick O'Shea was a strange choice to be running the nonprofit that owned Huntington House.

As I talked, Vargas had his BlackBerry out and was typing the information onto an e-page.

"I'll run him when I get back to the office," he said. "I've got some good sources."

"I already ran him. Nothing major. But trust me, the guy's slime."

Sabas nodded.

The address on Lupine Lane turned out to be a very large, new, Spanish hacienda–style house on about two acres with a front fountain and cobblestone drive located in an expensive new development. It looked like a hell of a lot of house for a guy who ran a charitable nonprofit corporation. The maroon Escalade I'd seen in the parking lot at Huntington House was parked out front.

"Maybe he's independently wealthy," Sabas said, reading my thoughts.

While we waited for O'Shea to leave his house so we could tail him, Sabas worked quietly on some legal documents in his briefcase. Occasionally, his BlackBerry would ring and he would speak softly to somebody in Spanish. The calls all seemed to involve a gang drive-by where he was defending two of the shooters.

He kept instructing the person he was talking to on which discovery motions he wanted filed first. He wasn't aware that I spoke Spanish. He thought he could have conversations in another language without my understanding. Maybe I could use that misconception to learn something that would come in handy down the line.

At about ten o'clock, it started to get warm in the car so I turned on the engine and the AC.

"Y'know, if we'd been both paying closer attention, maybe you and I coulda stopped this from happening," Sabas finally said, looking over at me.

"Right." I focused on the house, trying to keep his gaze out of mine. I didn't want him to see the pain I was hiding.

He was quiet for a minute, then he said, "You're right about my juvie record. I was at Huntington House in the early sixties. Twelve years old when I arrived. Already had a righteous one-eighty-seven on my yellow sheet. Back then I was working for a Latin Kings drug crew. I started out as a lookout at six years old. My set liked to use pee-wee G's for payback murders. It was how you got jumped in. The added benefit was, if one of us got caught, we'd only get juvie time.

"When I was nine it was finally my turn. I popped a Sureno over by one of our drug houses. The vato was only sixteen, but he hadda go 'cause he was doing corners on one of our blocks. The flute I used was a piece of rust. I'm amazed now it even fired. My cousin, Arturo, gave it to me, and 'cause I never owned my own burner, like an idiot I ditched it in my backyard. I wanted to keep it. Took the cops about ten minutes to find the damn thing.

"After I did my juvie CYA time, the courts assigned me to Huntington House. I found out later that Pop heard about my case and rigged that for me, got me out of the sheriff's honor rancho two years early. Once Pop was on a mission, there was no ducking him. He kept hammering on my juvie judge until she placed me there."

It was a familiar story. I'd heard different versions from other Huntington House grads.

Sabas went on. "When I arrived at Huntington House, I got put in Harbor Elementary. I had lotsa little homies in that *escuela*. With my bad-ass murder rep I was an instant big deal. A leader. I was down for my boys. But Pop was having none of it. As soon as he found out, he wouldn't let me see any of those kids, then he put me into a new school in Long Beach where I didn't have any vato brothers. Drove me all the way over there each morning himself. Pop got me out of my old set by force of will."

Vargas stopped his story and sat there thinking about it for a moment. "Y'know, I never got that dead Sureno off my conscience. It's been half a century and I still dream about that kid."

The overactive BlackBerry was now off and forgotten in his scarred hands. He turned to face me.

"Since he died, I've been seeing Pop in my memory, remembering him like he was back then. You ever do that?"

"All the time."

"He take you surfing?"

"Yeah."

"Losers on parade, right? I got to go a lot because I couldn't get out of my own way back then. Once we were alone, out beyond the break, Pop would be working to convince me I should take a better path. Nothing I did got him off my back. The man was on me like gel coat.

"I can still see him paddling out on that big ol' gun he used, that rhino chaser. Catchin' a pipe ride, getting vertical on his log, riding it 'til the curl collapsed. Then afterward, all of us on the beach having Cokes and sweet rolls. Me wondering what the fuck I'm gonna do with myself. How I'm gonna get through tomorrow. Wishin' someone would just save me the trouble and take me off the count." He stopped for a moment before he added, "Walt kept me alive. He got me all the way from there to here."

"Pretty much says it," I answered softly.

We sat there in silence, both dealing with separate memories.

Half an hour later the front door opened and Rick O'Shea came out. He was dressed in workout gear, carrying his gym bag. His muscles rippled.

"Yeah, this *pendejo* definitely came off the wrong

bus," Sabas said, watching as Rick O'Shea got into his car.

I let him pull away, then I put the MDX in gear, dropping in about a block and a half back. We followed the maroon Escalade onto the 118 and then all the way into downtown L.A.

CHAPTER 23

O'SHEA PARKED IN A LOT SOUTH of Broadway, six blocks from the financial center in a slum neighborhood full of discount clothing stores and run-down secondhand shops.

I pulled in, took a ticket, and parked a few lanes over. Sabas and I watched as he yanked his monogrammed gym bag out of the passenger seat and made his way across the cracked asphalt to a medium-sized brick storefront that faced the parking lot. It had a dirty, plate-glass, floor-to-ceiling window with alarm tape and small gold letters that said:

NHB INC.

"Wait here," I told Sabas, then got out of the Acura, went to the trunk, rummaged around, and found a Dodgers baseball cap. I pulled it out and put it on. Disguise. I crossed back to the passenger window and looked in at Vargas.

"Stay in the car, I'll be right back." I fished in my pocket for dark glasses.

"Whatta you gonna do?"

"Don't know yet. Keep an eye on my back."

I walked across the pavement toward the storefront, past a beautiful, modified red and white Indian motorcycle that had fancy leather saddlebags and was parked in a spot reserved for the manager of NHB. As I walked past the chopper, I wondered what I would find behind the grimy plate-glass window.

I pulled the baseball hat lower, put on my darks, opened the door, and walked inside.

It was a small gym, or more correctly, a fight-training center. Except for the plate glass in front there were no other windows. Most of the light came from old-style wire-enclosed ceiling fixtures. There was almost no concession to décor. The benches and workout machines were mismatched. What paint there was had chipped long ago. An octagon for cage fighting stood in the center of the room. Heavy bags and workout equipment dominated the perimeter. The smell of sweat lingered. It was very old school.

One or two experiments in chemistry were taking turns lifting the bar on a Smith machine over in one corner. The Smith was a weight-lifting apparatus also known as a hat rack because it has a rack that guides and supports the plates. We have a few in the police gym where I sometimes work out, but I'm a free-weight guy so I've never actually used one.

There were several poster-sized pictures of past mixed martial arts events hanging on the paint-peeled brick walls. I spotted one that showed Rick "Ricochet" O'Shea advertising something called "The Fall Brawl." In the shot, he was pushing his flat nose at an equally intimidating opponent. Underneath it read:

"RICOCHET" O'SHEA
VS.
KIMBO SLEDGE

ONLY ONE WILL WALK AWAY

There were posters showing pictures of other gym celebrities—Raymond "Stingray" Jackson was a big black guy with a shaved head, Gary "The Great" White was aptly named. A huge glowering blond guy with a Mohawk named Dane Vanderheiden called himself "The Striking Viking." Never heard of any of them, but I don't follow ultimate fighting so that didn't mean anything.

All of them looked like they'd be serious competition in a brawl.

I moved behind a power rack, out of sight of the two fighters on the weight machine, and tried to spot where Rick O'Shea had gone, but he'd disappeared into the back somewhere.

"Whatta ya want?" a pissed-off voice behind me said. I swung around and found myself facing a six-foot-three pile of pale white gristle with a serious V-taper. He had sixty-inch shoulders and a monstrous set of lats that sloped down from his armpits to a thirty-two-inch waist. He was wearing a loose-fitting, low-cut sweatshirt that said *NHB* on the front. Under that were words that defined the letters: *NO HOLDS BARRED.* He had a shaved, torpedo-shaped head to go with his scowl.

"I was thinking maybe I'd get into MMA," I said, smiling. "You got a program I could join? A trainer who could work me out, show me some striking and ground-fighting techniques?"

"Private gym," he said. "We only train club professionals. No cardio bunnies. Take it down the street."

I pointed at the posters on the wall. "These the guys you train? Pretty impressive."

He gave me nothing. No expression. No personal connection. He just stood with massive bowling-pin forearms crossed, looking like an ad for a toilet-bowl product. A facial muscle high on his cheek began to twitch.

"And you are?" I asked.

"Getting angry," he answered.

"I really like this place," I persisted. "It's near where I work in the financial district. I'd only come in on lunch breaks two or three times a week for an hour. I'm really serious about this. I can pay whatever it takes."

"How many times I gotta tell you we're a private gym? We don't deal with the public."

"Tell you what, let me write down my number so you can call me if you change your mind."

"Get the fuck outta here," he growled.

Just then, Rick O'Shea came out of the back.

"Hey, Chris, you seen the shot kit? I left it in the lockup, but Brian's been in there cleaning up again. Everything's moved."

"In my desk," Chris answered. I pulled my ball cap lower, trying to keep my face turned away so I wouldn't get recognized. O'Shea had only seen me for a moment in Diamond Peterson's office, and that was two days ago. I was pretty sure, in my hot disguise, he wouldn't make me.

"Do I know you?" Rick said, immediately busting that hope. He moved closer to get a better look.

"Don't think so."

"You look familiar."

"I got one of those familiar-type faces."

I started toward the door, but he was moving along with me as I went.

"Wait a minute, wait a minute. You're the guy. With Diamond. From the home."

"Sorry I bothered you," I said to Chris. I had my hand on the door, but Rick O'Shea managed to get between me and the threshold, pushing my hand off the release bar. He suddenly snatched the ball cap off my head.

"What the fuck is this?" he said angrily. "You following me or something?"

I started to open the door again, but Rick slammed it shut. Turned the bolt.

I was armed and just seconds from giving this idiot a gun-sight tonsillectomy when some instinct told me I should hold on and try to BS my way out. Bad decision.

Without warning, Rick O'Shea hit me square in the forehead. I could feel my skin tear as a nasty cut opened up. I've been hit by some pretty good punchers, but this one rocked me, dimmed my lights, and sagged my knees. I went down, bowing before them.

"Get his wallet," Rick said. Chris grabbed my wallet from my pocket.

He was about to open it and find my badge when the plate-glass window of the gym suddenly exploded inward, raining glass shards all over us. It was followed an instant later by the entire front end of my car. Then Sabas Vargas was out of the driver's seat, swinging a tire iron, which I guess he'd gotten from the back of my SUV.

It happened so fast nobody had much time to react. Vargas bounced the metal bar off O'Shea's head, sending him to the floor. Then he dropped the iron and ripped a body shot at Chris's midsection, following it with an impressive uppercut. The big heavyweight was just turning toward him and didn't see it coming. He doubled over with the first blow, flew backward with the second. Both men were now spitting out blood and chipped teeth.

"Did you have something else you wanted to do or can we get the fuck out of here?" Sabas said.

I stumbled to my feet and started to get in the passenger seat of my idling car, which was parked over some workout mats halfway through the window.

I suddenly came to my senses and went back, pried my wallet out of Chris's hand, and relieved both of them of their wallets while Sabas got behind the wheel of my Acura. I half-limped, half-ran back to the passenger side of the car and tumbled in.

Sabas already had it in reverse and we squealed backward out of the gym. He smoked a U-turn in the parking lot, hitting the classic old Indian chopper that was parked out front, knocking it over on its side. Seconds later we were flying down Broadway, heading out of downtown.

CHAPTER 24

WE GOT OFF THE HOLLYWOOD Freeway at Santa Monica Boulevard and parked near Paramount Studios. Sabas kept the motor running. I was slumped in the passenger seat, dripping blood, looking down at a bunch of spaghetti wires hanging out from under my dash.

"What'd you do to my car?" I asked as blood drops continued to land sporadically in my lap.

"You had the keys. I needed to hot-wire the starter," he said. "Back in the day, I used to steal cars for my set, but those old ignition boxes were a lot easier to open."

"Why didn't you tell me you were such an animal? That was awesome," I said, looking over at him with new respect.

He smiled at me and started massaging his scarred knuckles, kneeding them as his entire right hand began to puff up.

"My punch has lost nothing, homes," he said, sounding like the vato g-ster he'd been fifty years ago. "My first agg-assault in two decades. I forgot how much fun it is, clocking guys."

"And you say I'm the one who runs stop signs and makes legal messes."

"I looked in the front window. I could see it was going bad. It was the best I could come up with." He grinned.

"It was great, Sabas. Perfect. I'm definitely takin' you on my next beat-down."

He kept smiling, pumped by his adrenaline rush, while my blood continued to run down the side of my face, ruining my trousers.

"You're making a mess. You better stop that bleeding. Looks like it might need stitches," he said.

I reached into the glove box, got some tissues, and pressed them hard onto the open cut on my forehead. After a few minutes, I stemmed the flow.

"Let's see what we got here." I pulled the two wallets out of my pocket with my free hand, handed one to Vargas, and took the other myself.

I had Baldy's ID. It turned out Chris was somebody named Christian Calabro. According to his DL, he was thirty-two, six three, and weighed two-sixty, so I'd definitely been fighting out of my weight class. He had four hundred in cash and half a dozen credit cards, including a Visa that was issued to him from some outfit called the Mesa Investment Group.

I went through the glassine section. Mostly business cards from personal trainers, nutritionists, and sports doctors. I found several business cards that said:

CHRIS "CLUBBER" CALABRO
MMA CHAMPION, TRAINER

"What's the Mesa Investment Group?" Sabas asked.

I looked over and saw that he had removed a similar Visa card from Rick O'Shea's wallet.

"Don't know."

He turned on his BlackBerry, went to the Internet, and accessed some Web site. Then he started typing in information. After a moment, he looked over.

"It's some kind of a money-management corporation with an address on Wilshire," he said. "Wanta go look?"

"Might as well go bleed on them for a while," I said.

We headed out on Santa Monica Boulevard, took a left on Highland to Wilshire, then drove another ten blocks or so to the edge of the Miracle Mile.

Sabas pulled the Acura up to the curb across the street from the address.

It was a huge steel and glass building with twenty-foot-high letters on the roof that said:

MESA INVESTMENT GROUP

There was a logo at the end of the name that looked like a desert mesa with a circle around it. The sign took up the whole east face of the building roof.

"I think we need to back off and think this over," I said.

"Don't want me driving your car through another lobby window?"

"One a day is plenty."

Forty minutes later Sabas parked behind his yellow '53 pickup truck next to my driveway in Venice. He didn't turn off the engine. There was a new easiness between us. We'd definitely bonded with our little fist-fight, even though I hadn't hit anybody yet.

"I wouldn't turn off the engine," he said. "I think I ruined the coil getting it started. You might not be able to get it running again. Sorry."

"Small price to pay for saving my life."

He was still massaging his swelling, almost clown-sized right hand.

"I think we should all meet again, right away," he said. "Like even as early as this evening. I'll have some people in my office do a run on the Mesa Investment Group, see what they're all about.

"I can promise you, those two dump trucks we clocked aren't moonlighting as corporate investment managers. We need to find out how all this affects Creative Solutions and Huntington House."

I didn't want to tell him what I really had planned and how after the new autopsy tomorrow, he and the rest of the pallbearers were no longer going to be dealing with this anymore. Instead, I said, "I don't feel too hot. My head is still ringing. Let's put that meeting off and talk in the morning. I'll call you and set it up."

He nodded, said good-bye, and got out of my car, leaving me there. After he drove off, I made a U-turn and headed to the freeway, then took the 10 back toward Parker Center.

I parked in my assigned space in the underground

garage, said the AAA prayer, then turned off the Acura. When I tried to start it up again, the ignition clicked at me. I had to make arrangements to get my car towed and check out a slick-back detective car from the motor pool.

I used my cell and set that up, then went to the men's room and cleaned up the blood as best I could. I took the elevator to Financial Crimes, which was on three, and looked up a civilian employee I knew who was assigned there. Her name is Trina Marks and she is one of those people who, if you give her any opening, will fill your ear with endless streams of personal and professional gossip. But she had a big heart, was always willing to do favors, and was a wiz on the computer. In the past she'd discovered things in the system that nobody else had found.

After I told her I'd cut my head in a traffic accident, I sat down beside her. I had my list ready and put it down on her console.

"You got a case number for this?" she asked.

"Use my badge," I said, laying it down in front of her. "I'm getting a fresh H-number tomorrow. I'll phone it down."

She punched in my badge number, then opened her LexisNexis file and started doing both civil as well as legal searches on the list of names I'd just given her.

While she worked, I heard about her nine-year-old nephew's All-Star game, her husband's hemorrhoids, her sister's breast reduction, and the juicy details on two messy cop divorces.

At six o'clock I left with some fairly provocative

questions and a ringing left ear, which was the one closest to her keyboard.

When I got home, I couldn't find a place to park. Alexa's car was in the drive, taking that space. The narrow alley, which usually had open spots, was packed. Somebody must have been having a party.

I put the department slick-back in the only spot I could find, half a block away. As I was walking back to our house, I started paying closer attention and spotted Jack's red and black Harley, Vicki's blue Camry, and Sabas's yellow '53 pickup.

When I walked inside my living room, I found out that I was the one having the party.

The entire Pallbearers' Murder Club was in the backyard, drinking beer with Alexa.

CHAPTER 25

THEY WERE ALL STARING AT me as I stood in the open sliding-glass door that leads to the backyard.

As soon as she saw me, Alexa got up and crossed the yard. "Sabas said you two got in a fight, but he didn't say you got injured," she said. She raised her hand and touched the nasty-looking cut on my forehead.

I had checked my reflection in the rearview mirror before getting out of my borrowed D-ride. The cut had an ugly Frankenstein quality—jagged, crusted, filled with dried blood.

"Sometimes to get difficult facts, I'll punch my head through things," I said, smiling. "It's how I investigate."

"That needs stitches," my wife said, frowning.

"I'll pull it together with a butterfly bandage. The scar will go nice with all the others."

I turned to the rest of the group. Diamond was seated at the garden table. Her shoulders were sagging, and she looked used up. Seriana was beside the barbecue, sitting ramrod straight. Vicki and Sabas were facing me, their backs to the canal. Jack, as usual, was tipped back arrogantly in one of our cast-iron patio chairs, feet up on a bench, studying me with his usual fuck-you smile.

Sabas had already filled them in, explaining how we'd followed Rick O'Shea to the NHB Gym and how it had ended up.

"Mr. O'Shea recognized you? What am I supposed to tell him when he asks?" Diamond seemed mortified.

"Shortly this is going to be a full-fledged homicide investigation. If O'Shea gets frisky, I'll pull him in as a material witness and hold him," I said. Diamond frowned. She didn't like it.

"Sabas says that you told him as soon as this becomes a police case, we can't be part of it anymore," Seriana said.

"I have bosses and LAPD protocol," I replied. "The department won't tolerate an unauthorized vigilante investigation."

Seriana said, "Shane, I have to redeploy soon and I don't want to leave the country not knowing what happened here."

Vargas crossed to the cooler that Alexa had pulled out of our hall closet and filled with ice. He reached inside with his swollen right hand and gingerly pulled out a beer, passing it over to me.

"I ran the Mesa Investment Group through a legal search program I use in my office," he said. "They're a pretty big deal. The founder and CEO is a guy named Eugene Charles Mesa. People call him E. C. He's only fifty and already close to a billionaire. Mesa Group mostly does acquisitions. They're turnaround experts who buy distressed companies, fix the problems, and then either run them for profit or sell them."

I already knew all that from Trina's computer run.

Vargas continued, "I also did a deep financial search and found out that Mesa owns that entire block where the NHB Gym is located downtown. It's scheduled for redevelopment next year. There's been a bunch of stories in the *L.A. Times*. The city is very excited about it. He's gonna put in two high-rise office towers."

All stuff I'd also learned an hour ago from Trina. As Sabas indicated, Eugene Mesa had a lot of political juice in L.A., with tentacles deep into city government. That meant he also probably had some pretty good leverage with my sixth-floor bosses at the LAPD. E. C. Mesa would need to be handled very carefully.

"I'm now working with Diamond," Vicki Lavicki announced, changing the subject. "You're looking at the new secretary-treasurer of Huntington House. I'm taking some sick days off from Kinney and Glass so I can devote myself full time to helping us get ready for that state audit."

"And not a moment too soon, girl. I was dying over there," Diamond said.

"Starting tomorrow, I'm gonna begin building old records going back two or three years to see if I can find out why there was never enough money to run that place."

"You're wasting time on that fucking audit," Jack said, suddenly taking his muddy feet down from my bench and sitting up straight. "This isn't even complicated. We need to hoist this Eugene Mesa guy up by his heels and start looking for wet spots."

"That's a bad idea," I said quickly. "We need to move very slow with those guys over at Mesa Group."

"Why?" Jack sneered. "We supposed to be afraid of a buncha guys with Princeton MBAs?"

"Shane's right," Alexa confirmed. "If we're not careful, Mesa could put us in a dangerous political situation."

From Jack's body language, it was obvious he didn't agree.

"I don't mean to throw you guys out," I said, "but I have a blinding headache. I think I might have sustained a minor concussion."

Everyone quickly finished their beers, and we agreed to meet at an IHOP pancake house up the street at 9:00 A.M. tomorrow.

After they left, Alexa wanted to call a doctor.

"I don't have a headache," I told her. "My head's been rated to break stone." I settled back into my chair and fished a fresh beer out of the ice chest. "I just wanted them out of here. I couldn't listen to any more of that. Fucking Jack thinks because he breaks the law, he understands it. Sabas thinks he should run the case because he's a lawyer. Vicki is an adrenaline junkie who packs a .44 Bulldog in her purse, and Seriana wants to rush a result just so she'll know what happened to Pop before she goes back to Iraq."

"They just want to help, Shane. I don't think you're being fair."

"So far all we've done is alert those muscle heads at the gym that we're onto them. I'm the one who screwed that up. Bad as that is, now Jack wants to brace Eugene Mesa. This case is moving in the wrong direction."

Then I asked, "How you doing with the ME? He gonna issue a new finding tomorrow? We need this case to become official fast so I can stop dealing with these people."

"That's going to be a little harder than we thought," she said.

"Why?"

"Rico from Pico wants to make the next cut." She was talking about our Chief Medical Examiner, Rico Comancho, who rose up from a ghetto in Pico Rivera, put himself through UCLA med school, and now headed the Medical Examiner's office for the city of L.A. "He took the case away from Ray Tsu," she concluded.

"Rico hasn't made a cut since he got promoted to Chief," I said. "What's with that?"

"Somebody leaked the whole thing about Walt to the *L.A. Times.* They're doing a major story on him and Huntington House for the Sunday 'Calendar' section, making this a high-profile deal. You know how Rico is. He feels he has to personally protect the integrity of his office. He was at an ME's convention in Vegas, but he's flying back over the weekend. The new autopsy is scheduled for next Monday. Sorry."

A few minutes later, Alexa went inside to get disinfectant and the butterfly bandages. Then, while I sat still, she stood over me and pulled the wound on my forehead together, taping the edges closed.

While she worked, I was thinking I could sure use some karmic intervention.

Come on, Walt, I pleaded silently to the heavens. *I'm doing this for you. Get busy and change my luck up there. Make something happen.*

CHAPTER 26

WHAT HAPPENED WASN'T GOOD.

It started with a phone call at 1:15 A.M. I rolled over and pulled my cell out of its charger. I didn't recognize the number on the screen as I fumbled it up to my ear.

"What?" I snarled. I don't wake up happy.

"Scully?" Whoever it was sounded like he was out of breath. Like he was running.

"Who is this?"

"It's Jack."

I heard something crash. Heard him groan. More heavy breathing. "Just a minute," he said. "Hang on. I got my hands full." It sounded as if he was running again, then he was breathing hard into the receiver.

"I think this is better. You still there?"

"Jack? What's going on? What're you doing?"

"Listen, dude. I got us something. I broke the case wide open. This is huge but I laid the bike down so I'm on foot. Near Park La Brea. I could really use a dust-off."

"You want me to pick you up?"

There was a long pause. "Well, *yeah*."

"What is it?" Alexa asked, rolling over and looking at me through tangled hair.

"I don't know yet. It's Jack."

"Scully." He was in my ear again. "Dude, you are gonna totally blaze when you see what I got for us."

"Where are you again?"

"Hang on a minute. There's a street sign up here. Lemme look." I heard what sounded like cycle boots running on concrete, then, "I'm on Hauser near Sixth Street in the La Brea district. You know where that is?"

"Sorta."

"Listen, Scully. Get your ass over here, pronto. This is huge. You're gonna love this."

"Now? It's after one in the morning!"

"Fuck yes, now. Come on, man. Oh, shit!" I heard running again and more heavy breathing, then Jack said, "Hey, I gotta get moving. I guess I won't be on Hauser after all. Get your ass in gear and come in this direction. I'll call back." Then he was gone.

"What was that all about?" Alexa said. She was now propped up on one elbow, watching me as I quickly dressed in old jeans and a T-shirt, then stepped into my flip-flops.

"I don't know. It's Jack. He says he's got something. He needs me to pick him up in Park La Brea. He was running, out of breath."

Alexa frowned. "I don't like the sound of that."

"Neither do I but I'll handle it. Stay here. I'm gonna

use your car. Is your new little Beretta automatic still in the glove box?"

"Yes. Did he say what was going on?"

"No." I leaned over and kissed her. "I told you these people were gonna make problems. I told you that, remember?"

"I remember."

She was still frowning as I ran out the door.

I wanted to use Alexa's BMW because I wasn't sure what Jack was up to and something told me that rolling around in a black and white department slick-back might be a little too high profile. It was the first of about six bad decisions I made in the next half hour.

Alexa's backup .25 automatic was in the glove box as she said. It was a tiny, palm-sized Beretta Bobcat with a seven-shot magazine and a pop-up barrel that took an eighth cartridge in the chamber. The way it worked was the escaping gas on the first shot chambered the subcompact so you could fire the rest of the magazine. When I checked, I found the gun was empty. No box of shells. I should have gone back inside for my own gun, but I didn't. Mistake number two.

I took off in the BMW instead, and by going Code Two I made it to Park La Brea in under twenty minutes. I was on 6th Street when my cell rang again. It was Jack.

"I'm almost there," I told him.

"Not on Hauser anymore," he panted. He was running again. "I'm gonna try to get into Pan Pacific Park. Meet me there."

"Jack, what the fuck is going on?"

"Can't really talk right now, dude. Later."

Just before he disconnected I thought I heard sirens in the background.

"Please don't let him be running from the cops," I pleaded to Alexa's dashboard.

I made it to the park. Between the buildings of the Park La Brea apartments, I spotted the giant Mesa Investment Group sign a few blocks south on Wilshire. I heard sirens getting closer, and the premonition of disaster struck. I should have turned around and gone home, but I didn't. Call that mistake number three.

I pulled Alexa's BMW to the curb, got out, left the car, and ran into the park.

I moved quietly through the semi-lit darkness. As I got closer to the small amphitheater, I heard a low whistle. I turned, and there was Jack, dressed as he was that afternoon, hiding behind a Dumpster, his face bathed in sweat. The police sirens in the background were definitely getting louder.

"Where you parked?" he whispered urgently. "We sorta need to jet out of here, man."

I could have arrested him right then, but I didn't. And of course, that was number four.

"What the fuck is going on, Jack?"

"Scully, you're gonna kiss me when you see what I got. I solved Pop's murder, but right now, we gotta book."

He started running back in the direction I'd just come. "Let's go. Where you parked?" he said as he sprinted past.

"Jack, what did you do?" I was loping along about ten yards behind him trying to stay up.

"I did what you should have done. I fucking broke this case wide open!" he yelled over his shoulder as he ran.

Then we were lit by a flashlight. The second it hit us, I knew it was one of the new department-issued mini-Maglites. Cops hated them because they put out a narrow beam.

The mini-Mags were just recently issued because of a lawsuit against the city filed by some special-interest group claiming that our old, foot-long, three-pound Maglites were unauthorized weapons. The idea was that the new ones were too small to use as bludgeons.

"Police! Stay where you are," the cop holding the mini-Maglite shouted.

"Let's go! This way!" Jack said veering right.

"Jack, come back here!" I shouted.

He suddenly spun around and headed back toward me. It was the first time I'd asked him to do something where he'd actually complied. Then I realized it wasn't me who'd turned him, but a fully lit X-car with its siren blaring. It careened around the corner and was charging across the grass right at us.

"Shit!" Now I actually started to run from my LAPD brothers. Mistake number five.

Jack flew past me, heading the other way, yelling, "Let's go! We gotta get outta here!" I made a grab for him but missed.

Then it got really strange. Four more squad cars

rounded into view and suddenly there were cops everywhere. All of them, out of their units with guns drawn, shouting at us. Jack and I were running around in the park, veering right, then left. The cops kept turning us, coming in on all sides. A big game of capture the flag with guns, batons, and Mace.

Jack was chased down and cornered first. Four cops descended on him, maced him, and started doing a bad-boy bongo on his head with their aluminum PR-24s. I was suddenly tackled from behind by two patrolmen, slammed to the ground, right onto my already-beaten face. I felt the cut on my forehead open up again. I tried to resist, and of course that was mistake number six.

I got maced for the effort, busted in the head, and finally, mercifully, I was handcuffed and it was over.

"I'm a cop!" I shouted. But even as I yelled this I knew it was going to be a hard sell. Both of my eyes were running thanks to the point-blank shot of Liquid Jesus. I had reopened the gash in my forehead and new blood was pouring down my cheek. The way I was dressed, in torn jeans and flip-flops with blood everywhere, the cop thing wasn't close to going over.

I was pushed into the back of a squad car. I looked over and saw Jack Straw in another black and white a few feet away. The insolent smile was finally gone. At least my brother officers had accomplished that much. He'd been pummeled and maced. His lip and head were bleeding.

Bad as all of this was, I could barely believe what happened next.

CHAPTER 27

THE UNIFORMS LEFT ME CUFFED and sitting in the back of the black and white while they dealt with Jack. Like most complete assholes in custody, he wouldn't stop running his mouth. He was saying all the dumb-ass things arrestees had been saying since law enforcement began.

"This is police harassment. You had no right to hit me. Wait'll my lawyer gets through with you."

Shut up, Jack, I thought.

They took his wallet, and one of the cops headed to another car to run him. They told him to be quiet or they were going to write him up as a 5150, which is our code for a head case. They threatened to call the EMTs and have him tranquilized. None of which slowed him down at all.

Finally, a weathered old Hispanic sergeant with five hash marks on his sleeve and whose nameplate said *S. Acosta* dropped anchor in the backseat beside me.

"Okay, sparky, what's your story?" He was already tired of me and we hadn't even started yet.

"I'm Shane Scully, an LAPD homicide detective."

"Then where's your wallet? Levinson says you don't have one. If you're a cop, then you obviously know it's mandated that all LAPD personnel carry their creds and a firearm at all times, on duty as well as off. Since you don't have either, as far as I'm concerned, that makes you a lying shitball."

"No. . . . I am a cop. I left my house so fast tonight I didn't remember to grab my badge case out of my desk."

"Or here's a better one," he said. "You learned while doing your last prison stretch that it's better not to carry ID when you're out capering so if you get caught, we can't run you or match you up to your old priors."

"I'm a police officer."

"You don't look like a police officer," he said, studying my still-bleeding forehead, torn jeans, and flip-flops. "You look like a guy out on a hot prowl who just came in second in an ass-kicking contest."

"My name is Shane Scully. Call my captain at Homicide Special."

"Right. We'll do that right after we notify the governor," he growled.

"You better do it now, Sergeant. I'm telling you I'm a homicide detective working out of Parker Center."

"No kidding." He pointed at Jack. "Then explain why your buddy over there did a B and E on the MIG building forty minutes ago."

"What's the MIG building?" I asked.

"Mesa Investment Group. He set off all the silent

alarms. We chased him on his motorcycle. Then, we lost him for about thirty minutes, and when he turns up again he's with you in the park. Start there."

"My wife is Alexa Scully. She's head of the LAPD Central Detective Bureau," I said. "I'll give you her number. You need to call her."

Before he could deal with that, another cop stuck his head in through the open back door and spoke to Sergeant Acosta.

"Sal, we just ran the other guy. Jack Straw has two outstanding warrants for federal bank robbery."

"He has *what*?" I said, astonished.

"Take both these humps to Men's Central Jail. Book Straw on the federal felonies and book this guy, whoever he is, as a John Doe material witness, until I can check his story or figure out something else."

Then a supervisor's car pulled up, and finally a cop I knew stepped out. He was a tall blond lieutenant named Gordon Moon. I used to play basketball with him when I was in Devonshire Division.

"Lieutenant Moon," I called out. He walked over to the squad car and looked in at me.

"Scully?" he said, with a puzzled look on his face. "What happened to your head? What're you doin' in there?"

"You know this guy?" Acosta said.

Moon opened the door and pulled me out. "Yeah."

"Don't tell me, he's really a cop," Acosta said. "I was just gonna transport him to MCJ."

"I sure wouldn't do that," Moon replied. "He's in

Homicide at the Glass House. What's the deal? What's going on here? Why's his head bleeding?"

Acosta ran through the basics of what had just happened. When he was finished, the lieutenant assured him again that I was who I said I was.

They took the cuffs off and one of the cops administered some first aid. I pressed a gauze pad on my reopened cut.

"Shit, man. Carry your fucking creds, why don't you?" Acosta said as I got the bleeding under control. I could see a worried frown on his face as he silently reviewed the violence his troops had already done.

"I'm taking back control of my arrestee," I said angrily.

"I'm sorry, you're what?" Acosta said.

"You heard me. Straw is my bust. I had him in custody when you guys blew in and fucked up my collar."

The squad of blues were all standing in a huddle around us, waiting to see how their sergeant was going to deal with this.

"Lieutenant Moon, I'm working Straw as a confidential informant on a big homicide case," I said. "It's imperative I retain control of my CI. I also want my car returned to me immediately."

Moon looked at Acosta. "What do you say, Sarge?" He grinned sheepishly. "The man really is in Homicide Special. His wife runs the entire Detective Division. I was you, I'd back off."

I handed Acosta the keys to the BMW, gave him the tag number, and told him where it was. A patrolman sprinted up the street and five minutes later returned with Alexa's car, parking it near where we stood.

Jack still didn't know what was going on. He was peering out the back window of the squad car parked next to us, mouthing questions at me that I didn't bother to answer.

Ten minutes later, he was pulled from the backseat of the X-car and put into the front seat of Alexa's BMW, still with his hands cuffed behind him.

"Whose cuffs are those?" I asked.

"Mine," a uniformed patrolman said.

"Give me the key and your business card. I'll have them returned in the morning."

After he gave them to me, I climbed behind the wheel. Jack started grinning despite the fact that he was bleeding from four nasty-looking lumps on his head. His bullshit gold-boxed tooth had somehow managed to survive the conflict.

"This is very slick, dude," he said as I pulled away.

"Shut up, Jack."

"Totally mint," he added. "Can we take these cuffs off now? That asshole cop put them on way too tight."

I didn't answer him. I didn't even look over. Then I remembered something I'd seen in the La Cienega Park playground a few weeks ago. I drove ten or twelve blocks and pulled into the parking lot that adjoined the park. It was just a half a mile west of Park La Brea. I pulled Jack out of the car.

"Where we going? What're you doin', dude?"

"You're a fugitive from the FBI?" I snarled. "I've

been running around for two days with a fucking bank robber?"

"Look . . . it's not as bad as it sounds," he said.

But it was.

In fact, it was much worse.

CHAPTER 28

I DRAGGED JACK ACROSS THE park and over to the children's play area, and stood him next to the twelve-foot-long metal teeter-totter. Then I reached under and checked the bar fastening that hooked the teeter-totter to its base. It was still broken.

I'd been to this park two weeks earlier on a field interview and had watched some kids unbolt the seat plank on this piece of equipment. They had put it across a five-foot-high metal brace on the jungle gym a few yards away. They were using it to go way up in the air. It was dangerous, so I'd reported it to the Department of Recreation and Parks as soon as I left. But like everything else with this budget crunch, it had yet to be fixed.

Since it hadn't been repaired, I pulled the twelve-foot-long aluminum plank off and carried it over to the jungle-gym brace, setting it across the top just as those kids had done. Then I grabbed Jack, pulled one end down, undid his cuffs, and redid them by looping the chain through the metal support under the seat.

"What the fuck is this?" he shrieked. "Whatta you doing?"

"Not the right question, Jack. The correct question is, what are *you* doing?"

"I was solving the case, asshole."

"I told you we needed to go slow with those Mesa guys, but you go ahead and pull a black-bag job on their office anyway. Don't you ever listen to anybody?"

I saw him trying to come up with a way to play me.

"I'm screwing around with you for two days, and all the time you're a federal bank fugitive? When did that happen? I thought you just got released. What'd you do, hit a bank up by Soledad on your way out of town?"

"I was broke. I needed cash. I had a disguise," he protested. "But they made me with a bank cam because of my arm tats."

"You must have sawdust for brains."

"Scully, you're focused on the wrong things. Wait'll you see what I got."

"Everything you took out of there is inadmissible!" I shouted. I was beginning to lose it. "You gotta have a search warrant to remove evidence in a police investigation."

"*You* gotta have a search warrant. All I need is a crowbar."

"You're fucking amazing." I went around to the other side of the teeter-totter and pulled the seat down, then got on it and lowered my end, hoisting him up by the handcuffs. His end was now almost eight feet in the air, and he was hanging under the seat, shrieking in distress, standing on his tippy-toes.

"Ow! Ow!" he bellowed. "This is police harassment!"

I bounced on the seat, pulling him a few inches off the ground with each bounce. He screamed in pain as the metal cuffs cut into his wrists. Then I lowered him back to his tiptoes again.

"Okay, Jack. Here's the deal. I wanta know everything you've done since yesterday. Everything you touched, every window you crawled through. I want your whole chicken-shit playbook."

"Nothing . . . I've done nothing."

"I figure you've been running amuck ever since this started. Tomorrow or the next day, I'm gonna be getting this case. I wanta know how much evidence you've lost or compromised, how many laws you've broken, how much of your shit I'm gonna be digging out of."

"Owww! Ow! Lemme down!" he screamed.

"You break into Diamond's office too?"

"No way! Lemme go!"

"You did, didn't you? You broke in there and went through her rebuilt files."

"No."

I bounced my seat a few times. He shot up and down, showing me his white belly like a prize bass on the end of a spruce fishing pole.

"Okay, okay. I did. But there was nothing there."

"How 'bout the NHB Gym? You pay them a little visit earlier tonight, before you went into the Mesa building?"

"Uh . . . okay, okay." He was squeaking slightly, hissing out the words through his teeth. "Put me down. I'll tell you everything. Please."

I lowered him until he was standing with both feet

under him, but his hands were still stretched high above his head.

"I'm listening," I said, looking up at him from the low end of the teeter-totter.

"Okay, I . . . I . . . okay, I went to the gym. Man, you and Vargas really fucked that place up. The front window was all boarded up. I had to pick the lock in back. Some guy's trashed Indian chopper was in the office, leakin' oil on the cement floor. But it's just a fight gym, man. Nothing there. I found some drugs in the back room, stole a Rolodex, that's it."

"What kind of drugs?"

"I don't know. Prescription shit."

I bounced a few times.

"Some kinda polypeptides," he blurted.

"Aren't they like human growth hormones?"

"The fuck would I know? I don't shoot drugs. I drink a little beer occasionally, couple a scotch shooters from time to time, but that's it. My body is my temple."

I looked at his temple dangling there, with numbers and pictures scrawled all over it. I took a minute and tried to assess the damage.

"Why would you break into Mesa Group after I specifically told you not to?"

"Because I've been trying to solve Pop's murder while you been sitting on your ass doing nothing."

"Eventually, I could have developed enough evidence to get a legitimate search warrant on that place. Now I can't use one thing you took! Everything you removed is inadmissible! Don't you get that?" I shouted.

"Scully, Scully, for chrissake, calm down and listen to me? Will you just listen?"

"I'm listening."

"Okay, look, you want the real truth? Here it is. I know you probably won't believe me but I wasn't the one who broke in there."

"The cops said you did."

"It wasn't me, okay? It was somebody else. Somebody I was following."

"You're a trip, Jack."

"I was following that MMA fighter guy you were talking about tonight. 'Ricochet' O'Shea. It wasn't something I planned. It just happened." He took a breath.

"Put me down."

I held him up there on his tippy-toes, then bounced him once to keep him talking.

"I was leaving the gym after going through their office and that Ricochet guy shows up for a late-night workout. He didn't know I was there so I hid. I wanted to see what his story was. He works the bags for an hour or so then leaves. I followed him. He went to the Mesa Investment Group building on Wilshire. It was almost midnight, and I'm thinking, what the fuck is this? So I decided to wait around outside.

"He musta tripped a silent alarm because half an hour after he went inside, two cop cars pull up and rattle the doors. A couple minutes later a security guard comes out and opens up for them. Five minutes later O'Shea comes flying out of the place through a side door. He gets in his car and books. I'm on the Harley, so I take off after him. He sees me back there and he throws something out of his car window, then escapes. It looked like a computer flash drive.

"I'm just gettin' set to pull over and pick it up when all of a sudden I'm in the middle of a major police action. I took off, but I laid my Harley down trying to get away. That's why I was on foot and why I called you for help, dude. I managed to ditch the cops for a while, but they're pulling in major backup. I'm ducking and jukin', running like a bastard, staying outta sight. Next thing I know, I see you in the park, and then ten seconds later we're both in the middle of a baton-and-pepper-spray party."

"That's your story?" I said.

"Yeah. What's wrong with it?"

I just glared at him.

"Swear to God, Scully. I'm not lying! It wasn't me who broke into Mesa Group. It was Rick O'Shea."

"Now you're just pissing me off." I sat down hard, yanking him high off the ground.

"Scully, I swear! It wasn't me!" he screamed.

"Right," I drawled.

"O'Shea threw the flash drive away!" he shrieked. "But Scully, I know where he threw it. We can go back there. We can get it."

"It's illegally obtained evidence. How many times do I have to say that?"

"How's it illegally obtained? It's just lying behind a Dumpster. You don't need a search warrant to find something some other asshole stole and ditched in an alley. C'mon, put me down."

I lowered him to his tiptoes again and studied him, hanging under the seat of the teeter-totter.

"I can't possibly look this stupid to you."

"Scully, you just gonna let the whole case disappear into some wino's pocket?"

"If you didn't see what was on the flash drive, how do you know it contains incriminating stuff we can use to solve Pop's murder?"

"Huh?"

"How do you know it's not just Rick O'Shea's Internet porn collection?"

"How?"

"Yeah, douche bag, how?"

"Because, because w-why else would he go in there at, at . . . at like midnight and like take something, unless he knew it was incriminating?" he stuttered.

I sat down hard again, lifting him for the third time off the ground. He was hanging by the cuffs, spinning around, shrieking.

"Okay, okay! Look, I know because I looked at the fucking thing, okay? I guess maybe it was me who broke in the Mesa building like you said at first, okay? The cops arrived. I downloaded the info and ran. Happy now?"

I dropped him back to his feet. Then I unhooked him from the teeter-totter and recuffed him with his hands behind his back.

I returned the long teeter-totter to its original location and led Jack back to Alexa's BMW. I got a beach towel out of the trunk and put it over the seat so he wouldn't bleed on her upholstery, then put him in the car. I got behind the wheel and looked off up the street.

"Whatta you doing?"

"Thinking."

He waited for a long moment, then said, "About what, dude?"

"I'm trying to decide whether to bury you on a beach up in Oxnard or just dump you in a shallow grave close by, like under the Hollywood sign."

"Funny."

"You think it's funny? You must not be picking up my vibe, *dude*."

After pondering this mess for another minute, I turned to look at him. "I don't know why the fuck I'm doing this, Jack, but okay. I'm gonna go retrieve those electronic records. You are gonna swear that you took them. Not me. After we take a look, I'm gonna book them as your personal property that you had in your possession when I arrested you for bank robbery. We'll worry about how, or *if*, they can ever be admitted as evidence in Pop's murder later."

"You're gonna book me on the federal bank charges?" he said, sounding incredulous. "I thought just now we were like in the zone or something, man, solving Pop's murder like a team. How can you take me in? That's pretty cheesy."

"Those cops turned you over to me. They're all witnesses to a custody exchange. You think I want to be an accessory after the fact on your two dumb-ass bank heists?"

"You could say I jumped you and got away."

I shook my head, and he sat there pouting. "You're not much of a friend," he said.

"You're finally seeing it," I shot back. "You're right. I'm not your friend. I don't want to have anything to do with you."

"I wasn't talking about me," he said softly. "I was talking about Pop."

CHAPTER 29

THE FLASH DRIVE WAS BEHIND a Dumpster in an alley off Spaulding Drive, about three blocks from the Mesa high-rise building. I gathered it up and got into the car beside Jack, who was sulking.

"What's on here?" I asked.

"Uh . . . it's like an audit or something."

"An audit or something?"

"Yeah. For Huntington House. A private audit done by some company named Randall Weis and Associates."

"So what's the audit say?"

"I don't know. I'm not a fucking accountant."

"I thought you said you broke the case while I was sitting on my ass."

"I said I *could've* broke the case while you were sitting on your ass."

"You said you broke it. You said it was huge. You don't even know what's on here? How 'bout finally telling the truth? I thought you said you cared about Pop."

"Okay, okay, stop with the nitpicks." He took a deep breath. "I followed O'Shea to the Mesa Building, went in behind him when he keyed his security card. He was accessing shit on the computer. When he was done the numb nut left the fucking thing on. There's all kinds of spreadsheets and shit. I just copied the pages. I didn't have time to sit around scrolling columns of figures. The file was marked Huntington House Audit 2005–2008 so I took it, but I musta tripped a silent alarm when I split. Are you happy now?"

I called Vargas and got him out of bed. I told him I wanted a meeting with everyone in an hour at Huntington House.

"Jeez, Scully, can't it wait until morning?" he complained sleepily.

"No, it can't. And make sure that Vicki is there. I need somebody who can understand a complex fiscal audit."

After I hung up, we headed to Huntington House. Jack was complaining all the way. "I don't see why you won't do me a solid and let me go."

"I won't let you go because I don't want to."

"We both went to Huntington as kids," he persisted. "We both got the same lousy start in life. I'll tell you, man, Pop really cared what happened to me. He would shit if he knew you were gonna bust me for those two nothing bank heists." It went on and on and on.

"Shut up, Jack," I kept saying, but it didn't slow him down.

He finally just ran out of gas. He had stopped sulking and was ignoring me.

We pulled up to Huntington House a little past 3:00 A.M. I took the cuffs off Jack while we waited for the rest of the pallbearers to show up. They all made it by four. The last to arrive was Vargas, but that was understandable because he had to call everybody else before he left and he had the farthest to drive.

Diamond unlocked the door, and we trooped into the makeshift office in the rec center. Vicki sat at the computer, which was set up on Diamond's card table, and opened the first file. All of us hunkered over her shoulder, peering at the screen as she began scrolling through spreadsheets and columns of numbers.

"Stand back, you're crowding me," she said.

We gave her some space, and after a minute she said, "This looks like it's an independent audit commissioned by Creative Solutions to cover the last four years. This first file lists some accounts payable and where the money went." She leaned forward, studied the screen, and frowned. "A lot of this references private loans that I have no record of. The documents probably all got lost in the fire."

She opened the next folder, scrolled through the files, and then did the same for the third and fourth. The first file of the final folder contained a summary letter from Randall Weis, who apparently did the audit.

"Uh-oh," Vicki said, as she started to scan the screen.

"What is it?" Diamond asked, moving closer.

Vicki turned off the monitor so she couldn't read it, then put her head in her hands.

I moved Vicki aside, sat down, then turned the monitor back on.

The letter was short. Under the accountant's letterhead it said:

Our audit of the disbursements made by Huntington House, LLC, for the fiscal years 2005 through 2008 uncovered numerous irregularities and charges without appropriate documentation. We also discovered several fraudulent loans. The totals of unaccounted-for losses by year are as follows:

2005	*$407,631*
2006	*$100,455*
2007	*$566,923*
2008	*$398,765*

The fraudulent transactions were initiated by the executive director, Walter Dix, who authorized payments to entities that were secretly controlled or owned by him, for services not rendered or goods not purchased. These fraudulent documents all contain his verified signature. Further, the executive director authorized loan repayments to himself, when in fact there was no evidence that any loans from Mr. Dix to Huntington House ever existed. A full analysis and documentation of these transactions has been scanned and appears on this disk.

Randall Weis, CPA

"What's it mean?" Seriana asked.

I turned to look at her, but her face told me she understood.

"According to this, Pop was stealing a lot of money from the home," I said.

"He wouldn't do that," Vicki protested. But this time she sounded less convinced.

"With the state audit coming, I guess Creative Solutions wanted to do their own audit in advance to find out what the state was going to come up with," Diamond said. "They must have done it during my vacation last month. During the weekend Pop went surfing in Mexico. Mr. O'Shea could have arranged it. He had the keys to the old office."

"That could explain why Pop called me," Vargas said. "With this state audit coming, he knew he was going to get caught. Criminal charges would be filed. He probably wanted to get legal advice."

"Pop didn't steal from this place," Jack asserted hotly. "I don't understand why you're all going along with this bullshit. If he was stealing and was about to be caught, I could maybe understand him committing suicide, but he didn't commit suicide. He was murdered. Explain that, why don't you?"

"Okay." I was trying hard to separate myself from my emotions, to work it like I would if it was any other murder.

"If Pop did take this money as this audit indicates, then where the hell is it?" I began. "He didn't have a new car or a new house. He lived on the cheap. His only vice was surfing, so where did it all go?"

"What are you saying?" Seriana said.

"Somebody might have known he took the money

and that person was looking for it. Maybe that's why Pop was beaten—why he inhaled his own blood before he died. Maybe somebody was trying to get him to tell them where a million and a half in missing cash was. Then after they found out, they blew his head off."

CHAPTER 30

ALEXA WOKE UP AS I SLID back into bed just before sunrise.

"Everything okay?" she asked, turning to me.

"It can wait. Talk to you in the morning," I said.

But I couldn't get to sleep. I couldn't imagine how Pop Dix, the ultimate giver, could turn up on that computer file as an embezzling thief.

My mind wouldn't stop chewing it. I was nowhere near going back to sleep, so I waited until Alexa was breathing evenly again and then slipped silently out of bed. I grabbed my clothes, dressed, and made myself a cup of microwave instant coffee. I walked into the backyard with a steaming mug and sat there waiting for the sun to come up.

The hour before dawn always reminded me of those times thirty-odd years ago when the group of us picked for sunrise surf patrol would sit in Pop's old Ford wagon with our boards stuffed in the back, watching the deserted streets of San Pedro slip by while we headed to the beach. We would listen silently while he talked about the morning surf report, fantasizing about the steeps.

Now that same ageless dawn was breaking over the ocean all these years later, just as it had when I was a boy. Pop was gone, and I was left behind to face a new day filled with sorrow at his passing and the dark suspicions that his unnatural death had produced.

Of course, I had questions. There were things that bothered me about all this. I certainly couldn't explain that accountant's letter. I couldn't explain the missing money, stolen with his own signatures.

But why would Pop steal almost a million and a half dollars from a place he fought so desperately to protect? For what purpose?

Only two things truly excited him—a northwest Mexican storm break with a six-foot swell and Huntington House.

When he told me two years ago about the new rubberized turf for the playground, his eyes had lit up at the thought of getting that new field for his kids. So why would he steal the very funds that might have provided it?

The answer for me was simple. He hadn't. Somebody else had. As I watched the morning sun climb in the sky, I ran through a growing list of inconsistencies that were beginning to add up and pester me.

Alexa found me out back a little after eight. She brought me a fresh mug of coffee and sat down in the nearest chair.

"What did Jack want?" she finally said. "And how much trouble did he manage to get himself into?"

"Plenty," I said. Then I filled her in on what had happened, leading her through Jack's wild-ass midnight raid at the Mesa building, the stolen evidence, and the police chase that followed. I told her about the fiasco outside Park La Brea, where I got arrested and learned about his two outstanding federal bank warrants, and took her through Jack's confession in La Cienega Park, leaving out the teeter-totter for obvious reasons. Next I described the pallbearers' meeting at four in the morning and the terrible information that we'd found on the stolen flash drive.

After I finished, she just sat there frowning. She said nothing for almost a full minute.

"I hate to say this, but you were right and I was wrong about letting them be involved," she admitted. "They've fucked this up completely, or at least Jack has."

"Yeah," I said, "but here's my problem."

She sat beside me quietly.

"That accounting report accused Pop of theft. I don't believe he would do it, but this Randall Weis accounting firm has the evidence. I saw computer scans of the phony loans with Pop's signature. Now that Pop's suicide is a murder, those files might contain the motive. He could have easily been killed over that missing million five, yet if I show up at the DA's office with stolen evidence, how do I explain where I got it?"

"The truth is sometimes a good ploy," she said sarcastically.

"Right. Throw Jack to the wolves. I should've thought of that."

She smiled ruefully.

"Here's some other stuff that's been bothering me," I continued. "Jack stole those computer files out of the offices of the Mesa Investment Group, but the audit was done for Creative Solutions, a freestanding nonprofit corporation. Since the files were in the Mesa office computer network, I'm wondering what the connection is between a billionaire's investment firm and this little nonprofit that owns Huntington House."

"You're right. That's a false beat."

"It's hard for me to believe that a wealthy guy like Eugene C. Mesa has anything to do with this. But his company had possession of the audit files, so I need to find out why. The accountant that Creative Solutions hired discovered almost a million and a half dollars missing over four years from '05 to '08. That's chump change for E. C. Mesa, but it would be big bucks for a high school dropout like Rick O'Shea.

"Both O'Shea and that other guy, Chris Calabro, had Visa cards issued by Mesa in their wallets. O'Shea's living in a million-dollar house in Calabasas. He's driving a new Escalade, but he doesn't look smart enough to make a tossed salad. I'm wondering what the connection is between these MMA fighters and Mesa Investment Group."

"All good questions, Shane."

I looked at my watch. "I got trapped into another meeting with the pallbearers at ten this morning, so I gotta go. They're upset. Deep down they don't believe Pop did this. They want to keep working it."

"Given what Jack did last night, that's probably not a good move."

"Yeah, except Vargas knows until the coroner assigns an H-number to this case, I can't stop them. He's put himself in charge. Team Huntington. They probably already have a sign-up sheet and jerseys."

"You need to stop that from happening," she said, coming completely around to my point of view.

"I also gotta put Jack in Men's Central Jail or I'm gonna have big FBI trouble over those two outstanding bank warrants. Trouble is, I sorta get it. Jack loved Pop. Even though half the time I want to wring his neck, I still kind of respect the effort."

"I would have slammed him behind bars last night," Alexa said, frowning. "Where is he now?"

"In the wind. After we found that accounting statement, I was so upset I took my eye off him. He slipped out the back and got away on foot. I was too used up to go after him."

Then Alexa took my hand. "But I'm still here. I'm on vacation with lots of free time. What do you want me to do?"

"Come with me to the IHOP for breakfast with these people. See if you can get them to stop playing police. They won't listen to me, but maybe you can make them understand."

CHAPTER 31

NOBODY IN THE BACK BOOTH at IHOP looked like they'd gotten any sleep either since we all split up five hours ago.

The restaurant was packed with a noisy breakfast crowd. As Alexa and I slipped onto the curved bench, I saw that Vicki had a calculator in front of her and work papers spread around. Vargas had started a file labeled *Walter Dix*. They had ordered coffee and rolls for six.

"Anybody seen or heard from our federal bank fugitive?" I asked as soon as I was seated.

They all shook their heads and looked at me with blank stares.

"What Jack did last night was a game breaker that could completely undermine everything," I said. "Even though the department hasn't made this a homicide yet, everything we do now still affects any eventual court case we might want to bring against Pop's killer. We can't just be . . ."

"Stow it, Shane," Vicki interrupted. She was looking at me with hard gunfighter eyes. "We don't want to hear it, okay? Sabas told us until it becomes a murder case we aren't breaking any laws, so stop slapping everybody upside the head."

"You aren't breaking any laws, but you're very possibly trashing the end result," Alexa said, jumping to my defense. "Anything on that drive will be subject to a legal challenge should we ever attempt to use it."

"What's done is done," Seriana said. "I think it sucks that Jack went out and broke into those offices on his own, but Mr. Vargas has told us what we can do legally and what we can't. We've all agreed to follow his guidelines."

Vargas looked over at me and said, "Are you interested in any of the stuff we found out this morning, or are you just gonna sit there and bitch?"

"You've been running around doing more since I left you?" I said as my stomach sunk.

"Mostly Internet searches," Vicki said.

"Mostly?" Alexa had one eyebrow cocked, staring suspiciously over at her.

"Before I drove home, I went down to Kinney and Glass and ran a LexisNexis search on Creative Solutions. I came up with something interesting. We already knew that Creative Solutions owns Huntington House, but what we didn't know is it's also a holding corporation for six other nonprofits. They all have names that sound like new-age textbooks: Bridge to Tomorrow, Life Promises, Hopeful Journey. Each one of those nonprofits in turn controls its own foster-care facility.

There's six group homes located all over L.A. that are part of the Creative Solutions family. There's gotta be almost a hundred kids in their network."

"At six thousand dollars per month per child, that comes to a lot of money," Sabas said.

"It sure does," Vicki confirmed. "It nets out at seven and a half million a year from the California Child Welfare Services."

"You think every one of these group homes is embezzling money?" Diamond asked.

"I don't know," Vicki said. "Sounds a little far-fetched. What do you think of this, Shane?"

"As long as you don't go over and start talking to any of these people, compromising the investigation, it's a pretty good lead," I said begrudgingly.

"Well, I already sorta did," she said. "I live in the Marina. On the way over here, I made a little detour and went by the Centennial House in Compton. It's owned by a nonprofit foundation called New Beginnings. I talked to the executive director, a woman named Claire Whitlock. I told her I worked at Kinney and Glass and represented a charity that donates to nonprofits. She was sort of running around like crazy getting the kids on the vans that take them to school, but I got some fund-raiser information and brochures from her."

She handed me pamphlets describing the great works of both Centennial House and the New Beginnings Foundation.

I opened up the first brochure, and there, on the inside cover, was a nice airbrushed picture of Chris Calabro. In the picture, he didn't look like an overbuilt hair trigger with killer lats who called himself Clubber. In the brochure, he looked very pleasant, with a wide, inviting smile. You couldn't tell that under his blue blazer he was a rippling polypeptide experiment who shot human growth hormones like a heroin junkie.

"This is one of the guys we fought." I passed the brochure to Vargas, who nodded.

"Right. I hadda dump this clown so he wouldn't kill Scully."

"It's starting to come together," I said.

"Is that a veiled 'I'm sorry, Vicki'?" She was now sounding sort of snotty. "Are you saying you think I actually did something good here that might help?"

I sat there squirming, then looked over at Alexa, who shrugged. No help. But I can read her and under the shrug, she was saying, *Your case, your call.*

"I understand why you all want to do this," I said, beginning to reconsider my position. "I get it, okay? If I was where you are, I wouldn't want to be blocked out either."

"But . . ." Vargas said.

"But there's ways to go about this stuff. There's a technique to the way we build a homicide case." I looked directly at the lawyer. "Some of it doesn't have anything to do with the way you try one."

"What if we put you in charge?" Vargas said.

"Yesterday you told me you were gonna run it and there wasn't anything I could do to stop you."

"You got some street cred with me now, *esse.* I'm

good for you running it as long as you promise we don't get frozen out."

I thought about it for a moment before I said, "Okay, then I need a promise from you guys too. If we turn up something, before anybody does anything, you have to run it past me or Alexa for approval. After that, we can all decide on how to go forward. If we decide to make a move, Alexa or I have to be on point."

"Agreed," Sabas said, then looked at everyone and got their nods of approval.

"And if anybody sees or hears from Jack, you gotta tell me so I can get my hands on him," I added. "I can't have him tracking up this case with bad moves."

I held their gazes until they all nodded.

"Okay, then for now we'll call this the unofficial Pop Dix Homicide Steering Committee."

"Deal," they all said.

"Vicki, I want you to start an information run on the NHB Gym on Sixth Street. We need to know who owns it, who goes there, membership rosters, anything you can get online."

"I can do that," she said.

"Sabas, you come with me. We'll start checking out those foster homes. Seriana, you go with Alexa, visit all of the nonprofits, see if they have offices. Don't go inside, but if they have parking lots, write down all the license plate numbers so we can run them."

"What about me?" Diamond asked.

"Go back and keep working on the files at Huntington House. See if you can substantiate any of those phony loans or cash disbursements the auditor claimed Pop made.

"If Rick O'Shea shows up and starts asking questions about me, downplay it. Tell him I used to go there and I'm just some out-of-work guy with too much time on my hands who's poking around because I don't think Pop would have killed himself. Don't tell him I'm a cop, but if he gets goofy, give him my cell number and tell him to call me. Whatever we do, for the next few days we gotta keep this on the DL."

We broke up and left the IHOP. I settled in the passenger seat of Sabas's flamed '53 yellow pickup as he got behind the wheel. Alexa and Seriana drove out in Alexa's car to check on the addresses for the six nonprofits Vicki had given them.

"Where do you want to start, *jefe*?" Sabas said.

"Let's go see what a 'bridge to tomorrow' looks like." He pulled the floor shift toward him, putting the truck in gear, and we left the lot. As he turned onto the surface street, I couldn't help but wonder, while we were doing this, What kind of mischief was Jack Straw up to?

CHAPTER 32

I FOUND A COPY OF THE *Thomas Guide* in Vargas's truck and planned a route that would allow us to hit all of the group homes efficiently. We decided to stick with Vicki's scam of pretending to represent an entity interested in making donations to foster care.

Our first stop was a foster-care facility named Lincoln House, a collection of bungalows in the South Bay near Torrance. It was in bad need of a paint job and had no athletic field. There were twenty children living there. We got a quick tour from a bored employee who kept looking at his watch and talking about his coffee break.

The others seemed pretty much the same and were depressing reminders of my youth. By three o'clock, we'd hit them all. The last home was the Challenge House in La Mirada, owned by a foundation called Hopeful Journey. A young social worker named Barbosa Polverini showed us around.

"You got twenty-five children?" I asked, looking at the fact sheet she had given me in the office.

"Yeah, and it isn't easy, believe me." She sighed. "Like trying to keep a bunch of feral cats in a bathtub. This is a gang area. Half the time they're going out windows after lights-out to hook up with their homies."

"What's your ratio of staff to clients?" I asked. By then, Vargas and I had picked up some of the terms. A *client* we had learned was a child in foster care.

"Four to one," she replied.

Then Vargas said, "So your RCL is what, about five thousand per child?" We were smokin' with the lingo.

"Yeah. But it barely gets us there." Barbosa shook her head.

We thanked her and got back into Vargas's yellow pickup. We had collected half a dozen brochures from the group homes. None of the others had pictures of MMA fighters inside.

Both of us sat for a moment in the parking lot behind the Challenge House nursing our thoughts, realizing we'd learned very little.

"Wasted day," Vargas finally said.

"Not completely. These places are all struggling, and beyond that, staff morale sucks."

"So?"

"Perfect environment for an embezzler. I don't know how many of these places are missing money, but I'll bet a comprehensive audit on each one would be very illuminating."

I asked Vargas to take me to pick up my Acura,

which was being fixed in Venice, two blocks from my house. I'd received a text message from Larry, my mechanic, that it was ready.

As I was getting out of the truck in front of the garage, Vargas stopped me. He had a frown on his face. "When it looked like Pop killed himself, it was somehow easier. This murder thing is really wearing on me."

"Yeah."

"I'm having a hard time with your idea that Pop stole the money, then got killed for it."

"Me too," I agreed.

"But I thought that was your whole theory. You said somebody beat him to death to find the million-five."

"He was beaten before he died, so it certainly could have happened that way."

"But it didn't?"

"Listen, Sabas. You keep telling me the law is your beat, so answer me this. In a criminal defense when you don't know who's bullshitting, how do you find the truth?"

"You evaluate motive."

"Exactly."

"So?"

"Pop had no motive to steal that cash. It was already where he wanted it. It was in the Huntington House bank account."

"You're saying he was set up?"

"Yeah, maybe. State audit coming, lotta money missing. Frame Pop, kill him, make it look like a suicide, case closed."

He sat behind that oversized fifties steering wheel and just stared at me. Then he said, "You think Rick O'Shea?"

"I'm not putting the hat on anybody just yet, but he's certainly got a reserved spot near the top of my list. He could have easily got Pop to sign stuff without reading it. You know how Pop was. He was no businessman. Tell him he's signing a contract to repaint the gym and he wouldn't bother to read it, he'd just sign."

Vargas began to nod his head. "I like this a fuck of a lot better, homes."

"Good. But don't marry it, 'cause it could turn out to be dead wrong. It's just a theory. Like the missing money idea, we log it but keep moving." I hesitated, then said, "As long as we're on this, what's your take on Diamond Peterson?"

He thought carefully for a minute before he spoke. "Funny you should ask that. I've been worried about her a bit myself. She seems kinda half in and half out. Not really involved, sorta going through the motions."

"Yeah, that's been my take too." I went ahead and told him what I'd been thinking. "She worked in the office. She was with Pop all the time. She could have shoved those phony loan documents under his nose and got him to sign as easily as O'Shea."

"You think she's in on it?"

"In my job, it pays to be a skeptic, look at everyone. It's just a feeling. Could be nothing. Don't tell the others, but let's both watch her a little closer for a while and be careful about what we confide in her."

"Okay."

We bumped knuckles. I got out of the truck and Vargas drove off. I paid Larry the mechanic for the repaired ignition, got in the MDX, and headed for home.

Alexa's car wasn't in the driveway. She wasn't back yet. On my way into the house, I decided to pick up our mail. I opened the mailbox and saw a shoe box–sized package that barely fit inside. I pulled it out carefully and examined it. The box was wrapped in brown paper and had no address, which meant it had been hand delivered.

I'm a cop, and I don't like getting hand-delivered, paper-wrapped packages with no postal marks. I was thinking about calling the bomb squad when I noticed a small *J. Straw* written in ink on the top left corner where the return address should have been.

I took the package inside and set it down on the kitchen table.

"What are you up to now, Jack?" I said softly to the little wrapped box.

I took out a knife and opened it. Inside I found an old-style brown plastic Rolodex. It was from the NHB Gym. Jack had told me last night, when he'd been dangling from the teeter-totter, that he'd stolen it. I rolled the tumbler. It had about fifty names, numbers, and addresses inside. I saw Raymond "Stingray" Jackson. I also saw an address for Kimbo Sledge, who I remembered was on the Fall Brawl fight poster with O'Shea. The address for both Jackson and Sledge was identical: 1386 Avalon Terrace in Wilmington. Roommates?

There was also an SD memory card inside. No note.

"Not again," I muttered as I took it into the den, put

it into my computer, and waited for it to load. I was expecting it to contain more stolen accounting information, but this one contained a video.

The camera was set up on a hillside and was pointed down at a huge mansion in the Hollywood Hills. The house was sitting right on the edge of a land cut that overlooked all of West L.A. It was one of those big expensive Cliffside deals that dot Mulholland Drive. From the cool light and medium-length shadows, I estimated it to be mid-morning.

I watched a Rolls Royce pull into the drive and park. I could hear somebody near the camera mic breathing, but nobody spoke. Then the camera shut off.

It came on again a second later, recording from a different place. This time, from the short length of the shadows underneath a line of poplar trees bordering the stone drive. It looked like it was shortly before or after noon. I could hear birds singing.

In the next shot the camera position was now inside the compound of the same lush estate. The shot panned the grounds, showed the layout, then clicked off again. When it came back on, we were actually inside the house.

I groaned as I watched a moving point of view coming out of the kitchen into the living room. I could hear more quiet breathing and light footsteps on the marble floor. Jack was actually hot prowling this place in broad daylight. He panned the camera, taking in the rich decor.

Outside on the expansive pool deck, I caught sight of a short man sitting under a canopy, having lunch with a trophy blonde. The camera zoomed in. The two were chatting, laughing, drinking wine. The man was middle-aged with dark hair and a stocky build. He had an olive complexion and could have been Mediterranean. His hairline looked like it had been filled in with plugs. Then the camera went dark.

The next shot was inside a garage. Six or eight expensive cars—a Ferrari, a Porsche Boxster, a new Lamborghini. Off on the far end I saw four or five classic Indian motorcycles like the one Vargas hit coming out of the NHB Gym. The Rolls that I'd seen pulling into the drive in the first shot was parked in the foreground.

As the camera panned, I was able to read the rear license plate and wrote it down to run later. I wanted to confirm my suspicions, but I was already pretty sure this place belonged to E. C. Mesa.

The next shots were inside a sports-equipment room. From the similar walls and windows, I guessed it was probably off the garage. There were tennis rackets and golf clubs, as well as several ten-speed and mountain bikes hanging three or four feet off the floor on wall pegs.

Then the camera panned to show a door that had a brass plate that read *The Boardroom.* A gloved hand reached out, grabbed the knob, and turned it. Then the door was kicked open.

The room was full of surfboards. Most were standing in racks. Wet suits were hanging on plastic hangers. There were several short boards with their colorful, artistic gel coats, along with a few tri-fin thrusters with pin tails and some old light balsas from the fifties.

The camera panned to the far side of the room, and there it was, in a rack all by itself. Tail down, it stood alone in a place of honor. A big, old, classic cigar-box model.

The long, heavy antique was almost nine feet tall and pointed at both ends for maximum rail contact. It was the only board heavy enough to actually hang ten on, but nobody ever rode them anymore because they were a bitch to stay up on. Only Walt was willing to fight with one of those bastards, shuffling forward in his strange, hunched-over Quasimodo stance to finally grip his toes on the nose as he rode the wall of glass inside the curl.

I hadn't even seen a cigar-box board since Pop rode his during sunrise patrol years ago. So what was this one doing here?

Jack must have had the same question, because he zoomed in on it and held the shot for several long moments before the camera suddenly went dark.

CHAPTER 33

WHILE I WAITED FOR ALEXA to get home, I spent an hour on the computer researching MMA fighting.

She arrived at a little past six. After I showed her what Jack had left in our mailbox and informed her that the plate on the Rolls checked back to Eugene C. Mesa, I poured each of us a scotch, and we settled into our chairs in the backyard to deal with it.

"Fucking Straw," I vented. "How do I get a leash on that guy?"

"Better question is, What does it all mean?" Alexa countered.

"That cigar-box board is a classic—an antique, the kind Duke Kahanamoku rode in the nineteen thirties in Hawaii. Nobody surfs on those anymore. As far as I'm concerned, it's no coincidence that thing turns up in Mesa's garage."

"If nobody rides one, then why on earth would he have it?" she asked.

"I've been mulling that, and the only thing I can

come up with is maybe E. C. Mesa used to surf with Pop. I remember when I was a kid all kinds of random guys used to show up on that beach. Walt adopted everyone. Lotta people wanted to try and ride his rhino. Usually one wave convinced them to give it up. But maybe Walt showed Mesa how to use that oversized log, and, like Pop, he somehow got into it."

"And maybe, that's the connection between Creative Solutions and the Mesa Group," Alexa offered. "Eugene Mesa and Pop became surf buddies and later, when Pop needs money, E. C. sets up Creative Solutions to take over when Pop can't carry the financial pressure of Huntington House by himself anymore."

I nodded. "Yeah, maybe." It still didn't feel quite right, but who knows?

As we sat and sipped our drinks, Alexa kept peeking over, checking me out. She was still worried about the effect all of this was having on me. But I was through my depressed, sentimental period. I was now just kick-ass angry. I wanted to get whoever did this to Pop. The idea that they might have also framed him as a thief made me even madder.

"We still don't know what ties all these MMA fighters into this," I said, thinking out loud.

"Maybe this will help," Alexa ventured. She opened her slim wafer briefcase and pulled out a handwritten sheet with forty license plate numbers on it.

"These are the cars that Seriana and I found parked outside the nonprofit offices we visited. A lot of them probably were just using the lot and have nothing to do with this. We're gonna have to run them all, then check the names against that Rolodex that Jack stole and see who matches up."

It was a big job. We decided to skip dinner and our second drink and get right to it. The RTO on the horseshoe in the communications center began sounding frustrated with us as we kept reading off new plates for her to run.

"Damn good thing I'm a division commander," Alexa said, grinning, during one of our breaks.

I was jotting down names and addresses on index cards and began to notice the same address—1386 Avalon Terrace, Wilmington—kept showing up a lot. When I finished alphabetizing the cards, we began going through the gym Rolodex, looking for matches, eliminating the other names.

Here's what we ended up with.

Besides Rick O'Shea, who was the executive director of Creative Solutions and lived in a million-dollar house in Calabasas, and Christian Calabro, who held the same position at Bridge to Tomorrow and lived in North Hollywood, four of the remaining matches were also listed as living at 1386 Avalon Terrace in Wilmington.

They included the executive director of Hopeful Journey, Raymond "Stingray" Jackson, and Dane Vanderheiden, "The Striking Viking," who ran the nonprofit in Torrance.

There was someone named Jason Scott, a new name that I hadn't come across before. He was listed as running Life Promise. The last name was Gary White, referred to at NHB as "The Great" White. He was the director of Pure Emotions.

"Okay, so that gym is the nexus," Alexa said. "Wonder why?"

I picked up the phone in the den and called Vicki Lavicki. She answered on the first ring.

"Lavicki," she half shouted into the receiver. Her voice nearly split my eardrum. The woman had not one ounce of social rhythm or personal subtlety.

"How you coming with the computer run on No Holds Barred?" I asked.

"It's a small private gym," she said. "Basically, a fight club. Eight guys on the roster. They're managed by something called Team Ultima, Inc., which is also the name of the corporation that owns the gym.

"The address for Team Ultima is a post-office box in Delaware. I'm trying to get the list of directors, but because Delaware is a tax haven, their corporations are tough to penetrate and it's gonna take some time.

"Also, I've been trying to catch up on this MMA phenomena. I've read some recent Internet stories that say some of these fighters at Team Ultima are starting to show up in televised events on Spike TV and are getting some pretty big purses. Six figures and up. O'Shea and Calabro seem to be the gym's two big stars."

I read Vicki the names that Alexa and I had culled from the pilfered Rolodex.

Vicki said, "Yep. All of them plus two more. There's a guy called Brian Bravo and somebody named Ivan 'Ironhead' Brown."

I thanked her and hung up. Then Alexa and I ran Bravo and Brown through the Department of Motor

Vehicles. They were also listed as living at that same address in Wilmington.

After we hung up, it was still early, only a little past ten in the evening.

"Whatta you suppose is at 1386 Avalon Terrace?" I asked Alexa.

"Guess we better go take a look," she answered.

CHAPTER 34

WILMINGTON IS IN A STRANGE part of Los Angeles. It's basically a town that caters to the South Bay's large port facility and fishing fleet, but it's sandwiched between a growing Crips gang area in Compton and the docks of San Pedro. It's an oasis of fishermen and dockworkers inside a festering maw of residential poverty and gang violence.

The businesses and restaurants are all no-frills. Wood turn-of-the-century houses line the blocks around Avalon Boulevard all the way to Anaheim Street. Wilmington was right on the way to Seal Beach, where this had all started for me years ago.

Alexa drove her BMW while I sat silently beside her, watching the exact same streets I'd watched as a kid when Pop had made this trip to the shore down the Pacific Coast Highway.

We turned onto Avalon Boulevard looking for Avalon Terrace. The cross street was so small we overshot it before I called out to Alexa. She made a U and we drove down a seedy block, full of unkempt houses and old cars, until we arrived at 1386.

The house was a big, three-story, gone-to-seed, wood-sided Victorian that looked like it had been built in the late eighteen hundreds. It had a pitched roof, a sloping porch, and a loud party raging inside.

Alexa and I drove past and found a parking place up the street where we could observe the festivities.

There were a lot of run-down cars parked in front. A few yards from the house, I spotted Rick O'Shea's out-of-place, new, pimped-out maroon Escalade.

There were also half a dozen vintage Indian motorcycles parked off to the side on the dead front lawn. They all sported the popular Indian red and white or turquoise and white paint jobs. Most of the motorcycles were chromed and tricked out with studded saddlebags. Impressive rigs.

"Those look like the same bikes that were in Jack's video of E. C. Mesa's garage," I said.

Alexa reached across me, opened the glove box, and pulled out a pair of Bushnell binoculars. She put them to her eyes and studied the Indians, then shook her head. "Too far away for me to read those bike plates."

I pointed to her little Beretta Bobcat still in the open glove box. "You should keep that .25 loaded," I said.

"I wanted a new purse gun, but I wish I hadn't bought it," she said as she put the binocs down. "No stopping power. Won't blow an asshole out of his socks."

I smiled. Most guys don't have wives who could get away with a statement like that.

We've had this punch-versus-penetration handgun

argument before. Alexa favors big-bore Magnums and Super 9s that carry a wallop. When I was in patrol, I did too. Like everybody else, I packed Dirty Harry style. But now that I'm in homicide I go for lighter, easy-carry weapons.

As far as I'm concerned it's not the size of the gun but the quality of the shooter that counts. Goliath got dumped with a slingshot. You just have to know what you're doing.

I listened to the rap beat pounding out of the house, fouling the neighborhood. I wondered how long the residents on this street had been putting up with this. But it was going to take a real set of cojones to pound on the door and demand that these animals dial it down.

As we watched the house, we saw women and men dancing to the music through the living room window. My eyes shifted back to the Indian motorcycles. They're rare. You don't usually see so many gathered in one place.

Indians had big V-twin engines and looked a little like Harleys, but with long, deep-skirted fenders and distinctive fender lights. One thing separating the vintage Indians from their Harley competitor back in the day was the fact that the throttle and shifter were on the opposite side from where they were located on a Harley.

The people who loved Indians were fanatical about them, and I guess that included some of these fighters and, for some reason, Eugene C. Mesa.

Alexa put the binoculars back up to her eyes, scanned the cars on the block, and started calling out plate numbers, which I wrote down. After about ten minutes, we had all of the tags from the vehicles parked near the old Victorian.

"I'm gonna go check those bikes."

"Be careful," she said as I got out of the BMW.

I made my way across the street, staying in the shadows. Then I crept up onto the grass and approached the six bikes, which were tucked off on the far side of the dead lawn.

Plates on a motorcycle are about the size of an index card, which is why Alexa couldn't read them with binoculars from where we were parked half a block away. As I wrote down the numbers, I was even more sure than before that these were the same bikes I'd seen on Jack's DVD.

I was just finishing with the plate numbers when I heard another motorcycle coming down the street. Before I could duck down, the headlight swept across me as it turned up the drive. I was caught in its beam.

The bike's engine shut off and the headlight went dark. It took a second for my eyes to adjust, and I used the moment to pull my Taurus .38 snub-nosed Hy-Lite from its ankle holster.

When I could see, I got a shock. Standing in front of me, next to his pavement-scarred Harley, was Jack Straw. He pulled two six-packs of beer out of his saddlebags, and said, "Don't shoot. Strange as it seems I'm still on your side."

Part of me wanted to tackle him, put him under arrest, and drag him out of there. But any commotion on the lawn and I'd have the head-butt team from inside to deal with.

"Jack, what the fuck are you doing?" I whispered.

"Get out of here, Scully. This is a whack move."

Then the screen door opened, and I ducked back as I heard footsteps coming across the front porch to the railing.

"Hey, Jack, get yer ass up here with that beer. Where you been? You left over half an hour ago." It was Rick O'Shea.

I slid further away from Jack, out of sight under the porch, pushing myself quietly into the bushes that surrounded the house.

"Whatta you doing down there?" O'Shea said to Jack from the porch just over my head.

"I thought I saw something by the bikes. A huge rat of some kind." Jack smiled at me huddled ass down in the bushes.

"How big?" Rick replied. "Maybe it was just a possum. We got a lot of those around here."

"This was no possum, dude. It was a big, slimy, ungrateful rat."

I flipped him off as he turned and bounded up onto the porch with the beer and entered the house.

When I got back to the car, Alexa was looking worried.

"That looked like Jack," she said, the binoculars still in her hand.

"It was Jack." My heart was pounding from an adrenaline rush.

"Why didn't you arrest him?"

"Why didn't *you*?"

Both of us tensed, watching the party house.

"If we aren't up to our asses in trouble in the next two seconds, then I guess Jack is on the level," I told Alexa.

When nothing happened, I added, "It appears that our runaway bank robber is over here infiltrating these pecker-heads on our behalf."

"How's he gonna infiltrate this bunch?" Alexa said.

"Look at him, honey. He's one of them. He's just the kind of asshole they'd throw their arms around."

Nobody came out to hassle us. The party raged on. About twenty minutes later, Jack came out to stand on the front porch. He seemed to be motioning to us. I grabbed the binoculars and focused in on him.

All he was doing was giving me the finger.

CHAPTER 35

THE PARTY BROKE UP A LITTLE past 2:00 A.M. Men and women started coming off the front porch. I saw Rick O'Shea exit. He had a pretty, dark-haired girl in a Hooters T-shirt clinging to his arm. They got into his Escalade, and he revved the engine like a teenager before slamming it into gear and squealing away from the curb.

The partygoers were streaming out of the house, heading to their vehicles. Motorcycles and old cars with dented fenders started firing up all over the street. Alexa and I ducked down as they roared past. I noticed they all turned east at the end of the block.

I pulled my head up and spotted the short, middle-aged man with the hair plugs who had been out by the pool in Jack's video leaving the house with Chris Calabro. E. C. Mesa.

He looked slightly ridiculous the way he was dressed. A dumpy, middle-aged guy with obvious hair implants wearing a too-tight biker jacket, torn jeans, and three-inch Cuban-heeled boots. He and Calabro got on the last two Indian motorcycles and racked the starters.

Jack exited the house a few feet behind them, mounted his Harley, and jumped down on his starter. The two Indians roared across the lawn and bounced over the curb, with Jack just a few yards behind.

I ducked down quickly, but Jack saw me. A big, slimy lugie gobbed onto our side window as he roared passed.

"Thanks, Jack." I turned to Alexa and said, "Let's go."

"Where?"

"Everybody turned east at the end of the block. I'm no mathematician, but that defies even my meager understanding of the law of probability. Gotta all be going to the same place. The party ain't over yet."

Alexa put the car in gear and swung a U-turn. When we got to Alameda Street, everyone was about three blocks ahead just making a left. I could see the taillight of Jack's trailing Harley as it made the turn.

We hurried to catch up. Either Alexa was closing the gap or Jack's Harley was slowing, because as we sped down Alameda and made the next left, I could see we were much closer. It was soon obvious that Jack was deliberately dropping back. I rolled down the window as we came alongside.

"Get out of here, Scully!" he shouted over the roar of his engine.

"You're under arrest!" I yelled back.

Jack shook his head in disgust, then powered ahead.

We followed the party as it turned onto Pacific Coast

Highway, heading east, and crossed the Los Angeles River into the coastal town of Signal Hill.

We continued along the PCH into Long Beach and were soon in a run-down industrial section of town a few blocks from the San Gabriel River. Up ahead the motorcycles and cars were turning into the parking lot of a big, wooden, red barn–shaped building. As we neared, I could read the neon-lit sign on the roof:

HAYLOFT
BAR & NIGHTCLUB

The parking lot was about half full of cars and a smattering of Harley choppers. The party crowd we'd been following all pulled in and began backing and filling in the gravel lot, sending up clouds of dust that reflected in everybody's headlights.

As we rolled past, I heard car doors slamming and saw the tough-looking men from Avalon Terrace, along with their dates, walking toward a barn-sized front door. Alexa and I came to a stop a block past the club.

As soon as she parked, Alexa leaned across me to rummage in the glove box, quickly pulling out the little palm-sized Beretta Bobcat. Then she grabbed a box of .25 caliber ammo from a hiding place I hadn't found under her seat and began thumbing cartridges into the magazine.

"Don't go all Jane Wayne on me," I said, watching her load the gun, then slam the magazine home.

"Hey, pilgrim, I know how you plan your work. I'm going in there with you."

"Let's just settle down for a minute and talk this over."

"You talk it over." She got out of the BMW and headed up the street toward the parking lot.

"Shit," I said, and scrambled out after her.

We knelt behind some bushes a hundred yards from the Hayloft. It was now two thirty in the morning, and according to California law, the nightclub should have already been closed.

Then, as we watched, the neon sign on the roof flickered off. We could still hear the distant sound of a crowd cheering loudly.

"What on earth are they doing in there?" Alexa said.

"Underground fight."

"I'm sorry?"

"I read up on this stuff on the Internet before you got home. The younger, upcoming MMA fighters start their careers in unsanctioned bare-knuckle events. They're known as underground fights and they take place in gyms or bars after hours. Lots of MMA fighters, including Rampage Jackson, the ex-champ, got their start like that."

"A bar fight?" She looked at me. "I gotta see this." She started to rise.

I grabbed her arm. "Get back here."

She shook me off, then pulled her shirt out, unbuttoned the bottom, hiked it up, and knotted it. Of course, she's already a ten, but in navel-baring mode, she was a twelve.

"Alexa, I forbid this."

"I'm your boss, dummkopf."

Man, do I love this hard-headed woman.

"Okay, okay. Then at least let's get a plan of action."

"I already got it. The putz with the hair plugs has gotta be E. C. Mesa. I'm gonna seduce that little gnome. Take his temperature."

"Okay, that's not bad. You target him and see what you can find out. I'll be close by." I pulled out my Taurus snubbie. Alexa frowned at the light, magnesium-framed .38.

"We're better off not pulling these two little pop guns. They could die laughing. Put it away. I know how to do this." As I reholstered, she stuck the Bobcat down into her boot, then pulled her pant leg over it.

"Ready?" she asked.

"If something happens to you, I will start a riot. So be careful."

"Shane, I ran the Patrol Division in Southwest for eighteen months. That's the toughest division in the city. Stop mothering me."

Then she headed straight across the gravel lot toward the front door of the Hayloft.

CHAPTER 36

THERE WAS A BOUNCER ON the door who looked bright enough for the job, but, as it turned out, not quite.

"I'm a Shooto fighter from NHB," I said, pointing to the butterfly bandage and the ugly cut on my forehead.

He nodded and let us inside without even asking for ID. Maybe it was because he couldn't take his eyes off my wife.

"Hi," he said, as she walked past.

"Not yet." Alexa smiled seductively.

Once we were inside it was pretty easy to mingle. The club was large, the theme corny. The Hayloft had a few old, worn saddles on poles sprinkled around as barstools, and there were bales of hay piled up for people to sit on.

There was a crowd of at least seventy-five people, most of them shouting encouragement at two bare-knuckle fighters who were going at it inside an octagon cage that had been set up in the center of the room. It was so loud it was almost impossible to talk.

One of the fighters was a sumo-sized white guy—a big, sloppy, slow-moving, four-hundred pounder with ugly rolls of body fat and Teutonic folds of flesh on the back of his neck. He threw looping punches in slow motion that took forever to land. His opponent was only five foot nine or so and about half the weight. But he was quick.

"What a mismatch," Alexa yelled in my ear pointing at the two disproportionate combatants.

As we watched, it was clear the smaller man was scoring most of the points. After researching this today I now knew a little about the many different MMA fighting styles. The little guy was what this sport called a striker. He was using his speed to stay away from the giant grappler in the center of the cage, peppering him with brisk punches that landed efficiently on the big sumo's forehead. He'd already opened a nasty cut over his opponent's left eye.

Then the sumo made a sudden, unexpected charge. He grabbed the striker's legs, and both men went down. The crowd went wild.

"Get him, Fannon!" a tattooed bald guy next to me screamed.

"Which one is Fannon?" I yelled over at him.

"Little guy. Fannon Bradshaw," he yelled back. "Kenpo Karate guy. They call him the Cannon. Fast as shit with heavy hands. He's gonna eat that tub a lard for lunch."

That was pretty much exactly what happened. It only took him three and a half minutes.

Alexa and I found out that this underground match

was a no-holds-barred event. The gym in downtown L.A. owned by Team Ultima was obviously named after this fighting style.

It seemed like anything and everything was legal except hitting your opponent with a barstool. No gloves or weight classifications, and the most complete fighter, regardless of size or technique, should win. There were also no rounds, and different fighting styles were pitted against each other.

Alexa and I mingled. We found out from a bartender that Brian Bravo from Team Ultima was coming up shortly. We learned his fight name was "Little Bull" and that he was a middleweight who was the newest member of Team Ultima. The bartender told us this was only Brian's third unsanctioned fight.

Eugene Mesa was seated on a raised platform of tables in the back, surrounded by his peeps. His group had taken over four booths next to the rail.

"There he is," I told Alexa when I spotted him. We watched from a distance while a waitress took the Mesa group's order, then left.

"How're you gonna do this?" I asked. We had found a place near the fire exit where we were more or less out of the mix.

"I'm gonna be his cocktail server." Alexa smiled. Her eyes never left the waitress, who was a dumpy-looking ash blonde in tight short-shorts.

"Give me fifty dollars," Alexa said.

I dug into my pocket and handed her two twenties and a ten, then asked, "What are you up to?"

"Watch."

She waited for the waitress to fill her tray with drinks, then moved up and cut her off before she got ten steps from the end of the bar.

"Hey, is that for that group up in the back?" Alexa pointed at Mesa's tables, and the waitress nodded. "Can you do me a favor and let me deliver it? They're friends of mine."

"No way, sis. You'll get me fired," the waitress said.

Alexa put the fifty dollars on her tray.

The woman looked at the cash, had an abrupt change of heart, then handed the tray over. "Knock yourself out, honey."

Alexa took off with the drinks.

I moved in as close as I dared. O'Shea and Calabro knew me, and they were at the crowded tables with Mesa, not too far away from where I stood.

There was a fighter up there who was already stripped down to his fight trunks and was moving around on the platform nearby, ducking his head, bobbing and weaving, shadowboxing by the table, sweating profusely. The guy was way too pumped, overdosing on his own adrenaline. He looked to be about five seven and one fifty, with a ripped, conditioned body. Had to be Brian Bravo.

Alexa moved to the table and began flirting with the group as she served the drinks. The table got very animated as they all started competing for her attention. A couple of men grabbed for her, but she laughed and slipped around them as she handed out the last cocktail. Then they must have asked her to join them. She looked around as if she were trying to spot her boss, shrugged, and sat down.

I moved to a table that had just come empty several booths away and sat with my back to them, facing the octagon, where two ring attendants were wiping the sumo's blood off the mat. By using the antique mirror on the wall next to my table I could keep an eye on the action at Mesa's booth behind me.

I was scared to death for Alexa's safety, so I never took my eyes off the glass.

I already knew that there was something decidedly wrong with these characters from NHB. I didn't like seeing her sitting with Eugene Mesa surrounded by street fighters and easy women. But she seemed to be handling it. She was chatting them up, and from what I could see in the mirror, Eugene Mesa was clearly enchanted.

As time wore on, Mesa began getting bolder. He changed seats with Calabro. A few minutes later he tried to put his arm around my wife, who smiled but brushed off this clumsy advance.

I was too far away to hear anything, but Jack Straw had spotted me when he passed by my booth on his way back from the can.

After that, he kept leaving the Mesa crowd and going to the bar, where he turned and faced me from across the room.

I could see him trying to catch my attention. When our eyes met, he would start shaking his head slowly. Once he actually drew his index finger across his throat.

Just before Brian Bravo's fight began, I picked up some company at my table. Four dockworkers from San Pedro sat down uninvited. I didn't protest because being in a crowd called less attention to me than sitting alone.

When his fight finally started, Brian "Little Bull" Bravo only lasted four and a half minutes. He was a wrestler who also used tai chi, but according to my tablemates, who were deep into this sport, he was up against a very efficient Muay Thai practitioner who was undefeated and outweighed him by at least eighty pounds.

Brian Bravo didn't have a lot of cage experience and seemed burned out by all that prefight energy he'd wasted showing off at Mesa's table. He walked into a devastating short right and went down. The damage he sustained rendered him unconscious for the next five seconds.

After Brian Bravo was revived, Team Ultima made a mass exit. Alexa was pulled along with them.

I didn't know where they were heading, but I was damned if I was going to lose her in this crowd. I tried to stay close, but as they headed toward the exit, I got blocked.

A fistfight had unexpectedly broken out in the parking lot. People were clustered in the main threshold in front of me, yelling encouragement to the fighters, blocking my exit. Two guys I could barely see through the crowd were trading punches just outside the door. The bouncers swarmed in, trying to break it up.

I pushed a big tattooed ape out of the way and almost got flattened for the effort. But I ducked past him and made it out into the parking lot. By the time I got there one of the combatants, a big tattooed biker, was already down. The other fighter had disappeared.

I looked up and saw that Team Ultima was just pulling out of the lot. Their motorcycles and cars were all rolling. This time as they left, everyone turned in a different direction.

I couldn't tell which vehicle Alexa was in, or if she was on the back of one of the Indian motorcycles. Her car was parked a block away, and I was on foot.

My heart started pounding. I'd totally fucked this up. I'd lost her, which was the one thing I'd promised myself I wouldn't let happen.

I took off running toward her BMW.

I sprinted as fast as I could to the spot where we'd left the car. I didn't know how I would ever find her. I was too far behind. My only idea was to go back to Avalon Terrace and hope she was there. But then what? Go inside alone and throw down on this bunch of animals?

I snatched the hide-akey from the magnetic box in the rear wheel well, barking my knuckles and tearing skin in my haste. Then I fumbled the key out and into the lock. I yanked the door open and jumped behind the wheel.

As soon as I was inside I saw her sitting there.

She was leaning against the passenger door, still looking smoking hot.

"Where you been?" Alexa said, smiling.

CHAPTER 37

"I THOUGHT I'D LOST YOU," I blurted, my heart still pounding. I was sweating from my panic.

"Jack saved me," she said. "He saw me getting pulled out of there and started a fistfight with some Hell's Angel in the front entrance. I slipped away in the commotion."

"God bless Jack," I said softly.

"I don't know about you," she said, "but that guy's kinda beginning to grow on me."

"No kidding."

I started the car, and we pulled away from the curb, heading home. As I drove, I felt a blanket of heaviness start to come over me. My body was starting to crash. I'd only had four hours sleep in two days. The sudden adrenaline burn and days of sleep deprivation were now bringing on a case of fatigue. My mind was beginning to waiver.

"Wanta hear what I found out?" Alexa said.

"Go." I struggled to regroup.

"Eugene Mesa's hobby is MMA and he owns Team Ultima. He collects these guys like fighting pit bulls. Holds their contracts, manages them, controls that Delaware corp that owns the NHB Gym.

"They're all kissing his ass because he can snap his fingers and make their fight careers overnight. Turns out in his spare time he's becoming one of the best-known promoters in the sport and has the contacts to book them into big-money MMA events on TV.

"Rick O'Shea and Chris Calabro have each had fights on Spike TV with six-figure purses. TV fights are the brass ring. Everybody at Team Ultima is trying to be like those two.

"Tonight was a tune-up for Brian Bravo. He needed to win to impress the big man, but he lost. He doesn't know it yet, but while he was unconscious on the mat, Mesa decided Brian's gonna get cut."

"Why do they all live in the same house?"

"Nobody, except O'Shea and Calabro, has any real money yet, and that's only been in the last few months when they started fighting on TV. Mesa keeps all of his fighters financially solvent so they can train all day and not have to work. He gives them a monthly stipend to live on. That house on Avalon Terrace is a place where they can live for free. They call it Fight House.

"If Mesa likes you and if you kick ass like O'Shea and Calabro, he'll loan you one of his classic Indian motorcycles to ride. It's his thing. Took me a while to get the significance, but it finally dawned. *Indians* live up on *mesas*, get it?"

"You mean he doesn't love the bikes as much as he loves the name of the bikes?"

"Near as I can figure that's more or less it," she said.

I was wishing I'd let Alexa drive because as interesting as this all seemed, I was now really fighting to stay awake.

"Anything else?" I asked.

"Yeah. He likes me."

"It always was a long line," I said. "Even when I was in it."

She smiled. "He gave me his card and invited me to a party he's throwing on Sunday." She paused, then added, "One other thing. I found out they have a big competition coming up. Another fight club called Team Spartacus has challenged them to a match.

"Mesa told me the way a team match works, both clubs put up a purse. In this case, ten grand apiece. They pair off and have seven bouts. One point for each match, the team with the best total score wins all the money. The cash goes to help support the fighters and the gym.

"This challenge match is somewhere out of town. They're very jacked about it. Excluding Mesa, if you take all twenty IQs in that crowd and add them up, you don't have a four-digit number."

I finally made it home, parked the car in the drive, and we went inside. I was totally bushed, but I took Alexa into my arms.

"You are a very beautiful and sexy woman," I said. "You had me scared to death, but you got more in one hour than I would have in a week."

Fear must be an aphrodisiac because as wiped out as

I was, as I watched her undress, she was turning me on. Once the lights were out and we were under the covers, I reached for her.

"I thought you were sleep deprived," she teased.

"I can do this in my sleep."

I held her close as I entered her. Tired as I was, I was overcome with a powerful lust. We made love for a wonderful twenty minutes.

It was over as suddenly as it started, and then without warning, the bottom dropped out.

I slept until almost one o'clock the next afternoon.

CHAPTER 38

I WAS IN THE SHOWER, SOAKING under a hot spray, when Alexa tapped on the fogged door.

"You better wrap it up and come out here," she said through the glass.

"What's up?"

"We've got visitors."

"Who?"

"FBI. Two of 'em."

"Shit."

I toweled off, dressed, and put a fresh butterfly bandage on my forehead so I wouldn't have to try and BS our federal government with a leaking gash in my forehead.

When I walked out to my living room I was met by a Mutt and Jeff team of tired-looking feds wearing off-the-rack suits and comb-over hairstyles.

"Detective Scully?" the taller, thinner one said.

"Yes."

"I'm Agent Kurt Westfall. This is my partner, Agent Leo Faskin."

Faskin was a sour, short, lunchbox-shaped guy who looked like he hadn't smiled since the Reagan administration.

"'Sup, guys?" I said, playing it loose and friendly. Of course, I already knew it was about Jack.

"We understand that you took custody of a wanted federal bank robber named Jack Straw two days ago."

"Yep."

"Where is he?

"Sorry, that's classified," I said as Alexa moved in beside me.

"Unclassify it right now, or I'm gonna start making some phone calls. You won't like how they end," Westfall threatened.

"Can't," I said.

Westfall continued. "According to Sergeant Acosta and Lieutenant Moon, you took custody of Straw on Wednesday at two fifteen A.M. in West L.A. We have an open warrant on that guy. He robbed the First National Bank in Soledad then hit the B of A in Temecula the next day. The federal warrant is over two weeks old, and I'm under some heavy pressure to redeem it. A federal warrant definitely takes precedence over whatever it is you're investigating."

"For you, maybe. Not for me," I said.

Westfall took a step forward. "Do not fuck around with me, Detective."

"Excuse me," Alexa interjected.

Westfall shot her an angry look. "We're not talking to you, ma'am."

"No, but I'm talking to you," she replied. "I'm the

commander of the Central Detective Division of the LAPD and the classified case he's talking about is an important murder investigation that has a high police department priority. Mr. Straw is acting as a confidential informant in that situation. Our homicide investigation cannot be compromised. You'll have to wait until the LAPD case is resolved."

"You're commander of *what*?" Agent Faskin said. He was having trouble accepting the fact that such a beautiful woman could be in charge of anything more complicated than a shopping cart.

Alexa grabbed her purse off the chair and pulled out one of her business cards. She handed it to Westfall, who, after he read it, held the card like he'd just fished it out of a public toilet.

"I'm afraid that's not good enough," he finally said.

"Then I would suggest that you take this up with Chief Anthony Filosiani at your earliest convenience," Alexa replied firmly. "Until I hear from him to the contrary, this matter is closed. Was there anything else?"

Both feds stood there for a long moment, not sure how to deal with this. They had been prepared to just take the case from me. Now they had a sixth-floor LAPD commander to deal with, which momentarily trumped everything.

"You'll be hearing from our ASAC," Kurt Westfall said testily. Then he looked at Leo Faskin, and the two of them turned. Alexa held open the front door as they passed, then closed it firmly behind them.

When they were gone, she turned to me and said, "Of course, you know that will never stick."

"Come on. Why not? You told the truth. Jack's working undercover even though we didn't exactly sanction it. This is a high-profile murder just like you said. What's not to stick?"

"Honey, we have a new Homeland Security rule book. There's something in there called the interagency operational guideline. They aren't gonna accept that we're using their wanted federal bank robber as a protected UC. Those guys have open-felony paper on Jack. I'm going to be hearing from Deputy Chief Bradshaw within an hour. I know he's gonna demand we turn Straw over, but of course we haven't got a clue where he is. So we're sorta fucked."

"Finally, you see how easy it is to get in trouble with Internal Affairs." I grinned.

CHAPTER 39

I CALLED VARGAS TO TALK about Jack and the FBI development. We arranged to meet for a late lunch in Torrance, where he had a hearing at the courthouse. I had some time to kill before then, so I decided to run by Huntington House first to see if Vicki was making any progress with the financial records.

Alexa had decided to go downtown to Parker Center and head off the FBI by convincing Tony to go on offense. There was a fair chance she could talk our chief into stonewalling the bureau.

Of course, the problem was that I'd lied to Sergeant Acosta and Lieutenant Moon and now Jack was gone. I had a hunch on how to get him back but wasn't quite sure I wanted to. He was actually in a pretty good place right now to help us.

A gnawing feeling of gratitude for Jack had been building in me for the last two days. He was unorthodox, but he had guts. He was moving forward and risking everything, including his life and freedom, because he wanted to get some justice for Walter Dix. You had to respect it.

When I got to Huntington House, nobody was in the office. I walked the campus, once again flooded with memories of my time there. I never found Diamond or Vicki, so I finally got back into the MDX and headed out. I had just turned onto Western Avenue when I glanced in my rearview mirror and saw O'Shea's custom maroon Escalade ducking in and out of a line of traffic. Somehow I had missed seeing the car at Huntington House. It wasn't in the main lot, so O'Shea must have been parked on a side street and saw me coming out. He was about three car lengths back.

I had to decide very quickly how to play this. I didn't know if I wanted to pull over right now and confront O'Shea on a city street, taking a chance that this polypeptide junkie would park another right cross on my forehead, or if I wanted to try and be more devious.

Given all that had happened and the short time line I now found myself on with the FBI, being devious seemed like the better plan, even if it wasn't the bravest.

I was sure I couldn't outrun him in my Acura, so I started to search my mind for a terrain-friendly spot nearby where I could obtain a tactical advantage.

Then I remembered a maze of little short streets and cul-de-sacs by the Torrance Municipal Airport, which was only a few miles away.

I accelerated through a yellow light and headed in that direction. In the side mirror I saw the Escalade plow through the red light, blaring the horn, narrowly missing some oncoming traffic. I drove as quickly as I could, weaving through traffic.

I was just passing the airport on my right, when suddenly the Escalade moved up fast. It slammed into my back left bumper, executing a pretty good pit maneuver, which spun my car. I went off the road onto the shoulder and finally came to a jarring stop half on the road, half off.

I opened my door and stepped out as Rick O'Shea exited his car.

He was coming at me fast from about ten yards away with an ugly expression on his face.

"What's wrong with you?" I called out angrily, looking at the damaged front fender of his Escalade, then at the paint-scarred left side of my bumper.

"Get the fuck away from me," I said, trying to get to the .38 strapped low on my ankle. I was reaching down, trying to unhook the flap on the holster and draw my gun, but I already knew I wouldn't have near enough time.

What came next was so fast I didn't even know what happened. O'Shea took me down in less than a second with some sort of complex Brazilian jujitsu move, then, like a break-dancer on his back, wrapped himself around me.

His legs gripped my torso while he simultaneously pulled me toward him and twisted my arms up in some kind of joint-ruining arm bar.

I was suddenly helpless. He held me there, pinned and

totally compromised. Then, like an anaconda squeezing its prey, he slowly began to apply pressure.

O'Shea's complicated holds were tightening, bending my joints the wrong way, shooting unbearable pain through my entire body.

He had his mouth next to my ear and whispered, "Are you getting the point, friend?"

"Okay, enough," I pleaded.

He put more pressure on my left elbow, bending it further backward. My right wrist was screaming in pain.

"This is so you won't forget."

He bore down hard, and I heard a snap. My right forearm exploded in pain. Then he unwrapped himself, stood, and patted me down. He quickly found my gun and then my badge case. When he opened it, he cursed softly.

"You're a *cop*?"

"Yeah," I whispered through gritted teeth.

"*Fuck*!" he shouted in frustration, then stepped back and threw my Taurus Hy-Lite and shield twenty feet away before sprinting back to his car. He pulled out and drove off, squealing his tires as he went.

I remained on my back, lying very still. I was cradling my throbbing right arm in my aching left hand.

I was supposed to be tough. I had a rep around the LAPD as a hard guy to put down. But I'd been in two scraps with O'Shea and I'd lost them both. Elapsed time on both contests—less than fifteen seconds. Pretty damn pathetic.

I finally got to my feet painfully, holding my arm. My left wrist was aching, but at least it wasn't broken.

After I got the pain under control, I somehow picked up my badge and got my gun back in its holster. I needed to get to a hospital, but I'd be lucky if I could even drive.

CHAPTER 40

I MANAGED TO DRIVE MYSELF to the nearby Torrance Medical Center and went inside. There was a doctor there whose son was on Harvard Westlake's football team, and he'd set Chooch's finger after he broke it on a blitzing linebacker's helmet while throwing a pass during the last game of his junior year.

Dr. Raymond George was listed as on duty. Everyone from school called him Dr. Ray.

I spoke to the admitting nurse and told her I wanted to see him and that I needed to get my arm set. I was directed to the waiting room of the ER and was given patient insurance forms to fill out, which was a severe challenge using only my left hand.

I needed help on some of the more involved written stuff and kept pestering the nurse for assistance.

While I waited, a woman who looked like she'd been in a bar fight helped me dial my phone. I cradled my swelling right arm in my lap, held the cell in my left hand, then put it gingerly to my ear.

Alexa answered a few seconds later by saying, "What's going on, babe?"

I filled her in on what had happened with O'Shea and told her where I was. When I finished, she said, "He broke your arm?"

"Don't make me say it again. I already feel like a total pussy. The guy has taken me out twice in two days and hasn't even broken a sweat."

"I'm on my way."

"Not necessary. I'm okay, sorta. I'll meet you at home. How are you doing with Chief Filosiani?"

"I haven't even been in to see him yet. Maria's trying to fit me in between appointments."

"Stay there. I'm okay. I'll call you when I get out of here."

Dr. Ray met me in one of the ER exam rooms. He was a tall, skeletal guy with an infectious smile. I showed him my arm and told him I missed a step and fell down some stairs.

"Let's see what you did," he said. "Gonna have to take a picture."

He numbed the arm and took X-rays. Once he got them back, he showed me the results.

"You have a hairline fracture," he said, pointing to a slight crack in the bone visible on the X-ray. "It's gonna need a cast."

He opened a cabinet and pulled out some fiberglass casting tapes and put them in a bowl of water to moisten. Then he began to wrap the waterproof cast liner, starting down by my first knuckle.

"I need to be able to use my hand," I told him.

"Shane, to keep this stable I should immobilize the entire arm, wrist to shoulder," he said, holding the dripping tape in his hand.

"Yeah, but I need to be able to fill out my police reports. I'll be careful. I'll keep it in a sling."

He looked at me skeptically.

"Come on, you immobilize my whole arm and my boss will pull me outta the field and stick me on a desk answering phones. Don't do that to me. I'll die of boredom."

Reluctantly, Dr. Ray acquiesced.

When he was done, the cast went from just above my wrist, almost up to the elbow.

"You have to leave this in a sling. The arm needs the support."

"No problem," I said.

Then he checked my swollen left wrist and declared it a sprain.

"This is gonna be sore. I'm going to prescribe something for the pain."

"I don't want it," I said. "I deserve the pain."

He left the room to get the sling. As soon as he was gone, I got off the table, limped to the medical supply cabinet, and stole a fiberglass tape roll, jamming it down into my pocket. I had a devious notion of how to use it.

Dr. Ray came back with the sling. He fitted it around my neck and put my broken right arm inside, adjusting the straps.

"Pay the front desk," he instructed.

I went out and gave them my card. The computer hummed and blipped. My broken arm ached like a bitch.

CHAPTER 41

I HAD A VOICE DIAL ON THE MDX, so as I carefully held the steering wheel, I recited Vargas's cell number. Miraculously, I got him on the phone.

After I told him what happened, he said, "Are you telling me O'Shea beat you up *again*?"

"I'm getting real tired of saying this more than once."

I hesitated for a minute, swallowed my pride. "Look, we're running out of time. I got the FBI circling because of Jack. O'Shea knows I'm a cop and that's bound to produce bad results. We need to get the pallbearers together and pool our knowledge. If it's not too much trouble, I'd really appreciate it if we could meet at my house."

"What about Diamond?" he asked after another long pause.

"Invite her. She's okay."

"You sure?"

"Yeah. O'Shea didn't know I was a cop 'til he found

my badge. If Diamond was in on it, she certainly would have told him."

"I'm glad."

"Me too."

We set up the meeting for an hour from now. It would allow me time to get home, take some ibuprofen, ice my wrist, and try to get my head to start working again.

It was hard driving with one hand, but I made it. My sprained left wrist was throbbing almost as badly as my right arm by the time I pulled into my drive.

I put the MDX in park, which was no easy task with the wrong hand. Then I got out and lumbered into the house. I opened the refrigerator, fumbled some ice into a bowl, took it to the counter, and spent a frustrating ten minutes trying to get the cubes into a baggie. I tore off some adhesive tape using my teeth and made a clumsy ice-pack compress for my left wrist.

Next, I went into the bathroom, put the roll of fiberglass gauze in the medicine cabinet, and took the ibuprofen. As I was clinging to the sink, I got a distressing look at myself in the bathroom mirror.

I won't bother to describe my appearance except to say it was startling.

The pallbearers all showed up at a little past five. We sat in my living room. I stretched out painfully in the lounge chair, and then we discussed my broken arm, swollen wrist, and how Rick O'Shea had changed my tires for the second time in two days. I told them not to worry, it wasn't going to happen again. They settled into chairs in my living room and regarded the remark skeptically.

"Shane, you called this meeting, so I guess you're on," Sabas said.

Diamond, Vicki, and Seriana also sat there, waiting for me to dispense some wisdom. I almost couldn't summon enough energy to start talking.

"Some stuff happened since we split up," I began slowly. Then I told them about the gift Jack had left for me in my mailbox. I handed Sabas the SD card, and he loaded it into my computer. They all watched it, then turned to face me.

"Mesa's house?" Vicki asked, and after I nodded she said, "He's got a long board just like Pop?"

They spent a few minutes discussing that, and I gave them my theory about Pop and E. C. Mesa maybe being surfing buddies. Then I told them how Alexa and I had culled the Rolodex and about last night's trip to the house on Avalon Terrace, which led to the underground fight at the Hayloft. Lastly I filled them in on everything Alexa had learned at Mesa's table. After I finished, the room was quiet.

Sabas finally said, "I thought we agreed we were gonna all work this together. You couldn't make a call and let us in on what you were up to?"

"It was sort of a spur-of-the-moment decision," I defended. "We were only going to check it out but when we saw that party, it sort of developed into something else."

"You aren't the only one who needs closure on Pop's murder, Shane. We're all hurtin'. You gave us your word if we let you call the shots, you wouldn't freeze us out. But you went ahead and did this on your own anyway."

I'd had a bad morning. I was starting to get annoyed. "It was late, almost eleven P.M. when we got there," I said. "Last time I called and woke you up you chewed my head off."

"Boys, boys, boys," Vicki said. "Let's stop bickering and deal with what Shane and Alexa found out. What's it mean?"

"I don't know," I admitted, taking a breath to cool down. "Haven't a clue. But we need to review everything we know. See how quickly we can unpack this and figure what the elements were that really got Pop killed."

So we began.

Some of it was just theory, some of it was feelings. A lot was sad memories and regrets about Pop.

Diamond kept asking why E. C. Mesa might have that big, rhino-chaser cigar-box board in his garage. Seriana wondered if it could be a coincidence.

"In law enforcement, the rule is never trust a coincidence," I told her.

Vicki said, "The suicide note seemed like hooey even when we still thought Pop had killed himself. Now that we know he was murdered, it's gotta be bullshit."

I got up and limped over to the desk and found my copy of the note. I handed it to Vicki and lowered myself painfully back into the lounge chair.

She began reading a few parts aloud. " 'Got pulled down by leash drag'? 'Sorry about the yard sale'? 'If you need the reason, tap the source, Walt'? That doesn't sound right to me at all. Who writes a last note that sounds like that? But if somebody was forcing him to write it, Pop might have been trying to send a secret communication."

"You mean maybe it's like a code or something?" Diamond said.

Vicki looked at us and nodded. "If he knew he was going to die and somebody was making him write this, then maybe he was using all this surf lingo to tell us something."

I didn't give that idea much credence. We were beginning to grasp at fringe theories.

"Here's something that's been bothering me," Seriana said. "Why the six of us? I loved Pop, and I certainly owed him, but I don't think I was more special to him than a lot of other kids who were at the home when I was."

"Most people don't pick their own pallbearers," I said, nodding. "But Walt wrote that letter a week before he was killed, naming the six of us."

"Why would he do that?" Vicki asked.

"Alexa thinks Pop must have already known he was in some danger the week before he was killed and chose his pallbearers because he knew the kind of people we are."

"Which is?" Diamond said.

"Well, except for you, Diamond, we're nonconformists who don't do what we're told. Alexa thinks maybe Walt picked us because in the event he got murdered, he knew we wouldn't accept the official version of his death and would keep looking until we found out what really happened."

"That's one fucking smart lady you got there, hoss," Vicki said.

"So you buy it?" I asked, looking around the room at everyone.

"I've also been wondering the same thing," Vargas said, nodding. "I always felt special in Walt's eyes, but then so did everyone else. I keep thinking, out of all the hundreds of people who went to Huntington House, why was I one of six that he wanted to carry his coffin? I feel the same as Seriana. There were so many others that he could have chosen."

Diamond broke the silence that followed. "So what's our next move?"

"I was waiting to go back and look at Pop's house until the coroner assigned a homicide number to the case," I said. "My idea was to take a forensic unit over to his house and redo the entire crime-scene investigation."

"Come on, that's nuts," Sabas sniped. "It's been a week and a half. There've been cops and newspaper people traipsing through there. That's a totally contaminated site."

I didn't have much patience for his tone. Despite a promising start after that fight at the gym, we were now getting on each other's nerves.

"I agree," I said, struggling to control my irritation. "So instead of waiting, let's go now. We knew Pop better than the cops who investigated this. Let's use our knowledge of him to see if we can find something they missed."

I rode with Sabas in the yellow truck. Halfway there, he looked over, staring at me with vato eyes. In that moment I could see remnants of the little nine-year-old shooter who had killed to protect his drug turf.

"Don't freeze me out," he warned. "Next time you torch me like that, I'll just take this into my own hands."

"Sabas, I wasn't leaving you out. We turned up the address on Avalon Terrace late at night. We didn't know there'd be a party and that Jack would be there. Why can't you cut me a little slack?"

"Why should I? Lookit you, you been getting beat worse than a birthday piñata. You ain't inspiring much confidence."

I decided not to argue with him. Despite all the mistakes I'd made, I felt I was on the verge of something. The answer seemed near. It was like the feeling I always got as a kid on sunrise patrol just before a big set rolled in.

As we neared Walt's old bungalow, in my subconscious I could hear Walt talking to me, using that crazy pidgin Hawaiian. *Paddle hard, bra. We be in da zone fo shur.*

The crinkly smile, the seawater-blue eyes, counting on me to get him to shore.

CHAPTER 42

POP'S HOUSE WAS A WHITE bungalow with a red tile roof in a middle-class neighborhood not too far from Huntington House, and it was exactly as I had remembered. After his wife, Elizabeth, died, Pop had continued to live there alone.

He always kept the hide-a-key in the same place—inside the feed drawer in the base of a large wooden birdcage that now hung empty from a chain on the far end of his front porch.

He used to sit out here on summer nights while a big green and yellow parrot sat in that cage squawking loudly. The bird spoke only pidgin and was named Hang Six. Pop had bought him in the early seventies on the Hawaiian North Shore. Hang Six had to be at least forty by now, if he was still alive.

On nights when some of us were over here visiting Pop, having one of Elizabeth's home-cooked meals, we were always fascinated by the bird's island patois.

"Hey hapa haole, boy. Surf's up, bra!" He would screech that stuff incessantly.

I thought it interesting that despite our age difference, every one of us knew that the hide-a-key was always kept in the feed drawer under the cage. Pop hadn't bothered to change its location in almost four decades.

That told me he hadn't been too worried about security. If his killer knew him, then he probably also knew where the key was and could have used it to get in here and lie in wait.

We opened the front door, turned on the lights, and stood in Pop's small living room. There was a lot of surfer art adorning this space. Over the fireplace hung a large painting of a forty-foot windswept wave, a magnificent aqua green crescent with white foam blowing off the leading edge. There were all kinds of surfer knickknacks on the walls, along with half a dozen photographs under glass of huge storm breaks on the North Shore of Oahu.

Hang Six's indoor cage was also empty, standing in the corner. Diamond said the cops had taken him to animal control after Pop died.

"Where do you want to start?" Sabas asked.

"Yard sale. Let's look at the backyard," Vicki suggested.

I was sort of humoring this idea as we all trooped to the back and stood on Walt's wood porch, the same porch where he'd died.

"You know, I used to come here from time to time

with two or three of the other kids," Seriana said wistfully. "It was ten years ago, when I was thirteen. We'd sit on this porch and drink lemonade. It was such a treat to be chosen to come. Before she died, Mrs. Dix would cook a meal for us. It felt for just a few hours like we had a real home."

"It's why Pop brought us here," Vicki said. "He wanted us to see what a normal family life was like."

Seriana nodded. "Did Pop ever let you take Hang Six out of his cage?"

"Yeah," Diamond said. "He'd sit on our shoulders while Pop told stories about Hawaii."

"Sometimes when I was here, we'd get to help him shape one of his surfboards," Vicki remembered.

The garage was Pop's board shop.

"Let's go see. Maybe that's the yard sale—the boards," Seriana said.

We wandered across the little patch of lawn. Since Pop died, nobody had been watering it. We stopped in front of the garage.

"Where'd he keep the key?" Sabas asked.

"Never locked it," Diamond said.

Sabas tried the door, and found it was open.

We entered and turned on the overhead light. In front of us, lying across two sawhorses, was a newly shaped, almost finished, nine-foot cigar-box board. It had already been sanded, and the first coat of varnish had been applied. It looked as if it had been left there to dry. I crossed to the board and traced the rough, unsanded first coat of varnish with the fingers of my good hand.

"Leash drag," Diamond said. "He kept those in here."

She crossed to a cupboard where Pop's surf equipment was stored and opened it. Inside were some old leather-and-rope ankle leashes, some board resin and wax, half a dozen small-sized wet suits for kids. There was nothing else inside the cabinet. We all stood there, beginning to feel a growing sense of futility.

"These big old rhino chasers have large air pockets in the front to keep them from being too nose heavy," Vicki finally said. "I remember Pop had to drain them at the end of each day. Maybe he built this to hide something in there."

Sabas walked over to the board and tapped his knuckles on the nose. It sounded hollow. Empty.

"Kinda hate to bust it open," he said. "It seems kinda special. The last board Pop ever worked on."

"We can come back to it if we don't find anything," I suggested. "I could probably arrange for somebody at CSI to get it x-rayed."

I wanted to get them off the idea that Walt's suicide note contained a message. What I really wanted was to do a thorough search of this place, looking for anomalies, some small piece of evidence that had been missed by Kovacevich and Cole but would make sense to the five of us.

I finally got that organized, and we began to look through the rest of the workshop. Then we searched the yard. After that we went back inside and searched the small two-bedroom house. We worked for an hour, and before long, failure to turn up anything was causing a pronounced loss of energy.

We took a break, and everyone gathered on the back

porch. Vargas and I leaned on the railing, Diamond sat on the wooden chair, Vicki and Seriana on the big porch swing.

We were all quiet, gazing out at the backyard and remembering those times when we came here as kids. As I looked out across the dying lawn, it just seemed so damned much smaller than it had when I was nine.

Vicki went inside to use the bathroom, and Sabas spoke to what all of us were feeling. "It's hard to believe Pop died right here on this porch," he said softly. "Maybe even in that very chair."

Everyone looked down at the wooden chair Diamond was sitting on. She got up quickly, abandoning it and moving over to the porch rail.

"I just never thought Pop would check out that way," Seriana said. "Never thought somebody so mellow could die so badly."

As we sat there, I began to feel a little lost. Looking out over the yard I had a sudden overpowering feeling that I had failed Pop again, that I had let him down now, just as I had during all those years when I'd rejected him. I looked at the faces of the other pallbearers and saw the same defeat reflected in their eyes.

"Hey, you guys. Come in here for a minute," Vicki called out from inside the house.

We trooped into the living room and saw that she had pulled a large Hawaiian kahuna tiki statue away from the wall where it had always stood. Kahunas were usually little shelf-sized figurines sold in surf shops. You could also buy replica good-luck kahunas that were inch-high wood carvings, often worn around a surfer's neck on a leather cord.

This one was much larger and stood almost three feet high. It was hand carved out of pinewood, with a big nose, oversized lips, and bushy hair made of dried straw.

"Something back there?" I asked, and moved over to look at the wall behind where the kahuna had always stood.

Sabas said, "I don't remember him from when I used to come over, but that was almost forty years ago."

"He was always here when I was a kid," I said. "It's a kahuna, the Hawaiian god of the surf."

"Isn't that what Pop always called the source?" Vicki asked.

I nodded. "Pop said Kahuna is the source of good waves. He lives in the middle of the ocean and makes the big double-overhead tube rides. He told me that when he was a kid, all the surfers on the North Shore would sit on the beach at night, smoking blunts, praying to this little guy for big rhino waves to ride."

"He said if we want the answers, we should tap the source," Vicki said. "That's how Walt signed his note, right? 'Tap the Source, Walt.' "

I shook my head. "I think all he meant was . . ."

"You don't know what the fuck he meant, Shane," she snapped. "Let's get this little asshole's head off and see what's inside."

Before anybody could stop her, she had leaned over the kahuna and was pulling and yanking on the statue's head, rocking it back and forth. Suddenly, it popped off and flew out of her hands and landed across the room next to the sofa.

There was a carved wooden peg that fit into the statue's torso to hold the head in place. Seriana removed the peg, revealing a hole.

We could all now see that the carved headless torso was hollow inside. Vicki stuck her small hand down through the opening, reaching deep into the body of the kahuna god, and began rummaging around.

When she pulled her slender hand out, she was holding a fat manila envelope.

I'll be damned, I thought.

CHAPTER 43

IT NEVER HAPPENS LIKE THIS in law enforcement—the whole resolution to a case hiding inside a vase or a statue.

Still, I couldn't keep myself from grinning.

But despite my elation, there was some part of me that distrusted it. On the other hand, *why not*? Why couldn't this have been Walt's plan all along? He'd picked the six of us because we were the nonconformist kids he had never given up on. And he know we wouldn't give up on him.

Maybe.

Vicki opened the manila envelope. Inside was what looked like a handwritten note on a piece of paper. It was in Pop's scrawling cursive.

1. *Never enough money to run home* . . . Why?
2. Open checks? Exact amounts? ✓
3. Rick O'Shea only receives $200.00 a month from H. H. How can he afford new Cadillac Escalade

and huge new house? Where does $ come from? MMA fights?

4. O'Shea's checkbook and stubs. Gym bag? ✓
5. Review accounts payable. ✓
6. Review last 2 years' H. H. tax returns. ✓
7. Correlate H. H. expenditures with R. O.'s personal deposits. ✓
8. *Why were we billed for the roof on Sharon Cross Hall when it never got repaired?*

The list was backed by a sheaf of papers, including photocopies of Rick O'Shea's personal-check stubs and his bank-deposit slips. Pop must have stolen the checkbook from O'Shea's gym bag and copied them. Certain numbers on O'Shea's bank deposits had been highlighted by Walt.

Vicki began sorting the photocopied pages, separating those that showed estimates or contracts for work projects to be done at Huntington House from bank withdrawals on Huntington House checks that bore Pop's signature.

"Look at this," she said.

She showed us what looked like a bogus roofing contract with a cheap letterhead that looked like it had been made up at Kinko's.

The contract was to redo the roof on Sharon Cross Hall for $10,280.00. With it was a canceled check made out to cash from Huntington House for the contracted amount signed by Pop. Presumably payment for the job. Then she showed us a deposit slip to Rick O'Shea's personal bank account for the exact same amount.

"You know anything about this?" I asked Diamond.

"We couldn't afford that new roof," she said. "I told Pop we were going to hold up all the maintenance contracts."

"O'Shea was the embezzler, not Pop," I said. "He set Pop up and somehow got his signature on all this so it would look like Pop was the thief. Alexa found out at the Hayloft that O'Shea only recently started making big purses on his MMA fights, so that obviously isn't the way he could afford that million-dollar house in Calabasas and the expensive SUV. *This* is what paid for that stuff."

Vicki said, "I'll have to go through all of this and see what else there is."

She pulled out another photocopy. "Here's another one. A bill for Huntington House employee and child health insurance for last year, totaling eighty-three thousand, nine-hundred-eighteen dollars and twenty-three cents." She found a corresponding canceled check made out to cash in the same amount with Pop's signature and matched it to one of O'Shea's deposit slips for his personal bank account. The amount was exactly the same, down to the penny.

"Since there are no coincidences in police work, these aren't coincidences," Seriana said.

I glanced over at her and saw a big wide smile. This one stayed on her face and made her beautiful.

"How the fuck could Pop be signing checks to cash and giving them to this dirtbag?" Vicki said, shaking her head in disbelief.

"Walt trusted people," Diamond answered. "It was just the way he was."

"*This* is why Pop wanted to see me," Sabas said softly, revising his reason for the third time. "He'd found all this. He discovered what O'Shea was doing. He wanted my advice on how to move forward. But I was too damn busy." There was pain and self-loathing on the lawyer's face.

"So here's the motive for the murder," I said. "Rick O'Shea was looking for evidence, not money. Pop had figured it out, had these documents proving O'Shea was guilty of embezzlement. Pop confronted him, told O'Shea he had the proof. O'Shea beat him to get Pop to tell him where this stuff was. When Pop wouldn't, O'Shea killed him."

Far from stealing from Huntington House, Pop had died protecting it. Shouldn't we have known that from the start?

"We need to put this on paper and deliver it to the DA's office," I said. "Then tomorrow we'll bust O'Shea. From there, it's wrap-up."

"Why do we have to wait 'til tomorrow?" Sabas said. "Let's go slam that asshole in cuffs right now."

"We can't do it tonight because we need an arrest warrant. I'll call Alexa. She can pull in some sixth-floor help. Vicki, you get these financial papers in order so they make enough sense for a judge to write us a warrant based on what they say. Tomorrow, it will be over."

CHAPTER 44

BY THE TIME ALEXA GOT HOME at six that night she had pretty much pulled the case together for me. She'd pestered Chief Filosiani until he finally agreed to throw a net over the FBI, telling the feds that Straw was off-limits until he was through helping us with our high-profile murder case. They had no choice but to stand down.

After Alexa finished giving me this news, she added, "Tony asked me if I had actual, physical custody of Jack."

"And you said, 'Of course I do, Chief. I wouldn't let that dirtbag out of my sight.'"

"Exactly. Flat-out lied to my boss. If this goes bad, I'm gonna get my ass kicked."

She was taking a huge chance for me, putting her own career in jeopardy. I took her hand. "I know you've been letting me run this, and I know it hasn't been my smoothest investigation. I want you to know how much I appreciate what you're doing."

"This is important to you. I can deal with the department fallout if it comes to that."

"I think we need to call a friendly judge and get the paperwork on Rick O'Shea going," I said. "I want to pick it up first thing in the morning. We can show the judge what Vicki has and move on O'Shea by ten A.M."

She tapped a nail against the kitchen table, deep in thought. "How come my instinct tells me this goes much deeper than Rick O'Shea?" she said. "Like all the way up to E. C. Mesa."

"Because it does. But we start with Rick. Since I've already got a decent prima facie case against him, and he's two pickles short of a full sandwich, we'll lay it on him, he'll get confused and give up everybody else. Cop 101."

Alexa said she knew a judge who would write our warrant for O'Shea and picked up the kitchen phone to call him.

I went outside and settled into my chair in the backyard to rest my aching body and watch the sun go down. I looked out at the still canal and thought about Walt. I wondered if I'd finally evened our debt. If arresting O'Shea made up for my not being there. Deep down, I knew it hadn't. It felt strangely incomplete.

I noticed some movement at the edge of the yard, leaned forward, and spotted our adopted cat, Franco, watching me from under an oleander bush. It was ladycat season and he'd been away from the house for the last day or so. Now he was back with a smirk on his face, satisfaction burning in his big yellow eyes.

"Been out getting some?" I asked him.

He's not a cuddly cat, but he can read my needs. If I'm feeling bad, he lets me know he cares.

He walked over and wound around my ankles, then jumped up into my lap and plopped down. He sniffed at my cast, turned his head, and gave me a withering look.

"I know, it's disappointing."

Franco put his head down and began to purr.

As I looked down at him, my thoughts started along a new path.

We'd ended up with Franco because I'd failed to move quickly enough to save his original owner, Carol White, and she'd been murdered. Now I'd also failed to save Pop. In the end I'd made Carol's killer pay. Tomorrow I was determined to do the same for Walt.

This memory started a chain of thoughts that led me, once again, back to those early mornings, kneeling in the sand beside Pop on Seal Beach.

I suddenly remembered something that had happened over thirty years ago. We'd been out beyond the surf line just before dawn. It was only my first or second time, and I was still nervous about being in the ocean. I was sitting on my short board in my beavertail wet suit, facing Pop in the water, when I felt something bite my bare leg. I freaked out.

"A fish is biting me!" I yelled. "A shark!"

Of course it wasn't a shark, but I was scared, and I wanted to go back to shore. Pop wouldn't let me.

"That fish didn't bite you, bra. He kissed you. The old Hawaiians say that's a sure sign that you are at one with your aumakua."

Pop proceeded to explain that according to Hawaiian legend, aumakuas were our heavenly ancestors, who were godlike and always watching over their family. It was a hard concept for me because I had never known who my family was. Then he smiled at me.

"Animals, even fish, know when you've found your true center. That fish is telling you that you're at one with your maker. He's one of God's creatures, and when you're right with God, he kisses you. You gotta relax, bra, and say thank you." He was smiling as he told me this.

Of course, to a street-hardened throwaway like me, this was total bullshit. I was a tough guy, a cynic. For that reason, I never paid too much attention to Pop's Zen surfer chatter, and over the years I'd sort of learned to dial him out. But on this one thing, some part of me always wondered.

So sometimes when I was out on the board before sunup, I would try to do like Pop, center myself and Zen out. I was looking for inner peace, although I'd never felt any.

I was a little nine-year-old, mad as hell, sitting on a short board, dangling my legs in the water, trying to find an emotional center I was positive didn't exist.

But nonetheless, whenever I was backwalling, waiting for a big rhino, I would tone down the aggression and try to be at one with my aumakuas, whoever the hell they were, because I'd been dumped at a hospital and had no ancestors that I knew about. I'd sit there trying to feel good about myself and about a life where nothing ever seemed to be going right. I finally got to where I could sort of do it. At least I could go some-place else and leave some of that blind anger behind.

Then, one morning I was out there, feeling kinda spiritual. The sun was just coming up. Good sets were rolling in from Mexico. The sky was a beautiful red-orange. I was filled with a sense of well-being. For once I was almost happy.

And then it happened again.

A little fish, a perch or a bass, came up and nibbled my toe. I sat very still and wondered what force of nature existed that would put me at one with a tiny fish in this cold, vast ocean. Was there more going on in the universe than I had ever stopped to consider?

The next morning when I woke up, I began to wonder about God.

CHAPTER 45

THE NEXT MORNING MY RIGHT arm was aching less and my left wrist was almost back to its normal size. I was feeling much better.

After I dressed, I went to my closet to get a new backup gun. I had two. The S&W .38 caliber Airweight had an aluminum alloy frame. Alexa said it was another underpowered pop gun just like my Taurus. Because I was going to serve a warrant on Rick O'Shea and because of my recent embarrassing history with him, I decided to pack heavy this morning and instead chose my Charter Arms .357 magnum Pug. It shoots 124-grain JHP ammo and will drop a charging elephant.

I called Vargas and told him that we had a warrant and that Alexa and I were going to arrest O'Shea for murder. I had checked in with him as a courtesy and to try and put it back together. I never thought that he'd give me an argument.

"The rest of us talked it over," he said. "And we all want to be there when you slam the cuffs on."

"It's a police action, Sabas. It's not a ride at Disneyland."

"Don't insult me with shit like that," he snapped. "We all did this. We did it for Pop. This is our victory as much as yours, but you're not letting us have it."

"Right." I wasn't going to argue. "Do me a favor and call Vicki. Tell her I'm on the way to her office right now to pick up her financial breakdown sheets. I'll be at Kinney and Glass in half an hour."

I hung up. I couldn't believe he was angry with me over this. He wanted to take a bunch of civilians out to stand on the sidewalk and watch an arrest for first-degree murder? Didn't he know how stupid that was?

On second thought, I guess if you have a California law degree and you're still willing on a second's notice to hit a guy in the head with a tire iron, you're not exactly going to be posing for the cover of *Lawyer Magazine.*

I left Alexa in our living room; she was getting ready to head to the courthouse in the Valley. I agreed to meet her there by nine thirty.

Kinney and Glass was one of those big Century City high-rise outfits. Too much chrome in the sterile marble entry, which was also hung with huge, ultraexpensive, modern paintings that looked like they'd been done by some fifth-grade class with finger paint.

Amana and Frigidaire people who walked as if they had Ping-Pong balls stuffed up their asses passed me on their way into work. While I waited for Vicki, I wondered how a hotheaded woman who kept a short-nose Bulldog in her purse could survive in such a frosty environment.

Vicki finally came out and handed me the paperwork. "Vargas thinks we should be allowed to watch this go down," she said.

"Where did you guys get this idea that law enforcement is a game with rubber guns and whistles?" I said sourly.

"Vargas thinks it's his fault Walt got murdered. He's blaming himself."

"Yeah, I get that 'cause I'm blaming myself too. But if I took any of you guys out there and O'Shea went hot and injured or killed someone, it would go down very hard. I'll stream some video on my iPhone, and we'll all watch it in a bar later, but I'm not taking you out there."

"No, I think you're right," she said. "I agree with you, Shane. We're not cops. We're . . . we're . . . what the hell are we?"

"Pallbearers," I said.

I made it to the courthouse in thirty-five minutes, which was great time. Alexa and I showed the judge the redone autopsy from Oakcrest, Vicki's spreadsheets, and the corresponding deposit slips from O'Shea's personal bank account and explained how this material was the motive for Pop's homicide. The judge agreed we had sufficient evidence and signed arrest warrants for felony business fraud and first-degree murder.

We left my car at the courthouse and took Alexa's because I was still having trouble driving. We exited the freeway in Calabasas, and I gave Alexa directions to O'Shea's large Spanish-style house on Lupine Lane. When we pulled up, there was a black and white parked on the side with two uniformed officers leaning against their front fender, waiting.

Given my history with O'Shea, I normally would have used a SWAT warrant-delivery team, but it usually takes a day to set that up, so we'd called the L.A. sheriff's department. As I walked up to the uniforms, I was hoping they would be enough backup.

I told the two officers how we wanted to serve the warrant. "This guy is a professional MMA fighter. If you don't think he can hit, take a close look at me. Every bit of this is his doing."

"We'll stay frosty," the lead officer, a big linebacker-sized deputy named Davila, assured me.

"Okay. Let's go hook him up."

We entered the property through the side gate and walked across the lawn to a path that led to the front porch. There was no sign of the maroon Escalade, but it was only a few minutes past 10:00 A.M., and I was hoping that it was still in the garage and that O'Shea was sleeping in.

I stood next to Deputy Davila, who rang the bell while Alexa and the other blue walked down the back drive to cover the rear entrance. Nothing happened.

We rang again.

Still no answer.

"This is a no-knock murder warrant," I told Davila. "Go ahead and kick it."

Then I stepped back so he could do the honors. I'd done my share of solid door kick-ins, and the last thing I needed right now was to add a sprained ankle to my growing list of injuries.

The deputy and I both unholstered, and then he let fly with two kicks up by the brass handle. The big oak door flew inward. No alarm sounded.

"Police!" I yelled out. Then we moved into the house.

Nothing. The downstairs looked like it had been done by a decorator with nothing out of place, like an expensive condo model.

"Let's clear this place," I instructed.

We let Alexa and the second deputy in through the back door, and began going room to room, covering each other, stepping inside and calling "clear," until we had checked the entire first level.

Then we went up the stairs. The second floor was completely empty of furniture. There was no sign of Rick O'Shea.

The master bedroom contained only a queen-sized bed, a dresser, and nothing else. I opened the walk-in closet, and it was obvious that O'Shea had left in a hurry. Hangers were strewn on the floor. He had also cleaned out his medicine cabinet and most of the dresser drawers.

"Shit," I said softly. "Bet he took off right after he saw my badge."

We finished searching the house and went downstairs to the front porch, where we all stood looking out at the half-acre front lawn.

"You need us for anything else, Lieutenant?" Deputy Davila asked Alexa.

"Nope. Thanks for the assist," she replied.

They walked back to their squad car and drove off.

"Want to hear plan B?" Alexa asked.

"We don't have a plan B."

"I do," she said. "I think I should go to Eugene Mesa's party on Sunday. I've been invited. There's a chance O'Shea will show up."

It was a good thought, but I couldn't protect her there because they all knew me and there was no way in hell I was going to let her go alone.

But as she'd already told me, she was my boss. That meant if I was going to prevent her from going to that party, I was going to have to come up with a much better idea.

CHAPTER 46

WE ALL MET AGAIN IN SABAS'S conference room, with its depressing view of the weed-choked backyard and empty pool. Five pallbearers plus Alexa were gathered around his folding table, sitting on uncomfortable metal chairs.

"I don't think it's safe for you to go to E. C. Mesa's party alone," Sabas said after Alexa told him her idea. "Besides, my guess is O'Shea's probably on the run, heading to Mexico."

I didn't think he was in Mexico, and I'd spent the last hour working on a better plan.

"Alexa told us that Team Ultima has a challenge fight coming up and that it's out of town somewhere," I said. "When is that?"

"Don't know. Soon," she said.

"Suppose we could get in touch with that other bunch—team—whatever."

"Spartacus," Alexa said.

"Right. Team Spartacus. We check them out, see if

they'll let us ride under their wing to that challenge match, wherever it is. Since it's out of town and because there's a big purse, my guess is O'Shea won't miss that fight. We'll have a SWAT team in reserve, and once they're all there, we make our move."

Diamond said, "You really think Rick O'Shea is gonna show up at that fight?"

"Yeah," I replied.

"Is he stupid?" Vicki asked.

"Very," Alexa said.

Everyone turned and looked at me, waiting for me to fill in the blanks, so I ran it down. "We got a warrant on Rick O'Shea, but as far as I'm concerned he's just one of many. I think all the guys who train at the NHB Gym are dirty. Chris Calabro and all the others who are running nonprofits are probably also embezzling from their group homes. That's how they're paying their bills. I don't know how much E. C. Mesa has to do with this, but if you ask me, he's involved."

"But what ties Mesa in, besides the fact the man owns that gym and manages its fighters?" Diamond asked. "That's hardly against the law."

"In police work you learn to trust your hunches, and my hunch says he's in this. I just don't have the connection yet."

As I looked around the table, I could sense that I was losing them. I was sitting here, wrapped in tape and fiberglass, looking like an extra in a war movie, trying to get them to follow me. I could subtly feel Vicki, Seriana, and Diamond turning from me toward Vargas. "Let's take it a step at a time," I said. "We start with

Team Spartacus. We find out where they train, go talk to them."

Vicki and Seriana, who had become our unofficial phone committee, started making calls. It didn't take long to find the gym.

Team Spartacus had an address on Atlanta Avenue in Huntington Beach. They worked out of a private gym named, appropriately enough, Gladiator School. After a short argument with Sabas, I agreed to let everyone come as long as either Alexa or I did all the talking. He nodded, but didn't comment.

We headed out of the conference room and stood quietly as Vargas gathered his things.

"I gotta pee," Vicki announced.

While his three chica office warriors glared at me, all of the women, including Alexa, trooped to the bathroom in girl formation, leaving me and Sabas facing each other.

"I couldn't be doing any worse than you," he reminded me.

"Good point," I admitted. "But I feel myself on an upward trajectory."

After the women rejoined us, we started through the front door. As we walked down the path outside, Alexa put something into my left hand. It was a .38 bullet. Somebody had filed a deep *X* on the nose.

"Where did you get this?" I whispered.

She pointed at Vicki, who was heading down the path a few yards ahead, clutching her purse. "After she came out of the bathroom, I found it on the floor under the toilet," Alexa said softly. "I think she was in there reloading her Bulldog with homemade dumdums."

CHAPTER 47

WE ALL RODE TO HUNTINGTON Beach together in Seriana's eight-passenger Dodge van.

Gladiator School was located about a mile from the ocean, just off Beach Boulevard on Atlanta Avenue. The building was a windowless, graffiti-tagged brick box with a scarred wooden door. It was between two abandoned storefronts and looked foreboding as hell.

I didn't want to roll into this place en masse. That wouldn't produce anything but blowback. In the spirit of cooperation, and in a renewed effort to keep them on my side, I needed to take at least one person in with me. But which one?

Sabas was a good puncher. He'd already proved that. But I was through fighting with these animals. This needed to be a finesse operation. Besides that, he was becoming difficult. Diamond was too passive and guileless. Vicki was packing that Charter Arms Bulldog, now fully loaded with dumdums. I couldn't trust her to stay cool. I needed Alexa to stay out here and police them, so that left Seriana.

"I'm thinking one person should go in with me as a group representative." I couldn't believe I was saying this, but they'd pushed me to the point where I was making bad decisions. "You up for it, Corporal Cotton?"

"Yes sir. By the way, in training we were taught three forms of martial arts. I'm not too bad, if that's helpful."

"Excellent. Let's tell them I'm your fight manager and that you're looking to start a professional career and want to train here. We have to get to the guy in charge. The promoter. Once we're talking to him, I'll take it from there."

Vargas didn't say anything because he had stopped talking to me.

I motioned to Seriana and she nodded, so I knocked on the wood door while the others took cover. After a moment, it was cracked open an inch. A huge black guy in workout sweats peered out at us.

"Yeah?" he said.

"Is this Gladiator School?" I asked. "It's the right address, but there's no sign."

"Yeah."

"She's interested in training here." I pointed at Seriana. "I manage her. I think it's time for her to turn pro."

"We're a private gym," the man said, but he was smiling at Seriana. He liked what he saw. "We only train current professionals," he added.

"What's your name?" Seriana asked, giving him one of her rare smiles. He seemed to melt under it.

"Joe Hardwick."

"Seriana Cotton. I'm trained in jujitsu, tae kwon do, and tai chi. I've had two amateur fights and won 'em both. Could I at least talk to somebody about a tryout?"

Joe Hardwick looked her over, more or less ignoring me. He wanted to let her in, but apparently there were rules he had to follow. "Only team members are supposed to be in here. But okay, I guess you being a fighter makes it an exception. Come on in. I'll get Mr. Mingo."

The Gladiator School was a slightly larger version of the NHB Center in downtown L.A. It had the same sweat-and-blood smell, the same bleak, overhead lighting and octagon fight ring.

There was one strange decorative note. Canvas mat covers from past cage bouts hung on the gym walls. Each bore the dried blood splatter from past contests. The Rorschach-like patterns of these old stains were memorialized by the felt-tip signatures of the combatants. Photos of various Gladiator School fighters who had performed in different events also hung on the walls.

I recognized two names from my earlier Internet research. Trent Subway and Jose Del Cristo. There was also a photo of Joe Hardwick on the wall. He was crouched in a fighting stance, bare knuckles in front of his face. His ring name was "Hammerhead."

There were six or seven fighters firing punches at heavy bags around the room. They were extremely dedicated, and none of them even paused their workouts to look at us when we entered.

"Stay here," Joe said. "I'll go get Mr. Mingo." He turned and went through a door in the back.

"I hope I don't really have to audition," Seriana said. "I don't want to have to fight one of these goons."

"Won't happen," I said. "So far we're doing great, but why don't you go hit one of those bags. Show 'em what you've got."

Seriana, in her slacks and polo shirt, walked to a heavy bag a few feet away and unleashed a variety of strikes and kicks. She was quick and efficient as her blows rang out on the leather. Now one or two of the other fighters stopped their workouts and turned to watch.

A minute later a very skinny sixty-year-old man with bushy white hair came out of the back with Joe Hardwick. He was one of those stringy Italian guys who was brown as a tobacco leaf, wearing a green silk short-sleeved shirt. He moved with a brisk, kinetic stride. An unlit cigar was stuffed in the corner of his mouth, making him look like he belonged in a Rocky movie.

As he approached us, he removed the cigar, then rocked back on his heels. He looked at Seriana still working the heavy bag, then at me, taking in my cut forehead and broken arm.

"Okay, okay. I see she can hit. Tell her to stop," the man said. Seriana quit punching the bag and turned to face us.

"This is Nate Mingo," Joe said. "He's the gym manager and our promoter."

He made no move to shake hands. When you're doing a field interview you have to make on-the-fly judgments. From his scowl and defensive body language,

I could tell that I was going to need some leverage to open him up.

Then I spotted what looked like several old, faded prison tattoos etched on his forearms. Like Jack's, the tats were done with handmade equipment, the drawings sketchy. The color was that same strange shade of blue-green ink the penal system uses.

"No matter how good she hits, this broad ain't gonna train in my gym," Mingo said. "Go find someplace else."

He started to turn away. I'd only spent an hour on the Internet and had very little background on this sport, but one of the things I'd read was that MMA TV events were sanctioned by the state. I was running out of time, so I took a shot.

"You guys fight on TV a lot, right?" I said. He turned back. "Spike TV? I understand those fights are all sanctioned by the California State Gaming Commission."

"Look, pal, I got things to do . . ."

"I know you're getting ready for an out-of-town fight. A challenge match with Team Ultima. That gonna be a sanctioned event?"

He studied me for a long moment before he said, "You're a fucking cop, aren't you?"

If it had to go in that direction, I was ready. I pulled out my creds. Mingo examined them quickly then handed them back.

"I don't talk to cops."

"You may want to adjust that," I said, smiling. "Where'd you do your time?"

"Go fuck yourself."

I pointed to the tattoos on his arms. "That's prison work. I can always run you, Nate, but it's gonna piss me off. You really wanta put me through that?"

"Soledad," he snapped. "It was twenty years back. I'm not on state paper anymore. My parole ran out nine years ago. Happy?"

"I got a little problem and I may need your help."

"Well, you ain't gettin' it." He started away again.

"The way I understand this, you guys need to be sanctioned by the state gaming commission to do organized fights. Last time I checked, an ex-con couldn't be involved in any state-sanctioned gambling event. I make a few calls, you could lose your manager's license. No more Gladiator School, no more Spike TV, no more Cuban cigars."

He just glared at me.

"I'm not here to make trouble, Nate. I'm just trying to solve a problem, but if you keep this up, I'm going to have to make some moves, and then what have either of us accomplished? Nothing, right?"

Mingo didn't speak for almost half a minute. Then he put the soggy cigar back in his mouth.

"Let's talk in my office," he said.

CHAPTER 48

THE FIGHT BETWEEN TEAM Ultima and Team Spartacus was being billed as "The Rage in the Cage." It was taking place at the Talking Stick Casino on the Tohono O'odham Indian Reservation outside of Tucson at eight tomorrow night.

Seriana and I reported all this to the pallbearers as we sat around a picnic table at Huntington Beach about two miles down Beach Boulevard from Gladiator School.

"An Arizona Indian reservation?" Vicki said. "Why there?"

"According to Nate Mingo, the casino has an active sports book and pari-mutuel betting. Besides the challenge purse, both fight teams split a ten percent cut of the casino's action off the top."

"You think you can trust that guy?" Seriana asked.

"My guess is he'd rather help me than lose his license to promote fights on TV."

"You've got a bigger problem than Mingo," Sabas

said. "If this fight is on an Indian reservation, you and Mrs. Scully got no jurisdiction." He looked pointedly at Alexa then back at me. "Indian reservations have treaty arrangements with the federal government. They're sovereign territories, governed by their own tribal councils and policed by Indian cops."

"I think we can . . ."

"I know what I'm talking about," he interrupted.

"What I was about to say is we can get plenty of cooperation. I've done it before. We just check in with the Indian police chief, show our warrant, accompany him while he makes the arrest."

"I still don't get why Rick O'Shea would show up there," Diamond said. "If he's on the run, isn't that taking a big chance?"

"It's out of state," Alexa said. "Plus he knows it's going to take time for us to get a warrant and get it served in Arizona by tomorrow. That's if we ever even figured out he was going to be there."

"According to Mingo, O'Shea hasn't pulled out of his match," I added. "He'll be there or his bout is a forfeit. It's probably way too big a payday for him to pass up. He'll take his share of the purse, then get out of the country."

Vargas finally broke the silence. "So we go to Arizona and pop him there. That's the plan?"

"No," I told them. "You guys aren't going. The Pop Dix Homicide Steering Committee is officially disbanded."

"Then let's get out of here," Sabas said.

"Just like that? No argument?" I said.

"No argument. I'm tired of fighting with you about this. Let the Indian police handle it if that's your plan. We'll just wait and get our payback at the L.A. arraignment."

I looked at Alexa. After a minute, she shrugged.

"Can we go now?" Sabas said. "I still have a law practice to run. I have a conference in my office at four."

Two hours later Alexa and I were back at our Venice house. I was sitting on one of the stools in the kitchen watching her prepare dinner.

"You want tomatoes and onions in this meat casserole?" she asked.

I nodded. "And garlic."

She peeled a clove then slammed the knife down on the cutting board and smashed the clove before chopping it and tossing the pieces into a sauté pan with some sizzling butter.

"I don't trust Vargas," I said.

"What makes you say that? The fact that he won't look you in the eye when he's lying to you, or that nervous little stutter when he got out of the van? Or the fact that he'd probably rather serve this warrant with a bunch of g-sters from Boyle Heights?"

"All the above. Plus, he's not used to being told he can't do what he wants. None of us are. After a promising start with that guy, it's sort of come apart."

"We've got bigger problems than Sabas Vargas," Alexa said. "I think we need to bring in the FBI. Vargas is wrong that only Indian cops have jurisdiction on a reservation. The feds can also make arrests in conjunction with Indian authority.

"Not that I don't trust the Tohono Nation PD, but I'm thinking it sure wouldn't hurt to have a few federal cops with guns around." Alexa put down the knife and faced me. "Here's something else that might help. When I was talking to Chief Filosiani, he said that their local ASAC seemed very upset with those two guys. Apparently Agents Westfall and Faskin had Jack in custody a few hours after the Temecula bank heist before he even got out of the Inland Empire.

"The highway patrol picked him up in a freeway speed trap, ran him, and made the arrest. Our two local heroes had Jack in the back of their car in cuffs and were transporting him to L.A. to get booked when somehow Jack managed to drain their car battery by pulling out the cigarette lighter in the backseat and cross-wiring it, or dead grounding it, or some damn thing."

My respect for Jack Straw took another leap forward.

Alexa continued. "I guess the way it happened, they pulled off the road to eat, took Jack out of the car and into the restaurant in cuffs, not noticing he'd rewired the cigarette lighter. They came back an hour later and the car wouldn't start."

"Ya gotta love that Jack," I said, smiling.

She nodded. "While Westfall and Faskin had the hood up trying to figure out what was wrong, Jack took off with their cuffs still on and escaped." She smiled at me. "Needless to say, this was not met with much enthusiasm at the 11000 building on Wilshire. Westfall and Faskin are cooking over a slow fire down there."

"And you think I should use this?" I said, smiling.

"No," she replied sarcastically. "Give it to TMZ or the *National Enquirer*, why don't you?"

CHAPTER 49

"WHAT'S THIS ALL ABOUT?" Kurt Westfall growled as I slid into a Denny's restaurant window booth directly across from chunky, red-faced Leo Faskin. It was a little past nine the same night. We were at Denny's because it was right across from the federal building on Wilshire, and they said on the phone they were hungry.

Since these two guys had already made it very clear they didn't like me, it didn't surprise me they'd already ordered. But I'd just eaten anyway, and if I played this right, maybe I could get them to lose their appetites.

I waved the waitress off as Leo Faskin poured about a half a pound of sugar into his coffee and Westfall shifted his string-bean body, trying to find a comfortable spot in the booth for his bony ass.

"Guys, I think what we need is a come-to-Jesus meeting," I said pleasantly.

"What we need is a fuck you meeting," Westfall shot back.

"C'mon, Kurt, that's a little extreme," I said, holding his gaze.

Agent Faskin leaned forward. "We been told Chief Filosiani wants us to back off, and for some reason, our wussy ASAC's going along. That means we're on the sidelines. What more do you want?"

"Here's the full and complete update on Jack Straw," I said. "Contrary to what you were told, I don't exactly have custody of him anymore."

"We know that, Scully," Westfall said. "You took him away from those cops on Wilshire last Wednesday night, and before sunup he gave you the slip. You been running all over L.A. like a blind rat trying to find him and so far don't have a clue. We're just waiting for this bag of shit to land on you where it belongs."

"I hope you guys have been playing fair and aren't abusing the Patriot Act, listening in on my phone calls."

Faskin set down the sugar and slid it angrily across the table, where it hit some napkins and stopped abruptly. "We don't have to tap your phones to know what an incompetent piece of shit you are."

"Have we finished with the fuck-you part of the meeting yet?"

"No we haven't," Westfall said. "That guy, Straw, popped two federal banks. He stole ten grand from one, fourteen from the other. He knocked out a sixty-year-old security guard during the Temecula heist. Poor old guy had to get twenty stitches. Straw is a bleeding sore with a yellow sheet that goes back ten years. He should be sitting in our cooler right now, but you cut him loose from Acosta and Moon and, dumb asshole that you are, promptly lost him. And *that*, my friend, is the full and complete update on Jack Straw."

"You left out the part where you two brain trusts let him hot-wire your backseat cigarette lighter and escape up in Temecula."

They both just sat glowering, their faces getting redder.

I leaned forward. "In the interest of lowering your blood pressure, I might be in a position to help. I know your ASAC is grinding you up over losing Jack. I also know firsthand what turds these administration guys can be. All they gotta do is come in late and make sure the Internet is connected. Field guys like us, we're the ones that do the real work, and if things don't go perfect, we always end up taking the heat."

"What do you want?" Westfall said. He'd clearly had enough of me.

"Even though I don't have physical custody, I know where Jack is. I'm willing to help you two get him back."

"Where is he?" Westfall asked.

"We're gonna need to work out some terms and conditions first."

Faskin said, "Hey, dickwad, if you've lost custody of Straw like you just said and you know where he is but don't tell us, then you're an accessory after the fact in those two bank heists."

"That's a slight exaggeration, don't you think?" I smiled blandly at him.

Just then the waitress brought their orders. Leo Faskin had ordered a patty melt with fries. Kurt Westfall had a cheese omelet with double hash browns. The Denny's high-cholesterol, artery-clogger special at taxpayer expense.

"Okay, so what's the pitch?" Westfall said. He seemed the more rational of the two.

"I want you guys to agree that if I get Jack back for you, we let bygones be bygones. You don't start making trouble for me after the fact at Parker Center, filing a bunch of interagency disciplinary requests."

"What else?"

"You go to Tucson, Arizona, on the midnight flight tonight. You hook up with the local feds there, wait for my call. Once I've got Jack in custody, I'll notify you, and we can make arrangements to turn him back over to the FBI."

"Why do we need to include the Tucson bureau?" Westfall asked. He had caught a whiff of my deception. There was nothing I could do but keep going.

"We need them because, while doable, getting Jack back may not be as easy as it appears on the surface. At some point I might need a scooch of backup."

"We're not gonna fly all the way to Tucson, scare up a federal posse without knowing why, and then hang around in some hotel 'til you call us," Faskin said.

"Fellas, I can deliver Jack, but I've got some department issues of my own I'm dealing with. I promise, if you go to Tucson and wait for my call, this time tomorrow we can all grab castanets and sing the Miranda at Jack's custody hearing."

They both started to pick listlessly at their food. I'd finally managed to ruin their appetites.

I got up and stood looking down at them.

"Is that gonna be a yes?" I said.

"Get the fuck away from us," Faskin replied.

"It's a yes," Westfall finally answered, then handed me his card.

CHAPTER 50

BY THE TIME I GOT HOME IT was after ten o'clock. As I was undressing for bed, I filled Alexa in on what had transpired with Faskin and Westfall. When I finished, she told me she'd been on the Internet since I'd left doing research on the Tohono O'odham Indian Reservation.

"The Tohono Indians are one of the Arizona Mesa Tribes, like the Hopis and Apaches. They're extremely poor, and most of their reservation is a rough, unsettled place," she said. "They've got a big Mexican illegal-immigration and drug-smuggling problem. This isn't just a footnote, it's a huge deal. The seven Mesa tribes spent ten million last year on border problems."

"Really?" I stopped undressing and looked over at her.

"The Tohono reservation is a big place," she went on. "About the size of Connecticut. It spans a seventy-five-mile border with Mexico, and because it's on both sides of the border, it's become a billion-dollar-a-year smuggling corridor. I checked with our drug-enforcement guys downtown, and they know all about Tohono O'odham. Homeland sends out briefing reports on it about once a month.

"According to Captain Summerland, there are over a hundred and sixty crossing points. Thirty of those have no barriers at all. The coyotes are running drugs and *braceros* unchecked.

"The Mexicans who are being smuggled in are so hungry and poor, they're looting everything the Indians own that isn't tied down. Stealing livestock and vehicles. Getting into gunfights with the Indian property owners. The tribal police are completely overrun with these shootings. According to Captain Summerland, it's the biggest corridor for illegal immigration and drugs in the U.S."

I sat on the bed and looked at her. "So does the drug and immigration thing tie in to Pop's murder somehow, or is it just a coincidence?"

"Aren't you the one who always says there are no coincidences in law enforcement?"

"So what's going on then?"

"I don't know. I called the main desk at the Talking Stick Hotel and Casino. I told them I was planning to come there on my vacation but was concerned because I'd read on the Internet that there were gunfights taking place between Indian landowners and smugglers. They assured me that the Talking Stick Resort is walled off and totally safe.

"The reservation has built a nine-foot-high barrier all the way around the two-hundred-acre hotel and golf course. The resort is heavily patrolled, and there are absolutely no guns allowed on the premises."

"Does that include us?"

"I think so. I asked, and she said no exceptions."

I sat there for a long moment; trying to absorb it.

"Drugs," I said softly, trying to get that to somehow jibe. How did a million-dollar embezzlement at Huntington House that led to Walt's murder also link to a billion-dollar drug corridor on an Arizona Indian reservation? I couldn't see the connection. My guess was, there wasn't one. But that didn't change the fact that, if I wanted to bust O'Shea, I had to go there. Making that arrest without jurisdiction on Tohono O'odham land only made it about ten times more difficult.

I finished getting undressed, then got into bed. Alexa joined me, and we turned off the lights.

"This doesn't feel right, does it?" she finally said in the dark.

"No," I said softly. "It doesn't."

As I lay there I kept turning it over in my mind. E. C. Mesa's connection to Pop's murder had always bothered me. I had other questions as well. Why would a rich, influential guy who buys and sells companies entertain himself with such a violent hobby as MMA fighting? Of course, there was nothing that said a multimillionaire couldn't have a fascination with combat arts, but nonetheless, it felt strange that he was hanging with O'Shea and Calabro and all the other thugs in that gym.

I also wondered why he was arranging challenge matches for his fight team two states away in Arizona, in a casino that sat on one of the biggest smuggling corridors on the U.S.-Mexican border. I didn't like where this seemed to be heading.

Instead of answers I was just turning up more questions, which is never a good sign this late in an investigation.

I finally forced my mind to stop dancing with it and tried to get some sleep. I was almost there when the bedside phone jangled. I rolled over and answered it.

"Scully?" a familiar voice said.

"Jack?"

Alexa propped herself up and looked over at me.

"Dude, we got trouble."

"Tell me."

"I'm in Arizona . . ."

"At the Talking Stick Casino?"

There was a moment, then Jack said, "Yeah. How'd you know?"

"I'm all-seeing. Talk to me, Jack."

"I'm with Team Ultima. I'm their unofficial roadie or gofer or some damn thing. You owe me for this, dude. These guys are a buncha steroid-popping morons. It's like hanging with the Sasquatch Towel Snap team. They're here in Arizona training for an event match tomorrow.

"At eight o'clock tonight I'm playing craps with a few of them in the casino and in walks Diamond Peterson. She's looking for O'Shea. He didn't come to Arizona with us so I didn't think he was here. But Chris called him on a cell, and ten minutes later in he walks.

"Once he and Diamond hook up, they have a big

screaming match. About as subtle as an inmate wedding. Security comes. It finally got calmed down, and O'Shea leaves with Diamond in tow. I don't know where he took her because I'm stuck getting beer and pretzels for these shitheads. I had to wait 'til they finally crashed half an hour ago so I could sneak away and call."

"What is it?" Alexa asked.

I covered the receiver with my left hand. "Jack's at the Talking Stick. Diamond just showed looking for O'Shea, who's also there. She may be in trouble."

Alexa was out of bed and getting dressed before I finished the last sentence.

"Okay, Jack. You got a number where I can call you back?"

"I'm not giving you my fucking number. These guys are all over me. You call and they pick it up, I'm toast. Just take care of this. I'm not staying in the same place with most of them anyway 'cause there's not enough room. These fuckheads have me and Brian Bravo sleeping in a reservation trailer. A total shit hole. Here comes Calabro. Gotta go." And he hung up.

I slammed down the receiver and started grabbing clothes. I still hadn't mastered getting dressed with one arm, so Alexa was way ahead of me.

"You think Westfall and Faskin are in Tucson yet?" she asked.

"I don't know. They should be, but I'm not sending those two donkeys in unsupervised."

Alexa was completely dressed while I was still fumbling with the laces of my tennis shoes. I was having trouble getting all ten fingers to work together.

"Let me help you with those," she said, and knelt down, tying them quickly.

When she finished she stood. "What do you want to do?"

"About what?"

"The others."

I must have been looking at her like she'd just lost her mind because she said, "We're kind of shorthanded. We could use some help, don't you think?"

"The pallbearers?" I said, astounded she would even suggest such a thing.

"Think about it. We don't have much time if Diamond is really in trouble. Sabas is good backup. Vicki is tough as rhinoceros skin, and Seriana's U.S. Army. We don't have any jurisdiction in Arizona, let alone on an Indian reservation. Out there you and I are just civilians. Since you don't completely trust Faskin and Westfall, then maybe these guys are our best choice."

I stood and gathered my jacket, keys, and money while I thought about it. I didn't want to take them, but I couldn't quite come up with a good reason why. Was Sabas right? Was I just being selfish? Was I using my cop status as an excuse to shut everybody else out?

"It's what Walt would want," Alexa prodded.

I knew she was right. He'd picked all six of us, not just me. "I'll call them," I said. "While I do that, you need to get us some transportation. The last commercial flights have already left. Unless you can scare us up something from the Air Support Division, we can't leave 'til morning."

"I'll get the chief's King Air," she said. "He's not using it."

I called all of Sabas's numbers but didn't get an answer. Everything went straight to voicemail. I left a message to call. I wasn't about to give the reason because I still didn't trust him not to take matters into his own hands.

Next, I spoke to Vicki and told her what had happened and what we planned to do. She didn't comment but said that she'd meet us at Van Nuys Airport in forty minutes. I gave her the hangar number for the LAPD Flight Department.

Then I called Seriana. When I finished telling her what had happened, she asked, "What kind of ordnance are you bringing?"

"Not much. Couple of 9s. But we might have to surrender our weapons at the reservation gate. Alexa checked, and they have a strict no-guns rule on resort property."

"I don't think it's smart to surrender your weapon, sir," she said.

"We'll just have to see how it goes when we get there."

While Alexa was on the phone, I went out to her car, opened the glove compartment, and pulled out her little Bobcat .25.

An idea had been festering ever since O'Shea broke my arm and I'd been sitting in that ER, wondering how I could deal with that thug given my growing list of debilitating injuries.

I went back inside the house and into the kitchen. I could hear Alexa still on the phone. It sounded like she had successfully arranged the flight because she was asking about ETAs.

I got a baggie out of a kitchen drawer, then headed into the master bath, where I opened the medicine cabinet and pulled down the cast tape I'd stolen from Dr. Ray's supply shelf in the ER exam room. Next, I turned on the faucet and filled the washbasin, putting the roll of tape into the water.

While it was soaking, I popped the barrel up and checked the breach on the little .25 automatic. Alexa had loaded it before we'd gone into the Hayloft. The magazine was full, and there was still one in the chamber.

I put the safety on, then stuffed the little palm-sized subcompact into the plastic baggie to protect it from the wet fiberglass. After the gun was in the bag, I palmed it into my right hand so that the barrel didn't go any further than my first row of knuckles. I pulled the wet tape out of the sink and started to wrap my wrist and palm to cover the gun. It was tough going, and I was making a mess.

"What the hell are you doing?" I heard Alexa say. I turned and she was standing in the bathroom door, hands on her hips, staring at me.

"Come give me a hand with this," I said.

She walked over and looked down at my project. "Are you out of your mind? You fire a gun inside an enclosed cast and the gas recoil will blow all your fingers off."

"That's something to bear in mind," I said, then handed her the gauze pad.

"I'm not doing that," she said.

"Honey, as you and everyone else continues to remind me, I've been destroyed by this ape twice in two days. Sad as it is for me to admit, I don't think I can take Rick O'Shea, let alone five more just like him. Especially with this busted wing. You should applaud this. I'm finally choosing guile over guts. It's a first. A sign of emotional growth."

"What a load of BS."

"Come on, help me out. If what you said is true, we're gonna have trouble packing guns into that resort as it is. Let's just call this my little insurance policy. What's it gonna hurt? Nobody's gonna check a cast for weapons. If it sets off a metal detector, I'll just say I have pins in there holding my bone together."

She cocked her head, looking at me askew.

"Honey, I promise I won't blow off my middle finger. I know how much you like that one."

She threw a wet washcloth at me but moved over and helped me finish the job.

When we were through, the Bobcat was safely hidden in the palm of my right hand. The new extended portion of the cast went down to my first set of knuckles, just the way Dr. Ray had wanted it to in the beginning.

I'd read the spec sheet when Alexa first bought the little Beretta. The seven-shot subcompact automatic was 4.9 inches long, nose to heel. It only weighed 11.5 ounces fully loaded and now fit invisibly under the wet fiberglass.

On my way out of the bedroom, I opened my dresser

drawer and retrieved my Swiss Army knife. It had eleven different features. I slid the tool into my pocket, grabbed my Charter Arms Magnum Pug out of the bedside table, and clipped it on the left side of my belt. Then Alexa and I left the house.

When we arrived at the Air Support Division hangar an hour later, Vicki was already waiting. Our pilot was a crew cut in a flight suit named Justin Cooper—Coop, for short. He had flown Alexa before, and they went inside the Air Support Division office to pick a landing field in Tucson and file the flight plan.

Seriana pulled up while Alexa was still inside. She unloaded a medium-sized nylon duffel from her green van. There was a suspicious-looking sharp object poking the fabric on one side as she slung the bag over her shoulder and approached us, then put the duffel in the luggage compartment, which Coop had left open in the nose of the King Air.

"What's in there?" Vicki asked her.

"Toys for boys," Seriana replied without humor.

Coop and Alexa came out of the FBO. He closed and latched the luggage bay as he said, "I've filed a flight plan for Tucson International Airport. With this southeast tailwind, we should be there in about an hour and thirty-six."

Ten minutes later, we were racing down the runway. The wheels came up, and we banked east into the cold night sky.

CHAPTER 51

I SLEPT ON THE SHORT FLIGHT because I've learned when you get to the end of a case, sleep is the one thing you can't plan for and never get enough of.

My eyes snapped open after a little over an hour, when the prop engine changed pitch and the King Air started to lose altitude for our gradual descent into Tucson.

I looked at my watch. If Coop's timetable was right, we had twenty minutes until touchdown.

The new portion of my cast was finally dry. I looked around the plane. Everybody was asleep, so I pulled out the Swiss Army knife, opened its little saber-tooth saw-blade, and began scoring the cast. I sawed a cut that was a quarter-inch deep from the knuckle of my right middle finger straight down across the palm where the Bobcat was hiding. I ended the cut at the heel of my hand, making certain it didn't go all the way through. Next I did the same thing at my wrist as I scored the fiberglass all the way around. When I was finished, the cast was substantially weakened, but still intact.

We touched down on the runway at Tucson International. Coop taxied up to the executive air FBO. Then he shut down the twin-engine prop, climbed out of the pilot's seat, and lowered the cabin door.

"I ordered up a car for you, Lieutenant," he told Alexa.

The four of us got off the airplane as our Lincoln Town Car pulled up. While Alexa was thanking Coop for the ride, Seriana walked to the luggage compartment in the nose of the plane, opened it up, and pulled out her duffel. Then she headed toward the terminal, where a young man wearing blue jeans and a polo shirt was standing next to the door, waiting. He had a crew cut and military bearing. Seriana embraced him briefly, then handed him the backpack. They spoke for a moment before she returned. Vicki had been watching this operation with a smile.

"What's she got in there? IEDs?"

"I'm trying not to ask," I replied.

"Interesting woman," she commented.

Like most of us, Alexa's strong link is connected to her weak one. Her strength is she values organization and rules. She believes in order. It was one of the reasons she had risen so fast in the department. However, her weak link was that same Girl Scout mentality. My strong link is a creative, loose working style that sometimes has me skirting the edges of the rule book. Obviously that's my weak link as well.

Technically, since I didn't know what was in Seriana's duffel, why make a public guess and draw a complaint?

Alexa told our pilot we wouldn't be needing him further and he could return to L.A. Then we entered the waiting Lincoln Town Car, with Alexa taking the front seat next to the chauffeur. Seriana, Vicki, and I all sat in back.

Our driver was a big African-American guy who had a neck and shoulders that said ex-jock. He introduced himself as Arthur. As we chatted, it turned out he'd been a defensive end at Arizona State.

"You know where the Talking Stick Casino is on the Tohono O'odham reservation?" I asked him.

"Yes, sir." He was talking to me, but I noticed when his eyes were in the rearview mirror, they rarely left Seriana.

We turned onto the Nogales Highway heading toward a chain of mountains, which Arthur told us was the Quinlan range, where the Kitt Peak National Observatory and its telescope were located.

The engine of the town car purred noiselessly, the headlights cutting through the desert darkness. Cactus and sand flashed past the side window as we raced along.

Alexa said to our driver, "I understand the reservation is very poor."

"It is," Arthur replied. "They have big problems out there. The diet these people eat is horrible. Half the tribe has diabetes. The average male life span is fifty-two years. Our governor is trying to do something to help them, but except for the casino, it's hard to find a way to get enough money to raise their standard of living."

"So what's the casino like?" I was expecting the worst.

"Brand new. You're gonna like it. 'Bout a thousand or fifteen hundred rooms. World-class golf course, tennis, pool right in the middle of a hundred square miles of desolate poverty. It's like somebody plopped a Ritz Carlton down in Honduras."

We entered the Tohono O'odham reservation a little past three in the morning. The road in from the highway was a wide four lane, which led us past run-down trailer parks and broken adobe houses. Junk was strewn everywhere. I could see the ghostlike hulks of rusting trucks parked on dead patches of dusty ground from which they would never move.

Then we arrived at the Talking Stick Casino property. The adobe barrier around the resort was nine feet high with decorative but lethal-looking wall spikes located at close intervals along the top. There was an elaborate guard shack at the entrance with a large computer check-in manned by several Tohono Nation security police officers.

We told our Indian gate guard we were going to rent hotel rooms and had to show our IDs and be put on the computer list. Since Alexa and I had creds that said we were police officers, the guard asked if we were carrying sidearms.

"We are," Alexa said.

"Sorry, but I'll have to collect your weapons," the guard said. "I'll give you a receipt and keep them in a gun locker right here. You can retrieve them when you exit."

"I've never been asked to surrender my weapon to a sister police department anywhere in the U.S.," I told him.

"You aren't in the U.S.," the guard replied. "This is the Tohono O'odham Indian Nation, a sovereign territory."

We all surrendered our weapons, including Vicki. Alexa glanced at my cast but said nothing.

Then we were passed onto the grounds.

As we drove on I saw an expansive eighteen-hole golf course off to the right and a lighted tennis center on the left. We drove past an aquatic park with water rides, then a riding stable and archery range, all of it new and beautifully maintained. This resort had it all. Up ahead the Talking Stick Casino came into view.

It was a big, artfully lit building with a huge five-story center section that was designed in a modern pueblo theme. Two large hotel wings stretched out on each side of the main structure and contained the thousand or more rooms our driver, Arthur, had mentioned.

The hotel casino was modern with clean lines, but along the roof of the main building were architectural cement parapets with decorative wooden poles extending from them, reminiscent of an Indian sweat lodge. The resort was modern and aesthetically pleasing but with a definite tribal flavor.

In the center of the circular drive by the front entrance was a fountain with a large lit statue of an Indian chieftain holding a crooked talking stick high above his war bonnet as water cascaded down, splashing on his bronzed head and shoulders.

A billboard nearby announced,

THE MAGIC OF CRISS ANGEL
IN THE TOHONO ROOM—MONDAY THROUGH FRIDAY
AND
THE RAGE IN THE CAGE
AT THE TALKING STICK EVENT CENTER—
8:00 P.M. SATURDAY

We pulled to a stop and got out. While we were standing under the huge porte cochere waiting for Alexa to pay Arthur, an overly polite, heavyset man in a dark suit with Indian features approached.

"Welcome to the Talking Stick Hotel and Casino," he said. "I'm Graham, your casino host. May I direct you inside or help you to find anything?"

"I think we'll just check in and get to bed," I said.

Alexa moved up to join us, and Graham led us to the registration desk.

The lobby was almost deserted at this hour, with only a few tables working in the adjoining casino.

There were four of us, so it was cheaper to rent a two-bedroom suite instead of three separate rooms. In order to avoid detection, we had already decided to take the suite under Seriana's name. She showed her ID, we were registered, and Alexa paid for one night in cash.

Because we had no luggage other than briefcases and purses, we followed a bellman, carrying our own gear down a first-floor hallway carpeted with a new, Indian-style patterned rug. We stopped in front of 1477, which had a brass plaque that read:

THE PINTO SUITE

The bellman opened the room and showed us inside. I tipped him, then closed the door as he left.

The two-bedroom, ground-floor suite was done in desert-sand colors and furnished with expensive, plushly upholstered, Italian reproduction furniture.

"Not bad," Vicki said.

The others trooped out onto the patio, which adjoined the beautiful, semilit golf course, while I called the front desk and asked for Rick O'Shea's room. He wasn't registered. Neither was Diamond Peterson.

They refused to give me any information about Team Ultima, saying I should talk to the event center in the morning.

After I hung up, I went out on the patio to join the others.

I said, "It's almost four. We're not going to learn anything tonight. Let's get a few hours' sleep and start working on it at eight tomorrow."

"What about Diamond?" Vicki said.

Alexa said, "We won't find out anything tonight. Nobody's even up to talk to."

We selected our rooms, and I went to the writing desk, picked up the cordless phone, and set the wake-up call for 8:00 A.M.

After I finished, I replaced the phone next to the

heavy leather folder that held the room-service menu and hotel literature.

On the folder's front cover, embossed in gold, I saw the same little logo of a mesa with a circle around it that I'd seen on the roof of the building on Wilshire Boulevard.

I picked up a brochure.

The Talking Stick Hotel and Casino was a Eugene C. Mesa resort.

CHAPTER 52

IT SUDDENLY MADE A LOT MORE sense. I now knew why Mesa brought this challenge match all the way out here. He was also getting a casino cut of the action.

After I showed the others, Seriana said we were bivouaced in enemy territory. There was nothing we could do to change it, so we went to bed.

I couldn't sleep. I was churned up with worry about Diamond, and the fact that E. C. Mesa was popping up everywhere.

I decided to wait until everybody else was asleep and go on a scouting mission. I wanted to get a better feel for this place.

Alexa and I had the main bedroom. Seriana shared the suite's second room with Vicki. When I finally heard Alexa's even, steady breathing, I got carefully out of bed, grabbed my clothes, and quietly dressed in the darkened living room.

I started by going back to the main desk. According to the room clerk, nobody named Sabas Vargas was registered. After the call from Jack telling me he was living in a reservation trailer, I didn't expect him to be registered either. He wasn't.

As long as I was up, I decided to take a look at the Talking Stick Event Center. To get there, I had to walk through the almost-empty casino. I made a slow tour of that glitzy gambling oasis, looking at the few people who were still playing, but saw no familiar faces.

The event center was on the west side of the casino, located in a large new annex. A big sign by the main entrance announced "The Rage in the Cage" later that night.

Six fighters from Team Spartacus were billed with their pictures along with six from Team Ultima. Rick O'Shea was not among them. Brian Bravo was listed in his place.

Since Alexa told me Brian was being cut from the fight club, it seemed strange he would be here, unless he was just acting as a placeholder for O'Shea.

The massive room was at least twice the size of two basketball courts, and at this time of night was completely empty. It was outfitted with fixed overhead lighting and a Jumbotron, and had state-of-the-art metal detectors at each entrance.

The event center had been cleverly designed with two second-story decks that ran all the way around the entire room. The floor seating could be moved to accommodate proscenium-arch productions for concerts and plays or to feature an arena-style configuration for sporting events.

I checked the seven exits and walked down a supply

corridor that led to a concrete loading dock and staging area in the back of the annex. Band equipment and scenery could be loaded into the event room through this corridor.

After I had a pretty good idea of the layout, I still wasn't ready for bed. I found a place in the quiet lobby where I could think.

I still had Rick O'Shea's arrest warrant in my pocket. I had been intending to go to the tribal police and get them to help me serve it. However, now that I knew this whole resort was owned by E. C. Mesa, I wasn't sure that was such a hot idea anymore. Unless, that is, I could get an updated players' report.

I dug into my pocket with my left hand, got my cell phone, then dialed Sally Quinn.

"This better be fucking great, Shane," she said, obviously reading my name on her LCD screen.

"I need someone to give me the name of a cop I can trust with my life at the Tohono O'odham Indian Reservation. It's just outside of Tucson."

"You need what?" her voice getting sharper as she came awake.

"I have a judge's warrant for a prime murder suspect, but my doer is friends with the guy who owns this resort. I don't want to ask the reservation cops for help serving the warrant only to have them give me up to the perp."

"How do you spell it? That Indian name."

I gave her the spelling.

"Call you right back."

I hung up and looked around at the lush décor of the

casino and hotel lobby. This whole opulent resort was like a bad version of *Escape from New York*, walled off from the poverty and outlaws that surrounded it.

Then I remembered Alexa telling me that the Mesa Indians had spent millions of dollars on border issues last year. Since there are no coincidences in law enforcement, I wondered, how does a man named E. C. Mesa, who has a fascination for Indian motorcycles, own a lush resort on a Mesa Indian reservation right on the Southwest's main drug corridor?

My phone rang, interrupting this thought.

"Yeah?"

"Okay, the guy you want to talk to is Captain Thomas Ironwood," Sally said. "Calloway called a friend of his on the Phoenix PD who says Ironwood used to work there and he's a kick-ass cop. He checked with the reservation PD and found out Captain Ironwood works nights on that department because that's when all the action takes place. I got an old Phoenix PD Web site article here that says he's a full-blooded Tohono Indian who got recruited to the reservation PD from the Phoenix drug-enforcement squad. He's ex-military, Marine Corps. Captain Calloway's friend on the Phoenix PD says you can trust Ironwood all the way."

"Thanks. Go back to sleep. Sorry I woke you."

I got up and went back to the concierge desk and asked where the Tohono Nation Police Station was. I was told it was about a quarter mile down the road in New Town. The concierge offered to have the casino host drive me.

Graham met me outside, his permanent smile in place.

We climbed into his golf cart and headed down the road. The electric cart buzzed as the headlights sawed through the early-morning darkness.

New Town was a grouping of recently constructed homes, stores, and warehouses. It was located inside the nine-foot wall that protected the casino from the Mexican criminals and endless gunfights outside.

From the architecture, I estimated it had been constructed about the same time as the resort. There were several blocks of efficient but uninteresting boxy-looking one-story dwellings, which I guessed served as housing for the hotel and casino employees and their families.

The police station was a concrete-block building with microwave transmitters on the roof and four blue and white Tohono police cruisers parked out front. It was good equipment, well maintained.

I went inside, showed my creds to a desk sergeant, and asked to speak with Captain Thomas Ironwood, who, as Sally had said, was on duty, working nights. An overweight deputy led me to a small, neat office and told me to wait. After he left, I studied the room filled with pictures of a tall, lean sergeant in a marine uniform posed with a squad of soldiers in Iraq. There were at least half a dozen law-enforcement awards and plaques presented to Thomas Mitchell Ironwood from the Phoenix Rotary, PD, and city council.

A few minutes later a tall, well-built man about thirty-five years old with black, close-cropped hair and a neatly pressed uniform walked in.

"I'm Tom Ironwood," he said. "How can I help you?" He had a military bearing and command presence.

I showed him my police credentials.

"LAPD?" He looked up and cocked an eyebrow. He was dark skinned with black eyes. Not quite handsome, but close.

I told him I had an arrest warrant for Rick O'Shea and about Diamond Peterson and how I thought she might be in some danger.

"You have the O'Shea warrant on you?" he asked.

I handed it to him. "I think he's scheduled to be one of the MMA fighters at that 'Rage in the Cage' thing at the event center tomorrow night. He's not on the poster, but I think that's because he knows he's hot. I'm betting because of the size of the purse he'll show up anyway. If he does, I'd like your help serving this."

"I can already tell you that nobody named Rick O'Shea is on the reservation," Tom Ironwood said. "You're the second guy's come in here tonight asking about him. The other one didn't have a warrant, so there wasn't much we could do but take a look on the computer. Check the gate sign-ins."

"Another guy?"

"Mexican named Vargas." He looked at me carefully. "A lawyer. According to his gate log-in he's staying over at the old Blue Mountain Lodge on the northeast edge of the res. It's about four miles down the road outside the wall, off Highway Seven, across from the new waste dump in Old Town."

"Can you check and see if you have a record of Diamond Peterson arriving yesterday?" I asked.

He scanned his computer. "No," he said. "That means she's not here. With that wall and all our perimeter security there's no way in or out except through the main gate. If she was on the property, it would be listed here."

I didn't want to get into it with him, but according to Jack he was wrong about both Diamond and O'Shea. They were both in the casino earlier this evening.

I thanked him for his help. I wanted to ask him about E. C. Mesa. But some survival instinct told me not to. I went to the reception area and called Desert Taxi, then went outside to wait.

The sun was just breaking the horizon in the east. I watched as it rose slowly, its red and gold beams casting long fingers of light across the desert sand, just as it always had at dawn on Seal Beach thirty years ago.

The cab arrived, and I told the driver where I wanted to go.

Then I was traveling toward that red-gold ball of light with the ghost of Walter Dix right behind me. I could almost feel him on that big old cigar box, paddling hard, breathing through his mouth, hurrying to catch the curl.

Paddle fasta. Dis is our poundah, bra.

CHAPTER 53

THE BLUE MOUNTAIN LODGE was a concrete-block, one-story motel situated near a garbage-disposal pit.

The motel sat outside the resort security wall and, as a result, had paid a high price in broken windows, litter, and spray-can graffiti. It was about a half a mile down the road from Old Town, which, as I drove past, gave off the tired look of despair. The structures in Old Town were ramshackle with broken equipment advertising broken lives.

When we pulled into the parking lot, it was only a little past five, but as I got out of the cab, I was immediately hit by the toxic smell of garbage coming from the dump across the street.

I went to the front desk and showed my credentials to a tired-looking, overweight Indian woman with a lined face and rat-nest hair who was perched on a high-backed stool behind the desk. I gave her a twenty and asked her if Sabas Vargas was registered here. She never got up, but told me that Vargas was in room six.

I reached over her shoulder and plucked the room key off a peg.

"Do not call and announce me," I told her, then flashed my creds again to make the order stick.

I walked down the cracked cement walkway, past scarred wood doors, until I found room six. I unlocked without knocking and stepped inside. The room was threadbare and smelled of cooking grease and cigarette smoke.

Vargas was sprawled on the bed in his underwear. When he heard the door open he reared up on his elbows and squinted at me with unfocused eyes.

"What the fuck?" he growled.

I crossed the room, pulled his pants off the chair, and handed them to him. "Get dressed," I said.

"I'm through taking orders from you, Scully."

"Let's go. I'm buying breakfast."

He blinked a few times, then stood and put on his pants. He grabbed a denim shirt off another chair, then went into the bathroom and closed the door. I heard water running. When he returned to the bedroom he was wide awake but still trying to figure out what was going on.

"You have a rental car?" I asked.

"Yeah, the red Mustang out front."

"You're driving. Come on."

We exited the room and walked to his car. I waited while he fished around for his keys and unlocked the door. We got in and pulled out onto the highway.

"I saw a coffee shop a mile back," I said. "We gotta get away from this smell."

"Yeah . . . I didn't see the dump 'cause it was dark when I checked in and the wind was blowing the other way."

We drove to a small wood-sided restaurant on the highway that advertised a farm breakfast special: Eggs, potatoes, choice of chicken or fried steak.

We climbed the steps, went inside the half-full diner, and sat at an empty booth at the front window. An Indian waitress came over, poured our coffee, and left two menus. When she was gone, I leaned forward.

"Okay, Sabas. I'm only gonna say this once."

"I don't wanta hear it."

"Yes you do. It's an apology."

He sat back, not sure how to react.

"You were right," I said. "I was trying to shut you guys out. I wanted this to be just between Walt and me. All those years since I graduated Huntington House, I've been running away from him, Sabas. It was such a bad time in my life I didn't want to go back. I didn't want to deal with those old memories. If I'd gone over there, I would have seen this coming. I would've gotten a nose full of Rick O'Shea. I woulda sensed something and stopped him. Like you, I've been kicking myself."

We were silent, eyeing each other across a scarred linoleum tabletop. At first, his eyes were shiny black marbles, radiating distrust, but slowly, they softened.

"Sucks, doesn't it?" he said. "Knowing you could've saved Pop but were too wrapped up in your own bullshit to even try."

"Yeah." I sighed. "I've been dragging it around for a week. I just figured since I screwed up so bad, that it was my job to fix it. I didn't want help from the rest of you. I kept telling myself you were amateurs and you'd just screw it up. Maybe from a law-enforcement standpoint that was correct, but from an emotional one, it was selfish. I'm sorry. That's the whole apology. It's the best I can do."

Sabas reached across the table and put one of his big, scarred paws on my left hand and squeezed it once before letting go. "Apology accepted."

"Jack's still running with these guys," I told him. "He called last night and told me Diamond showed up here yesterday. She got into an argument with O'Shea in the casino. O'Shea pulled her out of there. Jack said it caused a big ruckus.

"According to the tribal police, there's no record of either of them being on the reservation, but since Jack saw them both yesterday they gotta be here. I'm worried about Diamond. Her name's not registered at the security gate, so I have no idea how she got in. But if Jack's right, then O'Shea got his hands on her, and I don't have a clue yet where she is."

"Maybe I do," Sabas said. He set his coffee down. "I saw Chris Calabro in the casino last night right after I first got here around seven. He was alone playing the slots. I hung back and watched. After he wiped out I followed him.

"He goes back to this little house that's about a half a mile down the road from the casino right on the golf course. I asked around and found out the casino has two or three bungalows that aren't listed on the room charts. They give them to the main acts who play the show rooms. The guys from Team Ultima are all staying in one of those. That's probably where they took her."

"Good stuff," I said.

He smiled. "So how do we do this?"

"I found out last night that E. C. Mesa owns the Talking Stick Hotel and Casino."

"Yeah, I learned that too. It's why I went down and registered at the Blue Mountain Lodge. But I can't put up with that smell another night."

"We're all at the resort under Seriana's name. We should be okay there 'til tonight. We've got plenty of room in our suite. Let's move you in with us. Then we can start working on a strategy."

He nodded, gazing out at the hot, dry Tohono O'odham reservation. Then he said, "It's turned into a fully developed sea, bra."

It was what Pop always called any dangerous sea where without warning, a riptide could sweep you far out into the bay with little chance of getting back to shore. Pop never let us surf when it was like that.

"I guess sometimes you just gotta take a chance and go out anyway," Sabas said softly.

CHAPTER 54

"WHERE THE HELL DID YOU GO?" Alexa demanded as I walked through the door. "I've been worried sick."

"Look who I found," I said.

Sabas walked into the Pinto Suite behind me. All of the women, including Alexa, hugged him.

We gathered in the suite over room-service coffee and studied a site map of the resort that I'd found in the leather-bound folder on the writing desk. Sabas pointed to the spot where he had followed Calabro. A small cluster of three bungalows were indicated halfway down the tenth fairway.

"Why don't we all sign up for golf," Alexa suggested. "Rent carts, go to the tenth fairway. Try and see inside."

It was a good plan, so we called and got an early tee time at 8:30 A.M. Next we arranged for club and shoe rentals. At the appointed hour, we signed in at the pro shop, got our equipment, and took off in two carts. I drove one, Sabas the other.

Once we were out of sight of the first tee and the

clubhouse, using a course map we'd picked up at the pro shop, we drove across the third and sixth fairways and shot off the cart path, through the rough, passing several other foursomes ahead of us.

The hot desert sun was making a slow climb in the clear blue sky. It was low enough so I could feel it shooting under the cart awning, heating the back of my neck and shoulders.

When we reached the tenth tee, we parked and waited. Nobody was coming up behind us, so we headed our carts on down the tenth fairway and pulled to a stop next to each other across from the bungalow Sabas had pointed out.

"You two guys have already been burned," Alexa said. She pulled a club out of her bag, dropped a ball, and sliced it over by the bungalow where Sabas had told us the fight team from NHB was staying. Then Alexa, Vicki, and Seriana walked toward the house and into the rough where they began searching for Alexa's ball. Sabas and I were backup, watching from twenty yards away.

Alexa moved toward the back fence of the target bungalow and began walking along the east side of the house. Then she turned and came back again.

"Not here," she called out to Vicki. "Try around to your right."

They continued to search, looking into the windows of the house from time to time as they traversed the back fence. Five minutes later they all turned and came quickly back to the carts. I could tell something was wrong.

Alexa got into my cart as Sabas pulled alongside with

Vicki and Seriana. Each woman wore a tight, strained expression.

"She's there," Vicki said angrily.

"You saw Diamond?" Sabas said.

"Yeah," Vicki said. "She's swimming in the pool. What kinda hostage gets to take a morning dip in the fucking pool? I was worried when Jack said she showed up here asking for O'Shea. I think this makes it pretty obvious the bitch is in on it!"

I looked at Alexa, who nodded.

"I don't get it," I said. "If she's one of them, then why didn't she tell O'Shea I was a cop?"

"Let's not deal with it now," Alexa said. "Let's just get out of here."

Sabas and I floored the little electric carts and, without another word, whizzed off down the fairway.

CHAPTER 55

WE WERE IN THE PINTO SUITE trying to deal with the idea that Diamond had betrayed us. But I was having trouble seeing it. Besides not telling O'Shea that I was a cop, she also hadn't burned Jack.

If she had scammed Pop into signing all those documents, then she was an accessory in his murder. She had a lot at stake. If she was an accomplice, she'd tell them. But Jack was still hanging with them, and that meant she hadn't.

Wouldn't she also tell O'Shea that we'd learned about the challenge match on this reservation and that we were planning on being here? Knowing that, why would O'Shea take the chance and show up here at all? Yet according to Jack, he had. So, what the hell was going on?

After I repeated these concerns to the others, we all sat around trying to come up with a reason that would fit the known facts. Nobody could do it.

Alexa finally looked at me and said, "The Black-Hole Rule."

"The what?" Sabas scowled.

Alexa said, "In astronomy, when the known astronomical facts don't fit the action of the planets, then there's usually a black hole you can't see creating the magnetic pull. Same is true in law enforcement. Since Diamond's actions don't fit our known facts, we have to assume there's an information hole we don't know about that's causing it."

Sabas said, "We gotta take some action. We can't just sit here and do nothing."

"Regardless of what we just saw, I think we still need to treat Diamond as a hostage," Alexa said. "We can't put her life at risk without having the answers to Shane's questions. That means we've got to come up with a way to rescue her before we attempt to arrest O'Shea."

"Whenever you have a split objective, the most efficient solution is to split your force and stagger the timetable," Seriana said. "Tactically, it weakens us, but on the plus side we have a relatively small AO and we should be able to divide up, put two people on that bungalow while the main group deploys in the event center. We stay in touch by phone. The bungalow team waits 'til all the MMA fighters leave that house for the event tonight. Then, if Diamond stays behind, we secure the house first and take her into custody. Debrief. Then the splinter group moves up in support."

"What the hell is an AO?" Vicki asked.

"Sorry, it's just the battlefield. Stands for Area of Operation."

"Then say it, okay? We can't afford a buncha misunderstandings."

Seriana nodded.

"I think Seriana's got a good idea," Alexa said. Then she looked at me. "What about Faskin and Westfall? Isn't it about time to pull them in?"

"Who are Faskin and Westfall?" Sabas demanded.

I told them about the two FBI agents and how I'd used Jack as bait to lure them out here.

"Jack's risking his life too," Vicki said. "You really gonna turn him over to the FBI?"

"He's guilty of sticking up two banks," I argued. "I'm still a cop. I'm supposed to turn my back on that?"

"Yeah," she said.

"Well, I'm not going to," I replied. But I certainly didn't feel very good about it.

Then I told them about my visit to see Tom Ironwood at the tribal police and that my boss, Jeb Calloway, said we could trust him.

What I didn't tell them was it concerned me that, despite his nine-foot wall and all that electronic security, Ironwood still didn't know Diamond and O'Shea were on his reservation. That meant he either had a large hole in his security or was careless or maybe even lying. But I didn't see any choice. I had to take a chance on him.

We went over our plan point by point. After we were finished, I wrote out some instructions for the concierge. Then I left the suite and went to the lobby, where I handed my sealed letter to the man behind the desk along with a fifty-dollar bill and some instructions on what I wanted him to do.

I showed him my LAPD credentials.

"Is this a police matter?" he asked.

"Yes, but I've already spoken to Captain Ironwood. We need you to follow the instructions inside exactly."

We ordered burgers for lunch from room service. After we ate, we put the final touches on our rescue-and-arrest plan.

When we were finished Seriana said, "We have eight hours. We should get some rest. Somebody needs to take the first watch."

"I'll do it," Vicki said. "I'm not tired."

We went to bed. Sabas pulled the drapes and stretched out on the couch in the living room.

As I lay on the bed I kept thinking how Chooch said that rarely are you able to pay your debts in full.

Tonight I was going to get a chance to try.

CHAPTER 56

I CAME AWAKE WHEN I HEARD Vicki outside yelling.

All hell was breaking loose in the living room.

I exploded out of bed, still half asleep, but somebody lunged into the bedroom, and I walked right into a sharp left hook, my third trip to the canvas in five days. When I struggled to push myself up, I got kicked in the head.

I could barely see my assailant because it was dark in the room, but from his gargantuan shape it looked like Chris Calabro.

As I went down again I saw Alexa being pulled out of the room by Kimbo Sledge. She was struggling to get free so he hit her. I lunged up to attack him, but with my collection of injuries and broken arm, it was a slow, lumbering charge, and Calabro ended it with a karate kick to my stomach.

I was quickly secured with plastic snap cuffs then dragged into the main room of the suite, where all six of the fighters from Team Ultima were standing over four of the five of us. Seriana was the only one missing. I had no idea where she was, but was praying she'd use her combat skill, and whatever she'd brought in that canvas duffel, to change this outcome.

I took a quick survey of the others' injuries. We all had our hands cuffed. Sabas had lost a tooth. Vicki had an ugly bruise forming on her jaw. Alexa looked dazed as she was pushed down on the sofa beside them.

Calabro threw me to the floor at Rick O'Shea's feet.

"Chris, get them out of here," O'Shea ordered. "I'll go through this place and find out what they've been up to."

I looked at the table clock. It was 6:00 P.M. We'd only been asleep for a couple of hours, but everyone had been so tired, we hadn't heard them come through the patio doors.

We were pulled outside. An electric golf-course maintenance vehicle with an enclosed metal flatbed was parked right by the edge of the patio. The roll-up back door was open, and we were pushed roughly inside and forced to sit on the floor. There was barely enough room for the four of us as we were jammed inside. The door was slammed closed and latched. Ten seconds later we were on the move.

"I'm sorry. My fault," Vicki said. "I was on watch. I didn't see them until it was too late."

"It's nobody's fault," I said. "Does anybody know where Seriana is?"

They all shook their heads.

"She said she was going to outpost, whatever that means," Vicki said.

We sat huddled in the small enclosed vehicle with our shoulders and knees touching as the little electric maintenance truck whizzed across the grass. Finally, we bounced up over a curb and were back on pavement.

We rode for about five more minutes before the truck pulled onto the grass again, slowed, and came to a stop. A minute later, the rear door was unlatched and pulled up. A flashlight was trained on us.

When my eyes adjusted to the light, I saw Jack Straw. He was standing just outside the truck, smiling at me.

CHAPTER 57

GARY WHITE, CHRIS CALABRO, and Kimbo Sledge were all with Jack at the rear of the truck.

"Get 'em inside," Calabro said to Jack. "Mesa's upstairs getting ready. I'll go tell him."

Jack pulled us roughly out of the truck, and Gary shoved us through a side gate in an eight-foot wall that guarded a mansion. A stocky young Indian kid in a green khaki uniform, packing a sidearm in a crisp new holster, stood by the gate.

This house was a huge, modern, two-story hacienda-style structure with a red tile roof. It was at least twenty thousand square feet, with its own private security force and perimeter wall.

We followed Gary single file along a walkway next to an Olympic-sized swimming pool. Jack walked beside me with Kimbo Sledge following. Nobody spoke.

Three young uniformed Indian security guards wearing sidearms in new leather holsters escorted us.

Alexa and the others were pushed off and herded toward the main house, but Jack grabbed my arm and pulled me toward the pool house. One guard followed us, never more than a few feet away.

I was pushed by Jack through the open sliding-glass door into a large entertainment room outfitted with a mahogany pool table, video-game consoles, big screen TVs, and a wet bar. The Indian guard followed. I looked around the spacious pool house. There were eight or ten changing cubicles along the perimeter of the room.

Jack shoved me up against the wet bar and turned to the young guard. "I got this," he said. "You can go."

"But Mr. Calabro said we should . . ."

"I got it!" Jack shouted. "Get the fuck outta here."

He wasn't moving, so Jack wheeled and hit me hard in the side of the head. I didn't see it coming, and with my hands tied, couldn't block the blow. The best I could do was try to roll with the punch. Even so, my knees buckled. I went down again.

Jack glared at the guard, who seemed shocked by this sudden assault. "You got the picture now?" Jack said. "I owe this shithead some payback. I wanta do it in private. Now get the fuck out of here."

The Indian guard was unnerved by Jack's behavior and quickly left. But he stood a few feet outside the closed glass door, where he could still observe us. Jack pulled me to my feet and leaned me against the bar.

"Too bad there ain't a teeter-totter," he whispered.

"Untie me. I gotta get to Alexa and the others."

"I can't untie you. This place is loaded with security.

That guy is right outside looking at us. Use your head, Scully."

"Where's Diamond?"

"I don't know. She's hanging by a thread with these guys. They don't trust her but they haven't decided what to do about it yet."

The guard was still at the window. Still watching through the closed sliding-glass door.

Jack followed my gaze and said, "Hold on, I gotta make this look right."

He hit me in the stomach, but pulled the punch as it landed. I doubled over, making a show of it. Out of the corner of my eye I saw the young security guard take a step back and shake his head in disgust. Then he moved further off and sat in a chair by the pool.

"What's Diamond up to?" I said as soon as the guard took his eyes off us. "None of this makes any sense."

"She's fucked up. She needed cash and struck a deal with O'Shea, got Pop to sign those documents for ten percent of his scam. She was playing the horses at Hollywood Park, got in debt to a loan shark or something. I don't have all of it but she started helping O'Shea siphon off money, and once she was guilty of that crime, she got threatened into helping O'Shea pin the missing cash on Pop."

"If she's in on it, why didn't she tell them I was a cop?"

"Because she never thought they'd kill Pop. She's as fucked up over his murder as the rest of us. She didn't rat you and me out because she was certain those guys would kill us too. She's not a killer. She's a good Catholic girl trying to have this both ways. It ain't working. She's shaking apart."

"How do we get out of here?"

"I don't know. Like I said, Mesa's got a ton of these Indian security cops. Most are just kids, but they got a few genuine tough guys who run things."

"O'Shea's pretty stupid, but you can bet Mesa will have some kinda workable plan if he intends to kill four people, two of them cops," I said.

"He's gonna stage a shootout that all of you are going to accidentally get caught in," Jack said. "It just might work. Last year they had a hundred shooting deaths on this reservation. Those *braceros* are robbing the Indians blind as they cross the border. There's shootouts almost every night. Mesa's hired some coyotes as triggers. They should be arriving anytime through a secret tunnel he has under this reservation's wall. It's how Diamond and O'Shea got in here. These coyotes are Mexican hard cases who will have no trouble pulling your drapes. The story will be that you and the others accidentally wandered into the line of fire."

"And Mesa can arrange that? What about the tribal police? Four U.S. citizens die and nobody asks any questions?"

"Fuckin-A right he can arrange it. Eugene C. Mesa was born on the Mexican side of the res. Half-Indian, half-Mexican, no parents. Growing up, he was a half-breed who nobody gave a shit about. He ran away when he was eight, but thirty years later he came back in a Gulfstream jet and built the Talking Stick Resort, the local school, a library, and just about anything else that's worth a shit around here. Even the tribal police chief is his man. He's like a god."

Before I could reply to that, the door opened and Rick O'Shea entered the pool house.

CHAPTER 58

"I WANT TO TALK TO MESA," I said once O'Shea was inside. "I know he's here."

"Gene doesn't waste time on dead men." He walked to a cabinet, pulled out his monogrammed gym bag, and started to leave.

"If Mesa intends to get past this stupid mess you've made, Rick, he needs to hear what I have to say."

He stopped at the door and looked back. "Right, I'm stupid and you're over there looking like an ad for adhesive tape. I gotta go get ready for tonight, but an hour from now you and me have an appointment. Sit on this guy 'til I get back, Jack."

He was almost out the door when I said, "The FBI already knows all about this. They have warrants. It changes everything."

O'Shea stopped again, his back to me. Then he slowly turned.

"The FBI can't do nothin' on Indian land," he said. "A reservation is like another country." A crafty, dumb look came into his eyes. "They got a treaty with the U.S. government or something. This place has its own courts and laws. Federal warrants are toilet paper here. We got immunity. The feds can't touch us. Nobody can."

"You shouldn't be practicing law without a license, Rick. You better let Mesa make that decision. At least he knows what he's doing."

O'Shea dropped his gym bag, crossed the room, cocked a fist, and shook it in my face.

"I see it, but hitting me won't solve this. You better be smart for once and tell Mesa. That's just the teaser. I've got more information to trade. He needs to hear it all."

"I'm totally on this guy, Ricky," Jack said. "I think you should go tell Gene. I got my own trouble with the FBI. Last thing I need is a buncha frisbees showing up."

"Mesa ain't gonna talk to you," O'Shea blustered. But he looked less sure. He crossed to the sliding-glass door and motioned to a new guard who had joined the other outside. This second man was much older and looked more competent. He had chevrons stitched on the sleeve of his rent-a-cop uniform.

"Hey, Arturo, get your ass in here and help Jack watch this turd." A minute later, the older, tougher-looking Indian guard entered the room with his gun out and stood by the door. As soon as he was inside, O'Shea snatched up his gym bag and left.

It was six forty. Nobody said anything. Jack and I watched the clock on the pool-house wall hit seven, then seven ten. The armed guard remained at the door, never taking his eyes off me.

Calabro had said that Mesa was upstairs getting ready for the event. But after half an hour had passed, I was beginning to wonder if O'Shea had even bothered to deliver my message.

Five minutes later, the glass door on the pool house slid open and E. C. Mesa stepped into the room. He was dressed all in black with his hair in a short ponytail. He looked like a crushed-down Steven Seagal.

"What's all this bullshit about the federal government?" he said. "I'm not wanted for any crime so the FBI hardly concerns me."

"But it concerns him," I said and nodded at Rick O'Shea, who had just slipped through the sliding-glass door and was standing in the pool house next to the older Indian guard.

"Let me worry about him," Mesa said.

"He's gonna get arrested. The FBI has a warrant. It's never a good idea to have a stupid accomplice standing between you and a DA. He'll start making selfish decisions."

"Rick, take Jack and Arturo outside for a minute," Mesa ordered.

O'Shea didn't move, but Jack pushed away from the bar and sauntered across the room. As Jack passed the Irish fighter, he said, "Let's go, dude. Orders." He pulled the slider closed after the three of them left. But they didn't go far. I could see them standing just outside the glass door.

Mesa and I were alone. He moved closer, stopping three feet away. "Your meeting," he said.

"He's wanted for murder," I said. "O'Shea killed Walter Dix. The arrest warrant has already been issued by an L.A. judge. When he crossed out of state and onto this reservation, it got turned over to the FBI. The feds will get the Tohono police to serve it. My guess is when Rick sees what a deep hole he's in, he's gonna fall all over himself giving you up, Gene. I don't think it's a good idea to add kidnapping and murder to this mess. Work with me and I'll work with you."

I still didn't know what the hell was going on with this guy. I couldn't figure out why an obviously astute, self-made billionaire who bought and sold huge companies all over the world was making what appeared to be so many stupid, emotional mistakes. There had to be a reason, and it had to come from somewhere deep inside him. However, he didn't seem too concerned with my threat.

"What I don't get is why you went after Walt Dix," I continued, trying to get him talking. "What could be in that Huntington House embezzlement for you?"

Mesa said nothing.

"You couldn't possibly care about a crummy one point five million dollars. There had to be something else." His expression remained blank. Now he wasn't even looking at me. His gaze had shifted to the plate-glass window and the three men standing just outside the closed sliding-glass door. "You surfed with him, right? Long boards."

After I said that, he shifted his weight and seemed to tense. When he turned back to me, his expression had changed slightly. There was a new tightness at the corners of his mouth and around his eyes. But still he said nothing.

"Those cigar-box boards are a bitch to stay up on," I said. "I know, 'cause I tried." I still had no idea where the hell this was leading, but I could tell it was upsetting him so I kept going. "Seal Beach. Six in the morning, right? Up by the Municipal Pier just before sunup, you and Walt kneeling in the sand with a buncha little kids. Walt timing the AWPs."

Mesa just stood there, but now his whole body was rigid. His dark face began to flush with blood. A vein started pulsing in the center of his forehead.

"You two musta been the only guys around who could stay up on a cigar box. Nose always pearling. Hard as shit to cut back on. I couldn't do it. Walt taught you, right? That was his thing, always helping the other guy."

Now Mesa's face twitched. "Shut the fuck up," he hissed angrily.

"So I'm right about that. He taught you to ride boards like he taught all of us. You met him before dawn at Ninth Street, tapping the source. So why steal from him? Why send O'Shea to kill him?"

"I didn't send Rick to kill him," Mesa said sharply. "It was a mistake."

"When you make a guy write a phony suicide note then blow his head off with a shotgun, it's hard to call it a mistake," I said.

His face was getting redder. His jaw clenched. He

didn't say anything more for almost a full minute, and I just stood there and watched him smolder. When he did talk, he changed the subject.

"You don't have anything that can hurt me," he began. "Even if you have a federal warrant for Ricky, all I have to do is get him across the reservation border into Mexico and that ends it. A little cash in the right hands down there and your warrant or any extradition gets crushed. As long as O'Shea doesn't do anything stupid, it's finished. If he screws up, he'll disappear. Nobody will ever see him again. Simple."

"Nothing in life is that simple, Gene."

"O'Shea's the one who killed Walt. So how's that my fault? I wasn't even there. It's on him, not me."

"That's gonna depend on how Rick decides to tell it," I said. "And then you got this multiple-kidnapping charge. You're holding four people at gunpoint against our will. If we end up dead, it's murder. Who you gonna blame for that?"

"You got lost wandering around out here at night, ended up on the wrong side of the border, got shot by cartel drug smugglers. I know how to control Mexican jurisprudence. I've got connections down there. It's not even close to being a problem."

I didn't like the sound of that. There's a lot of police corruption in the border provinces of Mexico, and with the right connections, my guess was he might actually pull that off.

"You've got nothing, Scully. I'm wasting my time talking to you." He turned and walked to the door but stopped unexpectedly and turned back. He had something more he wanted to say but was struggling to get it out.

"You probably loved Walt," he began. His voice was thick with emotion. "You were too fucking gullible to see what a selfish, egocentric prick he really was."

"Selfish?"

"All that cheap Zen philosophy, talking over everyone's head. Trying to make it sound like he had some kind of cosmic answer. Like my life was some kinda journey instead of what it really was—a nightmare created by selfish, angry people who didn't give a shit what happened. That worked great on most of you, but even back then I knew it was psychobabble. I was too smart for Walt's hype. My mind refused to log bullshit. I was always looking for the real answers. I could see what was really going on. I was too smart for him. Too smart for everybody. That's why I made it from a dirt hut in the desert to the top of corporate America. Nobody understood what I was thinking. I thought Walt did in the beginning, but then I found out he was just another guy with a program, working the system." He stopped talking, but the vein had not stopped pulsing in his forehead.

If I wanted to survive, I needed to get a handle on this guy fast.

"Why were you so angry at Walt? A guy you just surfed with?" I asked.

And then, without warning, he told me.

"Walt caught me stealing once," he said. "After it happened, he took me out to dinner. I remember thinking, What is this? I steal a bunch of money from the home, he catches me at it, then pays me back by buying me dinner in a big fancy restaurant.

"Asshole that Walt was, of course he had this bullshit Zen lesson for me. We're sitting there over inch-thick steaks, and he tells me that two wolves were fighting over my soul. I'm thinking, *wolves*? Gimme a fuckin' break. He says one wolf was evil and only wants to eat my heart, but the other was good and was fighting to protect my spirit. I remember getting more pissed by the minute. The guy was patronizing me. It wasn't about that. It was about need. It was about winning; getting the other guy before he could get you. So I finally asked him, Okay, if these wolves are fighting, which wolf will win? You know what he told me?"

"Yeah," I answered. "He said the wolf you feed will win." I remembered the story well. Walt had told it to me the second week I'd been there. The day he'd caught *me* stealing money from the office.

Mesa was silent for a minute, then he said, "Two months later Walt threw me out. Sent me back to child welfare. I was twelve."

"So you were at Huntington House just like the rest of us," I said. It was the piece I'd been missing. All along, I'd thought Walt had befriended him as an adult. Now it turned out Eugene Mesa was just another orphan. It was the emotional connection that had caused all of this. Anger, love, and betrayal were driving him. Revenge, not money, was the motive for Pop's murder.

I must have looked shocked because Mesa laughed before saying, "I thought you already knew."

"No."

"I was found in an alley in Long Beach by child services when I was nine years old. I lived at Huntington House for three and a half years."

"And that's why you framed him and tried to destroy his reputation? Because he threw you out for stealing?"

"He betrayed me," Mesa said, coldly. "Pop was a fool. After I made it, I called him, set up a meeting. He let me get close to him again all those years later. I formed Creative Solutions and bought Huntington House when he ran out of money in the mid-nineties. All the time I was helping him, he never realized all I ever wanted was to pay him back for what he'd done."

In that instant, I could see Eugene Mesa the way he was as a nine-year-old, full of hatred and fear. He had been exactly like me.

"I feel sorry for you, Gene," I said softly.

"Don't," he said. "As it turned out, I never needed anybody anyway." Then he opened the slider and left me.

CHAPTER 59

I WATCHED MESA TALKING to Rick O'Shea out on the deck, just outside the pool-house window. As soon as I was alone, I began trying to get the Swiss Army knife out of my right front pocket. I had my hands around to the side as far as they would go and thrust deep into my jeans. My fingertips could just barely touch the knife. I moved over to a barstool, and by rubbing on the edge of the seat, managed to shift the knife up half an inch inside my pocket. I hooked my little finger through the metal loop on the top of the handle and finally fished it out.

I was holding it in both cuffed hands behind me as O'Shea came back inside the pool house. He was now dressed in his fight trunks and wearing a white silk robe that had *RICOCHET* embroidered on the back. He closed the door and walked directly over. As he crossed, I managed to open the small blade behind my back and turned it in my hand so I could start sawing on the plastic band that bound my wrists, while trying to conceal my body motion as I worked.

"What makes you think you can prove I killed Walt?" he asked.

"We've got the motive, the accounting work papers Pop had, your bank transactions that match the exact amounts you embezzled. All the stuff you were trying to get from him when you accidentally beat him to death."

I was about halfway through the plastic cuffs when he suddenly stepped forward and hit me. The knife flew out of my hand and clattered on the floor behind me. I instantly tasted blood in my mouth. He hit me again, and I went down hard.

As soon as I hit the floor, the half-sawed plastic cuffs snapped and my hands came free.

I scrambled to my feet, with my fiberglass cast and one good fist in front of me, ready to defend myself for the third time. If I lost this round, it was going to cost me my life.

"This is gonna be fun," O'Shea said as he went into a fighting stance. "Just like before, you got no chance, Scully."

I slammed the cast down hard on the bar top. It hurt like hell, but the scored end cracked and immediately exposed the little Bobcat .25 in its protective baggie. I transferred the gun into my good left hand, ripped the baggie off, flipped off the safety, and fired.

I pulled the shot slightly and the bullet hit him high in the right shoulder.

"Fuck," he said, looking down at the wound. Blood

began spreading out, blossoming on the white silk robe around the bullet hole.

It looked like the .25 caliber slug had gone clean through without hitting a bone or doing any major damage.

Then O'Shea charged me, knocking the gun to the side as I fired a second shot, which missed him completely. In seconds he had me by the throat, and threw me to the floor.

It was the Torrance Airport all over again as he wrapped me up in some kind of bone-breaking, martial-arts hold. I managed to retain the Bobcat, got it up between us, and fired again. This one hit him in the groin and did a lot more damage. He screamed in pain, then let go of me as he grabbed his stomach with both hands.

"Hey, Scully. My turn."

It was Jack. He had rushed through the door at the sound of the first shot and was standing directly behind O'Shea with a pool cue he'd picked up off the center table. He swung from the heels and caught O'Shea behind the ear. Rick slumped on the floor, out cold.

I untangled myself and slowly stood. "We gotta tie him up. See if you can find something."

Jack picked up my Swiss Army knife and used it to cut down a drapery cord to bind O'Shea's hands, then handed it back to me.

"Somebody must've heard those shots," I said. "We gotta get outta here. Call the hotel desk. Ask to be connected to Captain Thomas Ironwood at the tribal police. Tell him to get some people out here fast, and tell him the FBI should be arriving any minute. They need to be included. Then get that maintenance truck and park it by the back gate behind the pool."

"Whatta you gonna do?"

"I'm gonna find the others and meet you out back in five minutes."

I headed out of the pool house, clutching Alexa's tiny Beretta in my left hand.

CHAPTER 60

ONCE I WAS OUTSIDE, I REALIZED that, despite the gunfire, miraculously, nobody was running out onto the pool deck. I sprinted across the pavement into the main house and started looking for the most logical place where Calabro would take the others. I saw a door leading to the subbasement and bounded down the stairs.

I was running recklessly down a narrow basement hallway, throwing open doors, looking for Alexa and the others when I turned a corner and suddenly collided with Kimbo Sledge and Gary White. They were also decked out in silk fight robes, their MMA ring names stitched on the back.

I raised the Bobcat and pointed it in their general direction. It's such a small weapon, it didn't seem to worry them at all, because they both simultaneously attacked me. I was trapped in close quarters and had just enough time to fire once. The .25 caught Gary White in the forehead. "The Great" White was off the ride and dead before he hit the floor.

I didn't have time to shoot Kimbo Sledge, who was instantly on me. His silk robe said *SLEDGEHAMMER*, and he began to prove it. The man was pretty much finishing up the job O'Shea had started on me five days ago.

Suddenly a corridor door flew open and Sabas Vargas came charging out and hit the pile. He'd somehow gotten his hands untied. All three of us were rolling on the ground. Both Vargas and I were pummeling Sledge, who had curled up and become a very difficult target composed of nothing but elbows and forearms. We weren't doing any damage when Alexa came through the same door, also untied. She held a heavy metal floor lamp in both hands. Without hesitation, she swung the base at Kimbo's head. He went down and out.

"How'd you get loose?" I asked them as I picked myself up off the floor.

"Jack came back a minute ago. He slipped me a kitchen knife," Vargas said.

"We've gotta find Vicki and Diamond, then get out of here fast," Alexa said. "I counted ten security. God knows how many more he has."

We left the "Sledgehammer" unconscious on the floor next to the late Gary White and ran down the basement corridors, throwing open doors until we reached a utility room, where we found Vicki tied to a water heater. Using my Swiss Army knife, I cut her loose.

"Where's Diamond?" I asked.

Nobody knew.

We spent another five minutes searching until we

heard cars pulling up outside. Doors were slamming and men were shouting orders.

"We gotta go now or we're not gonna get out at all," Alexa said.

We took off running up the basement stairs to the main floor. The pool area seemed clear. After checking outside, we ran out of the house and across the deck.

Then I spotted Eugene Mesa standing with his back to us on the second-floor balcony, screaming instructions at someone over his cell phone.

I grabbed Vargas's arm and stopped him.

"I want this guy," I said, pointing up at Mesa, who still hadn't seen us.

"Then let's get him," he said.

We doubled back toward the main house and scrambled up the outside staircase to the second-floor balcony, taking the steps two at a time. As soon as we reached the top, Mesa spun to face us as two young security cops stepped out of an upstairs doorway, blocking our path.

I took the nearest one, hitting him with the flat side of the Beretta, which I was holding in my good hand. He sagged to his knees, dropping his gun. Sabas unleashed a devastating combination, dropping the second. Mesa was staring at us a foot away, holding his cell phone in front of him as if it could somehow protect him.

"Looks like you're gonna have to do your own fighting this time, Gene."

I moved into punching range. He took a step back and started digging for a small compact gun that was in a holster at the small of his back. It was an awkward slow draw and I fired the Beretta before he could get it out. Either I was jerking my shots or the little Bobcat was pulling up and to the right because I hit him in about the same place I'd hit O'Shea, high in the right shoulder. Mesa's gun flew from his hand and clattered onto the pool deck one story below.

"Let's go," Sabas said, as armed men swarmed onto the pool deck beneath us. I grabbed Mesa's good arm. Vargas got a grip on his wounded arm and we pulled him off the balcony into the house just as gunfire erupted from below. Glass shattered but nobody got hit.

"Lemme go! Lemme go!" Mesa screamed, his eyes wide with fear.

Sabas and I pulled him downstairs toward the pool doors, then I shoved the Bobcat up into his ear.

"Okay, Gene, real easy question. How bad do you want to stay alive?"

"Don't kill me," he stuttered.

"Then do exactly as I say."

I nodded to Vargas, who kicked open the glass door, and we dragged the billionaire out onto the pool deck, which now contained almost fifteen armed men.

"Don't shoot!" Mesa yelled at his guards. "He's got a gun on me!"

We dragged him across the deck with the complement of gunmen trailing us like a pack of feral animals, all of them with their weapons at the ready, not sure of how to attack us without killing Mesa.

"Don't shoot, that's an order!" Mesa screamed at them in panic.

We pulled him out the back gate, where the golf

maintenance truck was sitting with the back door up and the electric engine running. Alexa was behind the wheel with Jack beside her. Vicki was in the back, motioning us to hurry. She held out her arms and helped pull us inside.

Just then the headlights from two vehicles swept around the side of the estate. As they neared, I could see that both were pickups. There were several Mexican men in the back with long rifles. As soon as they came into view, they began shooting over the truck cabs at us. I figured they must be the coyotes from the Mexican side of the res that Mesa had hired to kill us.

Bullets were pinging off the engine compartment and riddling the back of the maintenance truck. In a second we would be disabled or dead.

"Don't shoot!" Mesa screamed again. "I'm in here!" But this was already out of his control.

"Get going!" I yelled at Alexa. Bullets ripped into the truck. I feared it was already too late.

Then I picked up some movement off to my right side. I turned and saw Seriana Cotton. She had somehow followed us here and was running low in a shooter's crouch, with an ugly-looking Austrian Steyr machine pistol cradled in both hands.

She yelled out to us. "Get out of here!" Then she threw herself down in the dirt and started shooting at the pursuing trucks. Her machine pistol ripped the night, shattering windshields and headlights.

Alexa floored it and we were away. Seriana was alone on the golf course, left to deal with God knows how many assailants. There was nothing I could do but watch as we pulled away, leaving her there, her machine pistol tearing into the night.

What happened next is hard to describe. We were all being thrown around in the back of the maintenance truck as Alexa bounced over greens and sand traps, cutting across the course toward the main gate of the Tohono reservation. I could see about five sets of headlights still behind us, trying to catch up, but the little maintenance vehicle was pretty quick on grass. Still, as we kept going, I could see that the pursuers were beginning to narrow the gap. It was going to be close.

"How much farther to the gate?" I shouted.

"Right up ahead," Alexa called back. "I see a bunch of unmarked cars. Gotta be the feds."

"Then this is where I get off," Jack said.

"Jack! You stay put!" I yelled. "You're under arrest!"

He ignored me and leapt out of the moving maintenance truck, rolled on the grass, and came up running. I could see him sprinting toward a line of trees. In seconds, we had left him behind.

We couldn't stop. The pursuing vehicles were getting closer. Occasional gunshots again hit our truck, the bullets rattling around inside. Miraculously, none of us were hit. Alexa bounced over the curb and headed toward the main gate.

It was quite a welcoming committee. The Indian cops were in some kind of major jurisdictional argument with Faskin, Westfall, and about half a dozen FBI agents in Windbreakers. We skidded in, threw our gun out, and pushed E. C. Mesa from the truck. All of us kept our hands in the air.

The men in the pursuing vehicles didn't know what was in store and came boiling in behind us, their gun barrels still hot. The feds and Indian police swarmed.

Ten minutes later, everybody was in handcuffs.

"So where the fuck is he?" Leo Faskin demanded of me. He was standing near a tan sedan with government plates, glowering.

"Let's not worry about Jack," I said. "I've got people tied up and bleeding all over this resort. We need to start collecting the bodies."

"You're really something, Scully," Westfall said. "You played us. Jack was never here at all, was he? You just needed our badges so you'd have some clout with these tribal cops."

"It's still a great bust, guys. I'm seeing gold shields and federal merit citations all around."

Again, Westfall proved to be the wiser of the two as he asked, "So where's this Mesa guy's house again?"

CHAPTER 61

CAPTAIN IRONWOOD HANDPICKED four deputies and went with the six feds to collect what was left of Team Ultima. O'Shea was alive and transported by ambulance to the jail hospital in Tucson, where he was hooked to a machine and intubated. Kimbo Sledge and Chris Calabro tried to run but were arrested.

They found Seriana Cotton playing the slots in the Talking Stick Casino. She was scraped and bleeding but claimed she didn't have a clue what had happened out on the tenth fairway.

Mesa made no statement and hired Gerry Spence as his defense attorney, dispelling the myth that cowboys and Indians can't get along.

Everybody lawyered up and within hours it became obvious to me that Rick O'Shea wasn't going to be talking.

I had multiple kidnapping charges against Eugene Mesa, but with good lawyering, that might only be worth ten or fifteen years. Not nearly enough. Even worse, I still didn't have a murder case on Eugene Mesa for ordering Pop's death.

Diamond Peterson was among the missing. I had a very bad feeling about that. I didn't think we'd ever see her alive again.

Alexa and I got stuck in Tucson dealing with tribal law, the Arizona courts, state-to-state extradition papers, and a mile of related red tape. We didn't get back to Los Angeles until a few days later.

We arrived home the same day our two-week vacation to Hawaii was scheduled to end. We went out into the backyard, sat on our worn metal chairs, and sipped rum and Cokes with a dash of pineapple juice. It was the closest we had in our bar to the ingredients for a Mai Tai.

"Aloha," Alexa said as we clinked our glasses.

We talked about Hawaii, about Walter Dix, and about how disappointed I was that O'Shea hadn't flipped. It had been a long, painful journey, and in the end, despite everything, I still felt that I had failed Walt.

"Seriana reports for deployment back to Iraq tomorrow night," I told Alexa. "At least she got to see how it ended."

Alexa said, "Without her, we wouldn't have made it."

There was certainly no lack of truth in that statement. The pallbearers had been an unlikely team, but except for Diamond, in the end they had all earned my friendship and respect.

"Vicki's picking up Walt's ashes from the crematorium tonight," I said. "We're all going to say good-bye in the morning."

"Can I come?"

"Got a surfboard?"

She smiled. "No, but somebody has to make sandwiches and kiss your bruises."

"Then you're invited."

An hour later, I got a call from Kurt Westfall. He sounded angry.

"Still no sign of Straw," I told him.

"Fuck Straw. You hear about this shit from Gerry Spence's office?"

"No, what?"

"The Tohono O'odham Indian Reservation is claiming jurisdiction on Mesa's four kidnapping cases."

"So we try him there. What's the problem? He's not gonna beat it. You got five witnesses, two of whom are L.A. cops."

"Indian law ain't exactly like American law, Scully. They got all these tribal loopholes from some treaty that was signed in the eighteen hundreds. Add to that the fact that the Indian prosecutor went to law school on a Eugene Mesa tribal scholarship and Mesa is gonna pretty much skate on this whole thing. They're charging him with four counts of false imprisonment. A fucking misdemeanor."

"Come on," I said. I couldn't believe this was happening.

Westfall kept rolling out the bad news. "They're claiming no guns were used in the abduction and the statement you and your wife made confirms that fact, so it's not a kidnapping."

"False imprisonment? Isn't that like when a store

security cop holds some guy for stealing clothes he didn't steal? We were tied up, dragged out of our room, transported. . . . They threatened to kill us!"

"The transportation clause isn't valid on the reservation either, and they say nobody threatened your life."

I was holding the phone, feeling a deep sense of frustration.

Westfall heaved a deep sigh. "The Indian prosecutor has already accepted the false-imprisonment charges. It's a misdemeanor, so the fine will be around ten grand. If I'm ever arrested for killing my wife, hire Gerry Spence to represent me," he groaned.

After I hung up, I went to our bedroom and sat down heavily on the bed. I told Alexa what had just happened, and she came over to sit beside me. She took me into her arms and held me close. But there was very little she could do to comfort me.

An hour later, I was in bed, but couldn't sleep. I was looking at the ceiling, thinking about Eugene C. Mesa and how much alike we were. Neither of us knew who our parents were. I'd found out that Mesa wasn't his real name either. He'd picked it because he needed an identity and was a Mesa Indian.

A nurse at the hospital where I was left as an infant had picked my name for me. She chose it because she was a Dodger fan and loved Vin Scully.

Mesa and I had walked the same hallways at Huntington House as nine-year-olds. We'd both kneeled in the sand with Pop waiting for the sun to rise so we could "go catch some, bruddah."

Half my life, like E. C. Mesa, I'd also been feeding

the wrong wolf, and that wolf had almost beaten me. But then Alexa and Chooch had entered my life and everything changed.

As I lay there, I remembered that I'd seen Walt at our wedding and spoken to him briefly that day. Something quick and meaningless. "How you doing, man? I'm stoked you came." I'd not bothered to thank him for keeping me alive so I could make it from Huntington House to my wedding day.

Walt had never known Alexa. Not really. But he could see how she had made the difference for me and it made him happy.

He had been there for me when it counted, but I had failed to repay the favor. I had left all of this unfinished.

I looked at the ceiling and waited for him to whisper down that it was okay. That I had at least made the effort. That I had done my best. He didn't speak. He didn't relieve my burden, but I could feel him up there.

Watching.

Waiting.

TOMORROW

CHAPTER 62

IT WAS TWO HOURS BEFORE dawn. I was out behind the house at 4:00 A.M., wiping down my old short board. I'd painted Walt's crest logo on the nose twenty years earlier when I'd first bought it.

The board was yellow and red, but over the years had become badly scratched. One of the three fins had a small piece missing.

I didn't have any surf wax, but I was sure one of the group would bring some this morning. My broken arm was fortified by ibuprofen but ached slightly as I loaded the bat tail into the back of the MDX and then stuck my head inside the house.

"Come on, Alexa. We gotta go."

She hurried out carrying a cooler and put it in the back of the SUV. We pulled out and headed toward Seal Beach.

I had envisioned this day very differently. I'd never considered that we would fail. Alexa sat quietly beside me. She knew I was churning inside.

We pulled into the lot at 9th Street, a block down from the Seal Beach pier. I parked beside Vicki's blue Toyota Camry. Sabas's yellow pickup with the flame job was already there, and Seriana's green van was two spaces away.

We got out and unloaded the car. I handed Alexa the cooler, then pulled my board out of the back. We walked through the predawn mist to the sand about forty yards away.

I could see the three of them gathered in the dark, kneeling in the sand, each holding a surfboard, waiting for the sun to appear.

Next to Sabas was a decorative urn that held Walt's ashes. Someone had brought flowers. Rose petals in four glassine bags.

Hang Six sat in a portable cage in the sand at Vicki's side.

"Hey hapa haole, guy. Whatta matta you?" the parrot screeched loudly at me as I kneeled beside them.

"Where'd you find him?" I asked.

"Animal control. I'm taking him home with me," Vicki said.

I set down my board with the others. Alexa set down the cooler and joined us.

"How come you're late?" Sabas said. He seemed disappointed with me or even angry.

"I'm not late. You guys are just early," I replied.

Sunrise was still a half an hour away, and while we waited, I told them what had happened to the kidnapping charges against E. C. Mesa. No one knew what to say.

"The sets are stacking up," Vicki finally observed. She was looking at her surf watch, timing the sound of the breakers. "Ten and a half seconds."

"You feel him here?" Seriana asked a minute later. She was wearing a black wet suit with her hair slicked back. She sat with her muscular legs gathered underneath her. "I'd kind of like to feel he was here watching us when we give his ashes to the sea."

"I don't feel him at all," Vicki said sadly.

"Me neither," I said.

Sabas just grunted, but said nothing.

This whole thing felt so unfinished, but there was nothing we could do about it. This was just the way it had turned out.

Walt's murder was still an open L.A. case, but without O'Shea or somebody else turning state's evidence, Pop's work papers probably weren't going to be enough. They were just circumstantial evidence. I knew the DA didn't have enough to file.

None of us wanted to spread Walt's ashes in defeat, but that's what we were about to do. It was over.

Then I looked up and saw two figures walking toward us, coming out of a predawn mist. As they got closer, I could see both were carrying surfboards, both wore the newer-style Kull wet suits. As they approached, moving deliberately, I realized that it was Diamond and Jack.

I'd thought Diamond was gone forever, either murdered by coyote gunmen on that reservation or in the wind as a fugitive from justice. But here she was, walking up Seal Beach with Jack.

They finally got to where we were and knelt silently in the sand beside us. "Sorry we're late," Jack said.

"Hi," Diamond whispered, not engaging our eyes but looking into the sand instead.

"Surf's up," Hang Six screeched. Diamond and Jack looked over at the bird and both smiled.

"This surf's a little weak, buddy," Jack told the parrot.

We were all now looking out at the small three-foot steeps. "Like Pop said, we don't make 'em. We just take 'em," Jack observed.

Diamond was fighting back tears. Then she raised her head and looked directly at all of us. "I came here to tell you guys something," she said.

Nobody spoke.

"I know what I did. I'll never be able to forgive myself for it. Because of me, Pop's dead and we didn't get those guys for killing him." She stopped and wiped a tear away. "I'm the only one now who can change that. I was there. I was an accomplice. I know Mesa ordered it and helped them cover it up. I can testify against O'Shea, Mesa, and the others."

Everyone knelt quietly, trying to think of what to tell her. Nobody could come up with anything, so nobody spoke.

Diamond cleared her throat and continued. "Jack and I made a pact. We're gonna both turn ourselves in. We're doing it in Walt's memory because that's what he would have wanted. We're gonna do the right thing for him and ourselves. We've decided to take whatever comes."

After a minute, Sabas said, "If you want, I'll take

your cases at no charge." Then he turned to Diamond. "I think if you agree to testify, I can plead you down to a lesser charge. Shane and Alexa can testify to what Jack did on that reservation and that should mitigate those two bank stickups. Nobody is gonna work harder for you than we will."

"We'd like that," Jack said, answering for both of them. "But we're not looking for deals, we're just looking to get straight with ourselves."

"I never thought we'd see you guys again," Seriana said, giving us her rare but beautiful smile.

"Yeah, surprised the shit outta me too." Jack grinned.

As we knelt on the beach, we slowly began to realize that we had won. This was victory. It was a victory with consequences, but it was a victory nonetheless.

The sun began to peek over the horizon. Tomorrow had finally come.

"Let's go rhino chasing, bruddahs," Sabas said, echoing Pop's standard predawn challenge.

We gathered up the bags of flowers and the urn with Walt's ashes and trotted toward the meager three-foot surf while Alexa and Hang Six watched from the shore.

In the water, everyone laid flat and began to paddle out. Vicki had the urn balanced on the nose of her board, and the rest of us carried the flowers. I hadn't been out in years, and the board felt unstable beneath me.

When we were beyond the surf line we sat up, warming ourselves in the early morning sun. Then we got ready to spread Walt's ashes.

"I guess now is just as good a time as any," I said.

Vicki handed the urn to Diamond, who held it for a

moment, whispering something to Walt inside. Then she passed it to Seriana, who did the same. Each of the pallbearers in turn cradled Walt's ashes for a minute to say a silent good-bye. When the urn was finally in my hands all I could think of to tell him was "I'm sorry I never thanked you."

We poured the ashes into the sea and scattered the flowers around them.

The waves lifted us slowly up and down as the rhythm of the tide began to spread the last remains of the only man who had been there for us as children when nobody else had cared.

I sat on my board, feeling for the first time like I had actually paid my debt. We all had. I wondered if I was mellow enough for a fish to come up and nibble my toes. None did.

"Son of a bitch, look at this," Sabas said.

We all glanced back over our shoulders and saw a beautiful five-foot wave coming toward us. It was formed in a perfect crescent shape. A rhino. The kind of wave Pop always waited for. The swell was moving toward us, a rolling green gift from the center of the sea.

We proned out on our boards and started paddling hard. My broken, aching arm was completely forgotten as I hurried to catch the swell. The wave passed under us and lifted us high above the beach. Then we all stood to shoot the curl.

It was a perfect party wave, and all six of us were on it.

Halfway down the face, I felt Walt drop into the pocket beside me. I couldn't see him, but I knew he was over there, crouched down low, shuffling up on the nose Quasimodo style, riding that big, heavy cigar box.

We all stayed like that, shoulder to shoulder, shooting out of the green room and into the chop. All six of Pop's pallbearers escorting him back into shore.

Read on for an excerpt from
Stephen J. Cannell's next book

THE PROSTITUTES' BALL

Available in hardcover from St. Martin's Press

PROLOGUE

CHAPTER 1

THIS IS A STORY ABOUT A STORY.

It's also a story which, despite all my efforts to the contrary, seemed destined to become a major motion picture.

It started a few days before Christmas, but it's not a Christmas story. It's about lost generations and emotional desertion, and about a Los Angeles family with way too much money. So I guess at its heart, it's a story about greed, corruption, and loss.

With those themes, what better place to start than at an office Christmas party? But before we begin, just a few preliminary remarks.

I'm a homicide detective, and as such, I'm carefully schooled in the three concepts mentioned above. I work at an elite LAPD detective division known as Homicide Special. Our unit was reconstituted after the O.J. Simpson case, another L.A. story of greed, corruption, and loss.

After losing that high-profile media trial, it occurred to our command floor managers that maybe it wasn't such a good idea to have cops carrying evidence blood vials around at a crime scene where they could later be accused of planting it.

As a result, Homicide Special was completely reorganized and staffed with our most seasoned detectives. I'm lucky to be assigned there. It's a great gig.

My name is Shane Scully, and for this story I will be your host narrator. It's going to be a fast ride through L.A. with a lot of reckless driving. Look out for abrupt lane changes, freeway shootings, and dangerous hairpin turns. As a police officer, I'm required to advise you to fasten your seatbelts.

All set? Then let's go . . . Cue the opening theme music. Fade slowly up from black, and we'll begin at:

THE INCITING STORY EVENT

CHAPTER 2

THE CHIEF'S CHRISTMAS CELEBRATION was being held at the Magic Castle, an old, baroque mansion in the foothills just above Hollywood Boulevard. It was a private club that normally catered to L.A.'s large population of magicians, but was also available to rent out for special occasions such as this one.

Half a dozen professional sleight-of-hand performers were ripping up twenty-dollar bills or cutting apart ugly neckties, then magically restoring them before a crowd of half-lit captains and deputy chiefs who'd seen their share of deception and were squinting through alcohol filters, trying to bust these tricksters.

The party was for the chief's command staff and spouses. More than a few of the braided hats were getting seriously hammered at the open bar, sometimes uncovering their dark, competitive natures or revealing dangerous political aspirations. The music was about peace on earth, good will toward men, but most of the people in this room had seen too much street crime to believe it.

Our chief, Tony Filosiani, mingled happily, wearing a blue double-breasted pinstripe over his lunchbox-shaped frame. On his shiny bald head, a Santa hat. He moved through the room, grinning and slapping backs, the ridiculous red hat bobbing along, identifying his position like a hazard warning.

It was hard not to wonder what would happen once this half-lit badge-heavy crowd hit the street and ran into the poor stiffs in our Traffic Division.

As usual, my beautiful wife, Alexa, was the center of attention, her looks both a blessing and a curse. Gleaming black hair, reefwater blue eyes, and high fashion-model cheekbones made Alexa attractive in a way that drew people to her but also made it impossible for a few of the "old boy cops" in this room to accept her as a division commander. Some of their wives stared in jealousy, while others wondered openly about her.

I was only here as Alexa's husband and was haunting the corners of the room, trying for invisibility. I look like a middleweight club fighter with a nose broken too many times and short black hair that never quite lies down, so people stay out of my way. I had her back.

On that December night, Alexa was riding in a political wave of congratulatory remarks. The day before, it had been announced that she was being promoted to Captain and would finally be able to drop the word "Acting" from her title of Detective Bureau Commander.

For two years she'd been running the detective division, which supervised three hundred plainclothes cops. In L.A. only captains can head police divisions, but she had been a lieutenant and that adverb had been haunting her authority like an asterisk. With her appointment to captain came full-fledged membership in the department's double bar club.

I watched as a few of our more aggressive career assassins mingled and schmoozed, wearing big, deceptive grins. They cruised the party like ocean predators, their dangerous personalities barely visible, only the hiss of their dorsals giving them away.

"You ready yet?" I asked Alexa, trying for the third time to get us out of there. I'm a line officer, a Detective III. I don't mix well at these things. Because I was uncomfortable, I wasn't drinking alcohol, so I wouldn't inadvertently insult somebody who would later decide to wreck my career.

"In a minute," Alexa said, turning towards a florid-faced commander named Medavoy, who ran the Special Operations Support Division. I knew he had actively opposed Alexa's appointment to captain, but you'd never know it as he congratulated her, gave her a big, expansive hug, and told her she was the absolute best. The putz.

I wandered off to find a backwater as the music changed and the annoying strains of The Chipmunks singing "We Wish You a Merry Christmas" began to claw relentlessly at my brain.

"Shane?"

I turned to find Sally Quinn, my partner from Homicide Special.

"Sally! What're you doing here?" I was surprised to

see her because this was a command floor–only party and we both worked down in Homicide Special. Short, with a bob hairstyle and freckles, she looked as uncomfortable as I did.

"Cal invited me as kind of a going away thing," she said, referring to both Jeb Calloway, our captain at Homicide Special, and the bombshell she'd laid on me without warning that afternoon.

"I was hoping to get some time with you before I left tomorrow," she said.

Sally and I had been partners for three years, although much of that had been interrupted, first by her maternity leave and then by medical complications she'd had following the birth of her daughter. I got benched right after she got back because I'd been wounded and needed time off to recover. As a result, we'd only been working the job together for a little over eighteen months.

Earlier this afternoon, she'd informed me she was taking another family leave. Tragically, she and her husband had just learned that their little two-year-old daughter, Tara, had been diagnosed with autism. Sally had decided to stay home to work with her.

"Now that it's sunk in, I hope you're not too upset," she said. "You seemed a little quiet after I told you."

"Of course I'm not upset." I stopped, then took her hand. "I'm gonna miss having you as my partner is all. I thought we were finally through the medical stuff and ready to kick ass."

"I'm sorry we had such a choppy go. After the baby, I had more stuff going wrong than a Russian airline." She squeezed my hand. "I just wanted you to know I think you're a great partner and I'll be back once Thomas and I have a good support program set up."

"I'll be waiting," I told her.

"You know yet who Cal is going to assign to our desk?" she asked.

"Nope."

"I hope it's not Hitch. You deserve better than that."

"I doubt he'll put Hitchens with me." But the truth was, I'd been worrying about that ever since Sally told me she was taking another home leave.

Sumner Hitchens had been bouncing between partners, hitting the guard rail, getting slapped to the center, ringing all the tilt buzzers, before ending back in the return tray like the kinetically overshot pinball he was. We were currently the only two unattached detectives at Homicide Special.

A captain from Ad Vice jostled us as he made his way back to the bar. "These guys look sloshed," Sally commented. "It's dangerous to drink at these things."

"It's a Christmas party," I said noncommittally. "Hopefully, Yellow Cab's gonna make the difference."

Sally hugged me and we wished each other luck.

Twenty minutes later I had Alexa by the arm and we were mercifully out of there. We walked to the valet stand out front, followed by the faint sound of "Frosty the Snowman."

They pulled my black MDX up and we both got in. Alexa and I had ridden in together this morning because of the party. My wife never drinks at police events either, so with what was just about to happen, thankfully we were both completely sober.

I pulled out of the parking lot, headed down the hill, and took a left on Franklin, making my way toward the Hollywood freeway.

According to the Communications Division, the radio call we answered a few minutes later hit dispatch at 10:13 P.M.

It was December 23rd, two days before Christmas.

CHAPTER 3

LAPD PROTOCOL DEMANDED you always keep your police scanner on, even while off-duty. Alexa reached into the glove box as we hit the 101 freeway and flipped the switch. A steady stream of low value mistakes bubbled out at us, all of it delivered in a flat, rambling female monotone.

"One X-Ray Seven, meet L-Fifteen Code Six at the Market, 1256 Freemont," the RTO said. "Cross street is Olympic. Felony 211 suspect needs transport to MCJ for booking."

It went on like that. Nothing too big seemed to be going down at the moment.

Since it was relatively late, I was using the freeways, taking the long way home in miles, which at this hour should turn out to be the short way in minutes.

I was tooling along, glad to be out of that party, when Alexa said, "I saw you talking to Sally. What a shame about her little girl."

"Yeah, she thinks if they start working with specialists

right now, they can minimize the effect. Tara's so young, it's hard to test her so the doctors don't really know how severe it is yet."

Because Alexa ran the Detective Bureau, I couldn't help but wonder if she'd seen Captain Jeb Calloway's new Homicide Special partners list.

"I'd sure like to know who Jeb's gonna put with me. You heard anything?" I said, casually floating the question.

We were about five miles from the transition to the San Diego Freeway, which would take us to Venice Beach where our classic canal house was located on one of the waterways there. When she didn't answer, I glanced over.

I knew that expression. She was trying to make up her mind. It was always a problem for us when she knew something that affected me that she wasn't supposed to confide.

"I'm hoping it's not going to be Sumner Hitchens," I gently prodded.

Then she said, "I think Detective Hitchens is transferring to CAPS in the Valley. But please don't say anything because I don't think he's been told yet."

CAPS was Crimes Against Persons, and if that was true, it was a big demotion for him to go from the elite Homicide Special squad where he was currently assigned to some Valley purse-snatch detail.

Hitchens, or "Hitch" as he preferred to be called, had somehow gonzo'd his way into our unit, then had shot through three partners in less than a year. All of them eventually became so frustrated with him they demanded reassignment.

"You sure he's going to the Valley?" I asked.

"It's just something I think I heard," she responded vaguely.

"Okay, that's good. Actually, that's great. But it leaves us with an odd number up there. Means they'll have to transfer someone new in to partner up with me. Bobby Shepherd has been trying for the unit. I worked great with him when we were in patrol. You think you could put in a good word? I'd love to get Shep as my new partner."

She stared poker-faced at my dash.

"I hope making captain isn't going to fuck up that nice, easy management style you're so widely appreciated for." Trying to kid her along.

"Come on, Shane, you know who gets in that division is Jeb's call. I can't micromanage my commanders and then hold them responsible for their performance."

At that moment the radio call that put this story in motion burbled out of my scanner.

"All units and One Adam Twenty. A 415 with shots fired at 3151 Skyline Drive. Nearest cross street is Mulholland. One Adam Twenty, your call is Code Three."

"Isn't that about a mile or two up there?" Alexa said, pointing off at the hills to my left where some very pricey real estate was located. We'd both been patrol officers for five years and as a result had a pretty thorough knowledge of the city.

"Yeah," I said. "I think Skyline Drive is just off Mulholland near Laurel Canyon."

Alexa snatched up the mike and keyed it.

"This is Delta-15. Scully and Scully. Off-duty, but in the immediate vicinity. We will take the Skyline Drive 415 shots fired call."

"Roger that," the RTO replied. "All units, all frequencies, Delta-15 is in the vicinity of 3151 Skyline and is responding Code Three. All other units, your call is now Code Two."

Code Three is red lights and siren. I hit the switch and the strobes I'd had installed in the grill and back window of my Acura flashed on. Simultaneously Alexa reached out and flipped another toggle, and as the siren began to bray, I floored it.

A 415 radio call is a disturbance where the 911 caller is so hysterical or incoherent that dispatch doesn't know the exact reason or nature of the event. In the Patrol Division, 415s were dreaded calls because you could be rolling on anything from an old lady locked out of her house to something as deadly as the North Hollywood bank shootout.

One night, years ago, when I was still in an X-car, I got a "possible major 415 with knives and chains." It sounded like a riot. We squealed in with our adrenaline surging and our weapons out. It turned out to be two eighty-year-old men fighting over a garden hose. We were so keyed up, and the lighting in the backyard was so bad, we could have easily shot one of them by mistake.

You had to be extremely careful but ready for anything on 415s. The shots-fired tag definitely upped the stakes.

We got off the freeway on Laural Canyon and headed into the hills. Out of the corner of my eye I saw Alexa fishing in her purse for her 9mm Spanish Astra. I caught her eye just as she tromboned the slide, kicking a fresh round into the breach, then clicking her safety off.

"Merry Christmas," she deadpanned.

CHAPTER 4

WE POWERED UP LAUREL CANYON with the siren squealing and turned right onto Mulholland Drive, which runs for a way along the top of a mountain ridge that separates Hollywood from the Valley. The road was almost a thousand feet up and provided spectacular views of Studio City on the right and Hollywood to the left. The view was the reason so many multi-million-dollar estates dotted this hillside.

About a mile down Mulholland, we hit Skyline Drive. It cut in on the left, heading farther up into the mountains. As I made the turn, I almost hit a blue Maserati that was speeding down the hill. It flashed past, making the turn off Skyline onto Mulholland. Alexa snapped her head to look through our back window, but it had already disappeared.

"Didn't get it," she said, referring to the license plate.

The engine on the Acura roared loudly beneath my siren as we continued to speed up the grade, passing more cantilevered mansions that hung off the mountain like glass-walled crystal palaces. We were in the 2800 block, which meant we still had a ways to go.

Then a red Ferrari Mondial flashed past. There were two people inside. The savvy driver flashed his high beams up into our eyes so we couldn't read his plate.

"Didn't get that one, either," Alexa said. She was looking out the back window again but missed the rear plate because of the dark, underlit street.

We passed two bumper-chasing Escalades. Both had their headlights off and were screaming down the hill. No front plates. Next, a half-million-dollar Mercedes McLaren whipped past, its high beams blinding us, followed by a Bentley Azure, then another Maserati. This one was yellow with a maroon racing stripe.

"Nope," Alexa said, turning again. It was way too dark to see much.

"Cockroaches running for the baseboards," I muttered as I grabbed a curb number. 3140. The house we wanted was going to be near the top of the hill.

The last car to pass us was a new black Mercedes 350. It was also running without lights, but this time as Alexa spun around, she managed to get the first four letters on the back plate.

"4 L M C!" she exclaimed. "Didn't get any numbers."

We got to the address and I skidded the MDX to a stop, flipping off my emergency package as Alexa and I bailed.

I clawed my party gun, the backup Taurus Air Light .38, from my jacket-slimming ankle holster, and we both surveyed the scene, our hearts pounding.

3151 was at the very end of Skyline. The driveway looked like an extension of the street leading up a hill onto a large property dominated by a looming overgrown mansion on the left. We were the first unit on the scene.

The huge house was a big, rundown Spanish structure that looked like it was built in the early 1900s, well before the rest of the sixties-style neighborhood had filled in around it. The front yard had gone to seed. An old wooden gate was hanging crooked but standing open across the driveway. I could hear Christmas music coming from the back—Frank Sinatra singing "Silver Bells."

"Let's clear it," Alexa said.

I nodded and we passed through the open gate and up the drive with our guns at port arms, moving carefully, ready for anything.

The mansion was dark. As far as I could see, not one light was on inside. We walked up the steep drive, hugging the mansion's south wall, heading toward the sound of the music.

When we got to the top of the hill, a huge eight-car garage came into view, and we began to see lights coming from a large backyard area. We crested the drive and saw that the house sat right on a promontory point. A magnificent half-acre pool area with a spectacular view overlooked the lights of the Valley on the left and parts of Hollywood on the right.

There were two neighboring houses on either side, but they were newer and sat a little farther back from the point, allowing them views in only one direction or the other. This property was obviously the first estate up here and, as a result, had secured the prime location.

There was a pool house with Spanish arches that matched the old architecture of the estate, but the newer plate-glass windows told me it was a more recent addition. It looked empty but was ablaze in lights. The Christmas music seemed to be coming from a sound system located inside.

We kept our backs to the wall and edged around the corner to get a better look at the layout.

It was then that I saw two female bodies floating face down in the rectangular, Olympic-sized pool. Their tangled hair and colorful dresses were illuminated by the powerful underwater lights. Both appeared to be Caucasian, their inert bodies leaking large amounts of dark arterial blood into the green turquoise water.

Alexa and I continued to stand with our backs to the wall of the house, surveying the terrain for any sign of movement. In addition to the two women floating in the pool, I could now see a third person back there. A man was bent over the back of a pool chaise with his ass poking up in the air. His face was looking down at the green canvas chair pad as if it contained something of great interest to him.

"Police! Stay where you are! Put your hands in the air!" I shouted at the man.

He didn't move—didn't twitch. In that instant, he changed categories, going from potential adversary to victim number three.

"Go," Alexa directed.

While she covered me, I ducked through the gate

into the backyard and sprinted across the deck to the side of the pool house, throwing my back to the wall. From where I now stood, I could see the rest of the backyard. It looked deserted.

"Backyard looks clear," I called as I raised my gun into a firing position to cover Alexa. "Go!" I shouted and she sprinted across the lawn, past my position and into the pool house. I followed behind her and covered her back as she threw open changing-room doors, checking both bathrooms.

"Clear," she called.

Then I left her and sprinted to the far side of the house to check the north side of the property and the path that led back to the street. It was also empty, the pathway lit by an old, rusting, Spanish-style carriage lamp.

"North side clear," I shouted, then checked the back door of the house. It was fastened securely shut by a big commercial-sized Yale padlock. The bracket was bolted to the side of the house and attached to the door with two-inch bolts that went all the way through the solid oak.

I looked through the kitchen windows into a pantry. The house was dark but appeared deserted—more than deserted, it seemed in terrible disrepair. For some reason only the backyard and pool house of this estate had been maintained.

Next Alexa and I checked the mammoth garage. All eight pull-up doors and side entrances were securely padlocked.

Once we were finished we returned to the man who was still bent over the pool chaise, obviously very dead. He was a middle-aged Caucasian, and had three huge, grapefruit-sized exit wounds in his back. All of them were oozing thick arterial blood the consistency of ketchup but the deep purple reddish color of egg-plant. He'd been shot with some kind of large-bore weapon.

"I'll check on the others," Alexa said, moving toward the two women floating in the pool.

They looked young and fit, both in colorful strapless party dresses, which in death had floated up around shapely thighs. Their leaking wounds were now beginning to turn the Olympic-sized pool a weird, greenish pink.

Alexa grabbed the nearest one by the arm, pulled her over and checked for a pulse. Then she repeated the process with the second body.

"Both dead," she said, but made no attempt to pull them out of the water. We had to leave the scene pretty much as we found it for the homicide tech teams and photographers because our 415 with shots fired had just morphed into a triple 187.

As I looked down at the blood-stained man bent over the pool chaise, I noticed a wallet in his back pants pocket. I carefully fished it out using my thumb and index finger, then dropped it onto a nearby glass-top pool table and took a pen from my jacket.

I flipped the wallet open, revealing a driver's license encased in a plastic sleeve. The picture of a tanned, good-looking man smiled out from under the State of California seal. The date of birth on the license said he was fifty-five. Then I read the name.

"You won't believe who we have here," I called over to Alexa who was still by the pool. "This vic is Scott Berman."

Alexa stood, her face now drawn. "Then we're sitting on a full-blown disaster," she said.

Frank Sinatra didn't seem to get it. "Have Yourself a Merry Little Christmas," he sang happily.

This incident, I later learned, was something screenwriters call the inciting story event. But for me, it was the beginning of two weeks I'm going to call "Shane's Midlife Crisis."